Past Presence

Nicole Bross

Literary Wanderlust | Denver, Colorado

Published in the United States by Literary Wanderlust LLC, Denver, Colorado. www.LiteraryWanderlust.com

ISBN print: 978-1-942856-35-1
ISBN digital: 978-1-942856-38-2

Cover design by ebooklaunch.com

Printed in the United States of America

Dedication

For Darcy, Mairead and Finley
When the seas are stormy, you are the lighthouse
that gives me hope.

1

"It's been nice chatting with you, Miss Eames." The night coach driver offers me his hand, palm up, as I prepare to step down and off the bus. With a smile, I accept—careful not to put any weight onto his fingers, which look swollen and red with age and the decades he's been gripping the wheel.

He handed a woman, all swirling skirts, and ruffles, off the carriage-and-four. She was laughing at something her mother had said, but before she stepped up the gravel path leading to the doors of the grand estate, flung open to welcome guests to the ball within, she turned to give him a nod and a half-smile.

"Enjoy your evening, Miss." He returned her nod as the heat crept up under his stiff white collar, but she had already caught up with her mother, and he didn't

think she had heard him.

The way his hand clasps mine is the same. Some habits carry over from one lifetime to the next, as I've learned. The vision lingers in my mind even after I pull away and shoulder my duffel. The manor home looked English, and the woman's dress was definitely late Victorian.

The sun is cracking the horizon, bathing the village of Soberly, Oregon, all twelve streets of it, in a glow that changes from sepia to marigold. The bus pulls away behind me in a cloud of exhaust and fine yellow sand, off to the next tiny hamlet along the coastal highway, leaving me standing in the empty street.

My destination is clearly visible—there is only one hotel here, the sensible, if unoriginally named, Soberly Inn and Public House. Standing one block away, it faces the sea and even from here I can see how the salt spray has faded the once-cobalt blue paint to a dull cornflower over the years. For reasons I don't yet understand, the Soberly Inn now belongs to me, and I am here to claim it.

I had no idea my Aunt Roz had even owned the inn. The last time I saw her I was an awkward pre-teen, and she was less than twice my age. I sometimes remembered to email her on her birthday, but not, I'm ashamed to say, every year, although she never forgot mine. Yet despite our distant, superficial relationship, she had left this place to me, rather than the wife she left behind when she died of a rapidly progressing cancer ten days ago. Maybe she was an ex-wife now. I had no idea. We weren't even Facebook friends. The notification of her death had come via her lawyer, not my father, along with the news that, for the first time in my life, I was a property owner. The news had affected me deeply, more so than I expected. Now, looking at Roz's prize for the first time, the quiet ache in my chest ramps up to a throbbing spasm before fading again.

This was what my carefree aunt gave up her vagabond life for, and now she wanted me to do the same? I stare up at the building, taking note of the aged wooden siding where the paint has curled away in places, the cracked cedar shingles, and the plain-lettered sign swinging from two chains beside the entrance. 'Shabby' was the word that came to mind, and not "shabby chic," either. I could only imagine the interior was just as dusty and unremarkable as the exterior.

"What were you thinking, Roz?" I say under my breath. My feet are still planted in the same place because I don't know where to go. There isn't a soul in sight at this time of day, nor are any of the assortment of shops and businesses that line the main street open. I know there will almost certainly be someone at the front desk of the inn, but although I've come all this way, I'm not ready to make an appearance there yet, not without knowing what I want to say, something I'd neglected to plan on the long bus ride. I scuff one toe of my battered Chucks in the sand that's accumulated along the curb, stalling. It's been a while since I've seen the beach, I decide, as I step into the street with the rising sun at my back. The inn is a problem I delegate to Future Audrey. Right-now Audrey is going for a walk along the coast.

As it turns out, the only thing four hours of roaming the

beach does is add hunger and the intense need to find a bathroom to my problems. Possibly a sunburn as well, judging from the pinkish hue my skin is taking on. I've always felt the injustice of not inheriting the platinum blonde or fiery red hair color that usually accompanies my level of fair skin. There's nothing even remotely exotic or attention-getting about the flat, medium-brown I ended up with. At least I can be thankful it doesn't frizz in the humidity, otherwise, I'd look like a positive nightmare right now.

The sun is almost directly overhead when I make my way over the last dune to the boardwalk. Although the village's one cafe is now open and will serve my requirements, I trudge past it to the inn, standing a bit apart from the businesses surrounding it by virtue of its height, the only three-story building in a two-story town.

Faced with two doors, one into the inn itself and one into the pub, I choose the latter. It takes my eyes a moment to adjust to the dimness, but my stomach reacts to the environment immediately, growling audibly as the scent of fresh-fried fish greets me.

The pub is classic seaside kitsch, decorated with fishing nets and glass buoys, old traps, and a well-worn rowboat suspended upside-down from the ceiling. Maps of the coastline and faded photographs decorate the walls, as well as other assorted nautical ephemera, and together it paints a portrait of the rich coastal history of the town.

I'm still blinking away the daylight, taking this all in, when someone steps into my field of vision.

"Grab a seat wherever you want," a guy holding a large plastic tub says. He's clearing empty glasses and plates as he says it. I nod my acknowledgment because the pair of red Beats headphones he's wearing will certainly drown out any verbal reply. His head is bobbing in time to music only he can hear as he disappears through a door leading to what I assume is the kitchen.

I duck into the washroom first, eliminating one of my problems. The maritime theme continues, with signs for pirates and wenches on the doors, and mirrors framed to look like portholes. *Girls can be pirates too, and I don't see why boys can't be wenches. Geez, Roz. Sexist much?* She'd been an ardent feminist in her early twenties. Had she stopped caring, or was I reading too much into a couple of bathroom signs?

The only table free seats six, so I choose a high stool at the near-vacant bar instead. I've arrived right in the middle of the lunch rush, from the looks of it. I still don't know what to say to anyone here. "Hi, I'm the new owner," seems arrogant, especially since I have no intention of keeping the place.

A menu appears in front of me, startling me out of my ruminations. Across the polished walnut bar stands a man whose skin is a shade lighter than the wood he's resting his hands on. His smile widens as he stares at me expectantly.

"Sorry—what?" I shake my head, flustered. Who has teeth that straight, that white? Self-conscious, I half-cover my mouth with the back of my hand. Mine show clear evidence of my two-pot-a-day coffee habit. I don't know what I was expecting, maybe someone of the same vintage as the decor, but it definitely wasn't someone younger than me, although maybe only by a couple years.

"Drink?" he repeats, jerking his head at the long row of taps, each with a branded handle. Most of them I've never heard of, and I'm not a daytime drinker anyway. "This is a pub," he adds and winks. The bartender who's well aware of his good looks. I'm familiar with the type. I wouldn't go so far as to call it *my type,* but I'd gone home with enough of them over the years.

"Sweet tea," I say. "Extra ice."

"Sure you don't want a pint? Maybe a cold glass of white?"

I shake my head. "Tea's fine."

"G&T? I'll put lots of ice in it." He's polishing up a tumbler, reaching for the bottle of Bombay on the shelf behind him. I roll my eyes, but I can't keep the side of my mouth from twitching.

"Put that back. I just want the sweet tea. Are you on commission or something?"

"Nah, I just want to card you so I know your name," he says. Unrepentant, he points to the sign nailed to a pillar that states *We ID Anyone Under 25.*

"You're off the mark by a few years, my friend," I tell him. He's finally pouring my sweet tea from the soda tap into a massive glass full of ice.

"Bullshit." As soon as he sets it down in front of me, I'm chugging it back, not breathing until the glass is half-empty. He snags it back and refills it while I wipe my mouth with a cocktail napkin. What I want to do is scoop the ice out and rub it all over my arms and face, which are starting to feel alarmingly hot. *From all the sun,* I tell myself. Not from the attention of this cocky bartender.

"We ID for all food orders too, you know."

I lean in close and pause before speaking, making it clear I'm appraising him. "Maybe I'm not hungry."

"You are. I saw you drinking in the smell of the fryer when you walked in. You got this dreamy smile that said you knew exactly what you wanted. So, let's see it." He holds out his hand with a crooked, teasing smile, but I push it away with the menu I haven't even glanced at. He's right. I don't need to look at it at all, but I don't want to admit that he can read me so well.

"You don't have to show ID to order food here. You made that up."

"So what? I can make up the rules if I want."

"Oh, you must own the place?" I mirror his teasing tone, but I'm watching him closely, seeing how he'll respond. I expect a smart ass reply in the same vein as our banter, but a shadow crosses his face and the smile slips. *Shit. The owner just died, you idiot.* As usual, the words spilled out of my mouth before I had a chance to think them through.

"I'm not, actually," he says.

"I know. I'm sorry, that was stupid of me to say." I bite my lip and plunge forward. "I'm Audrey. Audrey Eames. Roz's niece. Umm, I'm the owner, I guess. So, they tell me. For now." The silence stretches out between us as he takes all this in, frozen in place while I sit there, feeling like an utter moron with my hand outstretched, waiting for him to shake it. I'm just about to withdraw it into my lap when a wide grin cracks his face. He grips my hand so our forearms touch and our elbows rest on the bar, like we're about to arm-wrestle. I'm drawn forward in the process so we're almost nose-to-nose.

A gaggle of children ran through the field ahead

of her and scrambled over the stile. They were jostling each other and shouting raucously, overjoyed to be free of the classroom for the afternoon. All but one, a small boy whose hand was clasped snugly into hers.

"Look, Miss Dean, a nest. The others missed it." The boy spoke with a thick country accent as he pointed up at the treetops.

"Good eye, Wil. What sort of bird do you think made it?"

"Something big. A kite, maybe." She nodded in agreement, and they continued on in companionable silence, following the sounds of laughter ahead.

"You totally played me, Audrey. I thought you were just another tumbleweed. I'm glad you're not. Kellen Greene. It's very nice to meet you." The vision of his past-self fades from my mind, and I wonder what qualities he and the teacher have in common.

"A tumbleweed?" He squeezes my hand before releasing it, the pad of his thumb tracing a line up the side of my index finger like he's trying to maintain contact up to the last possible second.

"Tourists that roll on through town with the wind, here and gone before you know it. They don't bring anything with them, and they don't take anything away either."

"My bag should have clued you in that I wasn't just passing through," I point out, kicking it where it rests at my feet.

"Ahh, but there's only one place to stay in Soberly," he nods toward the ceiling and the rooms above, "and it's full up, at least until Sunday." Kellen walks over to the door leading into the back and swings it open. "Hey, Ma," he shouts, drawing the attention of everyone in the pub. "Come meet your new boss."

I shoot lasers through my eyes at him, and he gives me another wink. This is payback, then. All eyes are now on me, and I smile weakly.

A woman who barely comes up to Kellen's chest emerges, wiping her hands on a dish towel. She has the same warm, dark amber skin as her son, and her hair, streaked with gray at the temples, is pulled back into a tight twist. Her eyes slide over me as she scans the room, and I wonder what picture she has in her mind of the new owner. Probably not a sunburned, disheveled, sleep-deprived woman who may or may not look young enough to fail the twenty-five-and-under ID test.

"Hi," I blurt, rising from my stool. "I'm Audrey. Roz's niece." A low murmur fills the pub. At least some of them must be locals who had known my aunt to find any of this interesting.

"My mother, and the inn's creator of gastronomical delights, Naomi Greene," Kellen says.

"In plain words, I'm the cook," she says. "Roslyn mentioned you to me several times."

"She did?" I'm in shock that Roz thought of me much at all, even before she got sick.

"Oh yes, she wanted to have you out here to visit, maybe to stay a spell," Naomi tells me. "Said you still hadn't found a place to call home."

"I—" Unbidden, tears rise to my eyes, and I stare up at the ceiling, willing them to recede.

"Ma, maybe you and Audrey can talk about Roslyn

later," Kellen says. He rests his hands on the broad straps of my tank top, fingers a bare millimeter from skimming my skin, a gesture that's comforting without feeling too familiar. "Audrey's hungry. Can you fix her up a plate?"

Naomi nods. "We'll chat another time, child. I'm sorry to meet you under such sad circumstances, but welcome to Soberly all the same. I'll have some food whipped up for you in a heartbeat." She disappears into the kitchen, and Kellen steers me back to my stool before slipping back behind the bar. He hands me a cocktail napkin, but I've regained my composure and use it to blot up the rings of condensation my glass has left on the bar top instead. Wordlessly, the gin and tonic Kellen offered me earlier appears in front of my downcast eyes. I'm thinking about my aunt, a woman who, by all accounts, barely knew me, yet seemed to have a plan for me—a plan she hoped would include her and this place. I wish desperately for the chance to have one more conversation with her, to get to know her as an adult, to see if that same bond we'd shared when I was young could be rekindled.

With a sigh, I decide that today would be a good day to take up daytime drinking and pick up the G&T. The first mouthful makes my eyes water, but I manage to swallow it back without choking. Once I stir it up a bit and squeeze the lime wedge into the glass, the second sip goes down easier.

"It's a double," Kellen says. "You looked like you needed it."

"Thanks. I did."

"So, you're homeless?"

I shoot him a wry half-smile. "No, I just move

around a lot. I'm a consulting historian, and most of my contracts are three to six months long."

"And what does a consulting historian do?" Kellen slices lemons as he talks, but his eyes never leave my face.

"Mostly research. I specialize in American history, particularly in smaller places like this. I might write up a history for a town's centennial, for example, or compile a detailed account of a particular historical event. My last contract was for a potter's guild, summarizing the history of pottery in the Southwest. I spend a lot of time in library archives and church basements, poring over musty old papers."

"Seems like it would be hard to put down roots."

"I'm not really a put down roots sort of person. Never have been." I stir the remainder of my drink with the straw as I speak. That's a bit of an understatement. More than nine months in one place, a year at the most, and the soles of my feet start to itch with the need to move on.

"Sounds like you just haven't found the right place yet."

There's no way to reply but with a shrug. Maybe I haven't. I'm fine if I never do. I'd never felt the draw of 'home' in my life—the desire to establish myself somewhere.

"Hey, no pressure, Audrey. I'm just saying it would be nice to get to know you a little. Roslyn must have believed there might be something here for you."

"The last time I saw her, I was twelve. I genuinely don't know what I'm doing here." *This is the part where the lonely traveler dumps all their troubles on the friendly bartender*. No doubt Kellen's met hundreds of people like me, with no one else to talk to, recounting their boring problems he couldn't care less about. I couldn't stand being in his shoes, and one of the best parts of being a historian was the fact that I seldom had to talk to people. Everyone I was interested in was dead.

"Here you go, child." Naomi sets an enormous plate in front of me. Two thick pieces of battered fish and potatoes so freshly fried I can still see the glisten of oil on them. That was the second time she'd called me child, a term that should have made me bristle and instinctively want to defend my adulthood. Coming from her, however, it felt like a term of affection. "Let the woman eat, Kellen," she adds. "Come help me in the kitchen for a spell, hmm? Just pop your head through the door if you need anything," she says to me and pulls Kellen away by the elbow. As he reaches the end of the bar he slides a bottle of ketchup in my direction, and I catch it right before it hits my plate.

"Thanks," I say around a mouthful of fish and homemade tartar sauce.

"Does Cora know you're here?" he asks, resisting his mother's pull for a moment. My mind registers a blank for a moment. *Roz's wife.* I shake my head.

"She's on the inn side. Want me to ring her and tell her to come over?"

"No." *A thousand times no.* "I'll go over when I'm done eating."

My trepidation must have shown on my face because he shakes himself free of Naomi's grip and resumes his position across the bar from me.

"Hey. It'll be fine, Audrey. Chin up. Don't even think

about sneaking away without saying goodbye, okay?" He covers my hand with his and gives it a squeeze.

He paced back and forth outside the door, wanting to stop his ears against the cries coming from within, but not as much as he wanted to burst through it and comfort his wife. The birthing room was no place for a man, the midwife had insisted. He would do anything to take Anna's pain away, to shoulder the burden for himself. She was so small, but she had the strongest will of anyone he knew.

Her screams tapered off, and he wondered if it was done and the child was here.

"Anna," the sharp voice of the midwife said. "Anna, open your eyes."

Something wasn't right. Despite the midwife's edict that he remain outside, he ran into the room, only to stop short just inside the door. The bed was covered with blood, and his wife lay reclining in the midst of it, her face as white as the sheets.

"The bleeding won't stop," the midwife said as she threw a wad of bright red bandages aside, replacing it with a fresh compress that soaked through in seconds.

"Anna?" he whispered. Her eyes fluttered open briefly but fell shut without any sign she had recognized him. "I'll go for the doctor," he told the midwife. It was only half an hour's hard ride to town.

"There isn't—it's too late for the doctor." Her words knocked the air out of his lungs.

"And the child?" The words sounded like they were coming from another man's mouth, someone far away.

The midwife said nothing, just pulled a clean sheet up over Anna's legs and stepped back.

"Anna..." he reached for her hand, folded it into his own. "Anna, don't leave me. Please, I need you. Don't leave me behind." She opened her eyes then, those warm brown eyes that had captivated him ever since they were schoolchildren together.

"Allen," she said, and the sides of her mouth turned up in a faint smile. "My love." Her fingers squeezed his and he smiled back, certain that she would be fine, she was poorly but she would fight through this. There would be more children. They were meant to spend the rest of their lives together. Her eyes flickered shut again, and her chest, which had been rising and falling rapidly, stilled. His own throat locked, and the room closed in on him, a darkness that threatened to extinguish everything around him.

"No, Anna, wait," he wailed, falling to his knees by the side of the bed, clutching her hand like a lifeline.

2

I can see into the past. Every human body, from the moment of their birth to their last breath, carries within them the memories of lives lived before, something that once existed in another time and will live on again in a new body when this one expires. The religious call it the soul. The non-believers call it consciousness. I call it curious, and when my flesh presses another's, I get a glimpse of it.

I wasn't born with the ability. When I was fourteen, I got sick with what I first assumed was the flu—high fever, body aches, especially my head. My father promised the Lord would heal me if I prayed hard enough. So, I prayed. Oh, how I prayed. I prayed until I screamed, and my mother screamed back for me to shut up because she couldn't hear herself think. I remember begging for the doctor and being called a filthy sinner. If I wanted to be delivered from my suffering, I had to repent and ask to be saved.

Some days later I woke up in the hospital. A concerned congregant at my father's church had stopped by to pray for me and, possessing the barest shred of common sense my parents were missing, called the ambulance.

Bacterial meningitis, they told me. Antibiotics would have cured me days earlier. As it was, I was lucky to be alive, although they feared there could be irreversible neurological damage. Rigorous testing failed to turn up any evidence of harm, however. My father, in a true bout of hypocrisy, called it a miracle and claimed that the parishioner had been sent by Jesus to save me. My mother never came to visit me once. Sick daughters were no competition for daytime TV and boxed wine. I left the hospital three weeks later with a clean bill of health and a standing monthly appointment with a social worker to check on my welfare.

What failed to show up on the scans and in the cognitive tests were the visions. I never was sure if it was the infection that caused them, damage from the fever, or something I brought back from the days when I'd been on the threshold of death's door. Every time a nurse held my arm to help me to the bathroom, or a doctor took my pulse, a short scene unfolded in my head of times long ago and places far away. Usually, they were only about half a minute long. The rational part of my mind wrote them off as the fantasies of a bored teenager stuck in a hospital bed. Except I couldn't make them stop. They flooded my mind against my will, every time I touched another person, and while they did no harm, nor were they useful.

There was a time when the belief that I must be delusional almost drove me to suicide. I did everything I could to prevent people from touching me so I wouldn't have these scenes forced upon me. Then, I found them. My parents, or who they had once been, according to the visions I'd collected of them from the past, which over time revealed their names, the village where they'd resided, and other clues which made me believe they might have really existed. Tracing one's roots was all the rage, and an online genealogy site took less than four clicks and twenty bucks to come back with a positive result. Friedrich Bauer, Sr. and Jr., a father and son who lived in the mid-1700s in a small town in northern Germany. They had been real. I never spoke a word of it to them, even when my fears of mental instability passed. A man who worshipped the Bible and a woman who worshipped Franzia would never believe me.

Over time, I found others, and learned that the energy making up our consciousness seeks out others it has been close to, again and again. We don't remember these past iterations of ourselves, but it's almost certain that the people we are closest to will have been with us through our lifetimes in some role or another. My parents, for example, were related by blood when their energies co-existed in that small German village. Others might be neighbors in one era, and siblings in the next. Gender doesn't seem to matter, nor does age. We find each other and love each other in whatever way best suits the bodies we are born into, as friends, family, or lovers.

There are other rules to the visions. I never see the same scene twice, and I am often given scenes from different lifetimes on successive contacts, rather than a series all from the same time and place. Visions usually correspond to major life events or something that parallels what's going on in the present. Curiously, I've never encountered anyone who offered me visions of more than six separate past lives lived. One of my most pressing unanswered questions is what happens after the seventh and present life meets its end. Does that consciousness move on to something else? Do souls not have the capacity to carry the memory of more lives than that? I'm not sure I'll ever know.

One thing that's been clear since the beginning is that people often follow the same path throughout their lives. Personality traits are frequently the same, both positive and negative. Just as we are drawn to the same consciousnesses, time and time again, so do we find ourselves drawn toward the same passions, even if they manifest in different ways.

If you find yourself unable to control what you eat and are obsessed with consuming as much food as possible, even at the expense of your health, I know it's because two lifetimes ago, you starved to death in a famine the preacher said was one of the seven signs of the apocalypse. In fact, I'm half-convinced the obesity epidemic in the Western world is caused by the hard times many people suffered in the past as much as it is by the fast-food culture. Or when you turn up on the doorstep of the shelter seeking sanctuary, battered and broken, only to return to the man who beat you, a simple handshake tells me it's because, in some distant age, your father instilled in you the deep belief that the best way for a man to discipline a woman is with his fists.

I'm also sorry to say if you consistently wind up trusting fools in this lifetime, you're probably going to do it in the next one, too. The end result might not be the same, but the tendency behind it is, as many times as not.

As for my own past? What sorts of lives have I lived throughout the centuries? I have yet to find out. I don't see any visions when I touch myself, and I've never been able to pick out anyone who might have been me through contact with others. Years ago, I started writing down all the details of my visions in a spiral-bound notebook, trying to find my own past amongst the people I encountered. I have close to a dozen notebooks filled with anecdotes, historical details, names, and descriptions, but I'm still no closer than the first day I woke up from the fever. In that sense, Roz might have been right—I still haven't found my home, the people whose essences I'm connected to on a deeper level. I hope I know them when we meet, just to relieve myself of the burden of seeking them.

I keep searching in the visions of other people's lives for someone with an interest in the past, someone who is interested in people despite feeling disconnected from them. Someone who is different, but longs to be the same. Someone who hasn't yet found their home.

3

I'm not in the mood for any more scenes from the past after Kellen's jarring vision, and I pull my arms back into my zip-up hoodie and stuff my hands deep into my pockets, despite the heat. I would have preferred to just slip out of the pub without a word but honored my promise to say goodbye to both him and Naomi by popping my head into the kitchen and giving a brief wave. People who had suffered a devastating loss in a past life usually clung tightly to their loved ones in the present, I've learned. Is that why he chooses to work in the same place as his mother? Sometimes visions create more questions than they answer.

I'm sure there's probably a path through the back of the pub leading to the inn side, but I step out the same door I entered instead and walk under the awning to the front entrance. A few seagulls barely make way for me as I pass, the prize of half a hot dog bun more important than whatever threat I might pose. Their squawks ring in my ears as the distance between the door and myself narrows. Suddenly I'm lightheaded, feeling the effects of the gin I'd gulped down combined with all the sun from the morning. I don't remember opening the door, but a blast of air conditioning revives me somewhat, and I'm inside before I can change my mind.

I was expecting your typical antiseptic hotel lobby, heavy on the marble, light on the brass, and inoffensively decorated in neutral shades. Instead, as the sound of the bell above the door fades, I find myself standing across from a spinet desk that might have come over with the Mayflower, judging from the way the corners are worn and the scars marring the carved legs. It's a beautiful piece, and my fingers ache to run along its edges to try and absorb some of its history. I've often wished I could discover the past from objects the same way I can from people.

While the desk is the oldest piece, the rest of the room is similarly furnished with well-cared-for antiques that evoke a Victorian style. Books stacked on spindle-legged end tables invite guests and visitors to relax on the brightly upholstered divan and lose themselves in a story. The artwork and curios continue the maritime theme found in the pub in a more subdued fashion. The smell of well-oiled furniture and hardbound books is a familiar comfort. It reminds me of some of the ancient libraries I've visited—Oxford, Trinity. Besides the paperbacks, the only modern concession is the sleek silver laptop with its glowing white logo sitting on the desk. I find myself smiling as I take in the welcoming atmosphere. This feels more like the Roz I knew.

A woman I peg to be in her mid-forties pops her head through the doorway behind the desk.

"Hello, dear, have a seat. I'll be with you in a flash." She disappears as quickly as she materializes, but not before I take note of her red-rimmed eyes, and the haphazard way her gray-streaked hair is fastened into a high bun. I nod, even though she can't see me, slip out of my hoodie, and settle onto the couch. This must be Roz's wife. When she emerges fully a couple minutes later, her hair is subdued into a tidier knot, and she has fresh concealer under her eyes.

"Now, what I can I do for you?" she asks as she settles into the high-back chair behind the desk.

"Are you Cora Veracruz?" She nods. "I'm Audrey Eames. Roz's niece." Her friendly expression slips slightly, her lips thinning into a less sincere smile. "I came as soon as I heard—the lawyer said he had a difficult time tracking me down because I'd moved. I'm so sorry for your loss. I wish I could have come sooner. I had no idea Roz was...sick."

"We didn't either until the headache started a few weeks ago. I took her to the hospital to have it checked out, and she never went home again."

"I'm sorry. That must have been terrible." We fall into an uneasy silence, looking at anything except each other. "How long were you married for?" I ask finally, at a loss for what else to say.

"We never got the chance to have a ceremony." Cora fiddles with the desk's drawers, moving pens in and out of them. "It was important to Roz that we wait until the federal court case was settled. She wanted our marriage to be legal all across the country. We'd planned on holding it later this summer."

My mouth quirks. "That sounds like her, although it was animal rights she was passionate about when she was younger. She used to tell me that as soon as she could get the money together, she was going to join Greenpeace or one of those anti-whaling ships. I don't think she ever did."

"When was the last time you saw her?" The unspoken question is clear from Cora's tone. *Why you?*

"When I was twelve. She came and stayed with us for a few days. Our house was small, so she had to share my room. She was incredibly patient with my girlish infatuation with her, and we stayed up for hours whispering in the dark about everything under the sun. I cried for hours when she left, it felt like I was losing my best friend even though she was eleven years older than me. She promised me when she was older, she'd come back for me, and we'd go off and have adventures together." The memory makes me smile and feel sad all at the same time. Roz had never come back for me. Our paths never crossed again, even though I lived like a nomad and had been as close as Seattle a couple years ago. She would have been in Soberly then, just a few hours' drive away, and if I'd known I would have definitely found the time to come visit. Maybe we could have rekindled that connection again. Maybe she'd just been humoring me the entire time, and my memories of her visit were tinted by the youthful naiveté that made me believe I truly was as important to her as she had been to me. Yet she'd brought me here now, all these years later, to hand over what must have been her most prized possession, her labor of love. It didn't make sense.

"Well." My disclosure hasn't answered what Cora wants to know.

"Did she—did Roz tell you what...why I'm here?"

"Not exactly." Cora's mouth thins into a frown, and her eyebrows pull together, revealing a deep vertical line in her forehead. "Only that it had always been her intention the inn should be hers and yours together. She decided all this after she got the diagnosis and knew there weren't any treatment options for her. I believe she wrote you a letter. It's with her attorney, along with all the paperwork to complete the transfer of ownership." Cora glances at the door behind me. I know a dismissal when I see one. My hopes that we might have any type of familial relationship start to fade.

"William Blackmoor. He was the one who notified me. Where can I find him?"

"It's not a big town, Audrey. His office is easy enough to find." She's tapping away on the laptop now, frowning at whatever she's reading. Her frigidness roots me in place, and I can't hold back the flinch. The breeze being circulated by the portable air conditioner humming in the window isn't the coldest thing in the room by far.

"One block north and one street over, on Lighthouse," she concedes, still not looking up from the screen.

"Look, I know you must be angry at me. You're probably almost as confused as I am. Maybe you feel betrayed—I think I would. Honestly, I don't want this.

Even if Roz was still here—this isn't my thing. I like my work. I'm not looking to make any big changes in my life, and I don't know the first thing about running an inn. If she'd gotten in touch with me before she—when she was making these plans, I would have told her to choose somebody else. I would have said it should go to you because you must have as much of your heart and soul in this place as she did."

Would you? Would you have refused her dying wish?

Yes, I argue. *I'd help her see what a crazy idea this is. Remind her it would hurt the people she was leaving behind.*

"Well." There's a lot of weight in the word, just like there was when she uttered it earlier. The creases in her forehead soften a fraction. "Maybe we can work something out then. Find a solution that makes everyone happy."

"That's all I want, honestly." I heave my canvas duffel onto my shoulder and turn to go. "I'm going to go talk to the lawyer and get it all sorted out."

"I'm sorry we had to meet under these circumstances." It's a peace offering, and I acknowledge it with a nod. "You have the look of her, you know. Not so much in your features, but in the way you smile, and the way I can see you taking in everything around you, filing it away for later. Roz was always one for the unusual details most other people don't notice. I think I can see why she liked you." Cora rises from the desk to show me out, and while her back is still ramrod straight, the smile on her face is the first genuine one I've seen from her.

"Thank you," I say. "That means a lot to me. I wish I'd had a chance to know her better, once I was older." A blast of heat slaps me in the face as I open the door.

"Make sure you get some aloe on this burn, the sooner the better," she says as she squeezes my arm just above the elbow. "It's shaping up to be a nasty one." The contact is over long before the vision is.

REGRESS

"Kolya, open the door, or we'll break it down."

He stood just on the other side of the thick beams, shivering. The meager heat of the hearth didn't reach this far, and they had precious little to burn. Only when night fell did they light it at all, and just long enough to heat the stones they placed under the blankets of their straw-tick bed. The rest of the time they spent wearing all they could layer on, wrapped in blankets and stamping their feet for warmth.

"My friends, there is no need for that," he said as he scanned the room, looking for any evidence, any clues that would give away the secret he kept. He must remember not to look at the false wall or the two floorboards in the corner that when lifted would reveal a small chamber. He must remember to look as

frightened and desperate as they no doubt were to be threatening violence upon him. His wife, Slava, sat in one of the single-room home's two chairs, her eyes wide with fear. He prayed she would not give them away, either, but he knew she would hold her tongue at least.

"This is your last chance, Kolya."

He forced himself to sound meek. "I'm only frightened, Evgeni. You are my neighbor, my friend. I do not know what I have done to anger you so. You have always been welcome in my home, and are welcome still if only you will assure me that you will not harm me."

"No harm will come to you if you have done nothing to earn it. Now open the door."

"I will, my friend. I will." He lifted the beam barring it and leaned it against the table, where he could grab it easily if he needed a weapon. Hunching forward, trying to make himself look small, he pulled open the door to face the three men on his doorstep. They all held makeshift weapons, and Evgeni's pitchfork looked the most lethal. Surely, he meant only to threaten. "Evgeni, Vadim, Pavel, please come in. Warm yourselves at my fire, small though it may be." He stepped aside and fought the urge to usher the men quickly in so he could keep what little heat was in the home from escaping. The cruel wind cut through his sweater, and this time when he shivered and clutched his arms around himself it was not an act. Always keeping the bar within arm's reach, he pushed the door shut once the three men trooped inside, their boots caked thick with snow none of them bothered to stamp off. At least it was now cold

enough that the clumps they left behind did not begin to melt, and he would be able to sweep them out later.

"We are not here to visit," Evgeni said as he pulled open the drawers of the wooden hutch, inspecting each one to the very back. The hutch would be the next thing they would have to burn. They had been feeding bits of their lives to the fire for the past month, ever since the firewood had run out, and the nearly-empty house was proof of the hardship they had endured and were still enduring. Slava said nothing, only looked miserable, as she was perpetually wont to do. In the end, Pavel's search turned up two potatoes and a few cabbage leaves wrapped around them, all from this week's ration.

"I assure you, my friends, I have nothing to hide. Just look about you. We have next to nothing." None of the men replied. Vadim was busy sifting through the quilts on the bed, stripping them off one at a time. Finally, he beat the straw-tick mattress with his hands, feeling each part of it. Kolya hoped he didn't cut into it and dump its contents, not because it hid anything, but because it would make an ungodly mess and would take most of the night for Slava to stitch up again. Vadim seemed satisfied with his cursory inspection, however.

There was precious else to search. The table held no drawers or compartments, and everything else had been lost in the service of fighting off the cold. Then Evgeni did what Kolya hoped least he would do—he turned to Slava.

"Stand, woman." Slava's eyes darted to Kolya, becoming impossibly wider. He met them with his own and nodded, a single jerk of his chin. Would they beat the truth out of her? "Shake out your skirts and turn out your pockets." Kolya fought back a sigh of relief, forced himself instead to maintain the mask of fear on his face. Evgeni thought Slava concealed their secret.

Slava obeyed wordlessly, even lifting her skirts above her knees, revealing her rough gray stockings, to show she held nothing beneath them.

"Evgeni, my friend," Kolya said, appealing to his neighbor. "Can't you see we're just as hungry and desperate as everyone else? We are not hiding anything. We have nothing to hide. You have seen with your own eyes. Check the shed. Check the chicken coop. You will find nothing in there either." Kolya knew they already had—it was the light of their torch spotted through the window that had given him the time to make sure all was concealed. He would have to be more careful from now on, lest there was another inspection in the future. "Why are you here, my friends? What have I done to earn your mistrust?"

"There was garlic on your breath yesterday. I smelled it myself, as did others. There has not been garlic in the rations in two months."

Inwardly, Kolya cursed Slava for insisting they flavor the soup. He could not deny it when so many people had detected the pungent scent. He needed to think quickly to pacify the men. "I gave all my food stores, all my grain, everything we had to the town council, just as you did, just as we all did," he said. "Two days ago, Slava was digging in the garden, hoping to find a potato or a parsnip we might have missed last autumn when she turned up a small head of garlic. It was half-rotten, only four small cloves, that we thought there was no point in adding it to the rations since it could never be divided up amongst us all. Perhaps that was wrong, but I was weak, and I gave two of the cloves to her and kept two for myself. We ate them raw. That's all it was, my friends. Forgive me, I should have handed it in." He bowed his head as though in shame.

Evgeni mulled this explanation over. Kolya and Slava had been careful not to eat too much from their secret store, lest they gave themselves away by remaining too fat as everyone else in their small village, locked in by a winter that seemed as though it would never end, starved. Besides, who knew if this winter would ever end? They needed to stretch their own supplies as far as they could. When the town council elders had declared that everyone must pool what food remained amongst them to ensure everyone received the same amount, Kolya had naturally held a portion back. Why should his hard work go to feed someone lazier or with less foresight? Why should he suffer so others may live? He built the false wall to store the grain, and the rough hole below the floor to house the vegetables, the dried fruits, the sacks of sugar and flour and the precious wheels of cheese, of which he still had almost one complete round left. They had both toiled hard to provide for themselves, and he would be damned if he saw it go to another while he himself starved.

"I apologize, Kolya," Evgeni said finally. "You can see how we had the right to be suspicious."

"Of course, my friend," Kolya replied. "There is

no harm done. Tell me, is it true Yegor snared a hare today?" All smiles now, a hopeful look on his face.

"Yes. A small one. The council made a stew from it for the children."

"That's wonderful. As it should be. We must protect the children above all." Kolya nodded vigorously as he spoke, hoping to convince the men he believed the sentiment.

"Goodnight, Kolya, Slava," Evgeni said, and he and the other two left without another word, although Pavel, his confidant, and sometime gambling partner, gave him a small shrug of apology. Once the door was barred again, and he could no longer hear the footsteps crunching through the snow, he allowed himself to relax and heaved a sigh of relief, shooting Slava an accusatory glare for getting them into the predicament in the first place. She stared at him mournfully and began piling the quilts back on the bed.

4

I walk down the street on auto-pilot, thankful the town is quiet enough I don't have to worry about dodging traffic or other pedestrians. I'm almost all the way to the lawyer's office before the vision finishes playing itself out in my head. It's definitely one of the longer ones I've had, and its tone disturbs me. I would not allow myself to jump to conclusions and assume that because she once had held something back in a past life, Cora was doing the same again. Not every event from history played out again to the letter. Maybe her spirit had recalled those events because it had felt similarly threatened by my appearance.

Lighthouse Street appears to serve as Soberly's main drag if such a small town could be said to have one. It's lined on both sides with brightly painted storefronts, their facades all meticulously maintained to reflect settlement times. Awnings provide intervals of shade along the sidewalk, and each shop has a wooden sign, all in the same style, announcing its name and trade. There's the requisite souvenir shop, an ice cream parlor, a cafe with a few round tables and folding chairs set out in front of it, an antique store, and a place selling beachwear, but nothing that would indicate a lawyer or any type of offices at all.

Naturally, I pick the antique shop to inquire. It draws me like a magnet. One never knows what hidden gems you'll find amongst the ships in bottles and endless incomplete sets of china.

A bell jingles above my head as I step inside. A woman maybe five years older than me sits behind the glass counter, which is stuffed full of costume jewelry. There's a wooden Indian to my immediate right, and long rows of shelves crammed full of old telephones, cameras, mason jars, leather-bound books, and all sorts of other detritus brought forth from the cellars of the locals over the years. All overpriced, no doubt.

"Can you tell me where I can find the offices of William Blackmoor?" I ask, telling myself this is not the time to get lost in a treasure hunt. My eyes roam the shelves almost compulsively, taking in the stock.

"You *must* be the new owner of the inn." The woman's voice goes up half an octave, and a smile breaks out on her face. "I heard you were here."

"Umm, what?" I drag my gaze away from the merchandise and toward her. How the hell did she find that out so fast?

"Oh, shit. I mean, my condolences. Roslyn was family of yours, wasn't she?" The woman looks chagrined.

"Yes, my aunt. How did you know?"

"Linda was eating lunch in the pub, and she texted Marnie next door at the pharmacy, who came over to tell me not five minutes ago. It only makes sense that you'd have to speak to Roslyn's lawyer about the will and everything. You're the most exciting thing to happen to this one-horse town since they found Marnie's daughter drunk, passed out in the trough outside Rooster's a couple months ago. Only *fourteen* years old."

"What trough? Who's Rooster?" My head is spinning, trying to follow this conversation.

"The general store around the corner, on Driftwood. It has a trough from when people used to tie their horses up outside. Thankfully, they keep it empty now, otherwise Kenzie would've drowned."

"Right." I have no idea what to make of any of this information, only that it has nothing to do with my mission. This Kenzie must be grateful she's no longer the most interesting person in Soberly. "Mr. Blackmoor's offices?" I've spied what I think is an emerald-green inkwell on one of the shelves, tucked in amongst a hodgepodge of old tonic and spice bottles, each worth no more than a couple bucks each. *Dammit.* If it's hand-blown, as I suspect it is from its imperfect shape, it could be worth a few hundred dollars. Trust treasure to find me precisely when I didn't want it. I like inkwells. They're small, which makes them easy to collect for someone who moves often and they come in an endless number of designs. I have one in a similar octagonal shape in cobalt blue. Ruthlessly I turn my eyes away. *Not today.*

"Bill's right across the street, the door next to the cafe's entrance is his. His office is upstairs, but don't rush out so fast. I didn't even get your name. I'm Sheena."

The Ramones start running unbidden through my head. "Audrey," I reply. This Sheena is the furthest thing from a punk rocker—her pin-straight blonde hair is cut in a reverse bob, and her style falls somewhere in the Anthropologie range. Sheena's behind the counter, and there's enough distance between us that I don't offer my hand to shake, nor does she. I'm still sifting through the details of the vision I received from Cora, and I don't feel like adding to the stew of thoughts in my head. "I have an appointment so I do have to go, but I'm sure I'll see you soon. It seems like that sort of town." I smile to take the sting out of my wry tone and ask silent forgiveness for the white lie. I want to get this business of the inn's ownership settled and read the letter Roz left to me.

"It pretty well is, but we're good people. I'm glad to meet you for myself."

"Nice to meet you too." I pause as I step over the threshold, and with an inward sigh, turn back. "Hey Sheena, know that green inkwell you've got in with the other glass on the shelf there?" She nods. "Do a bit more research on it. You can get a couple hundred bucks on eBay if it's in good condition, easy."

"Seriously? How do you know that? Mr. Maxwell brought it in with a bunch of other bottles he found when he ripped up his front porch a couple weeks ago. I didn't think it was anything special. I gave him five bucks for it, and I thought I was being generous."

"I'm a historian. Old stuff is what I know."

"You come back some night and tell me what else I'm missing, and I'll provide all the wine and fried clams you can handle," she calls after me. I doubt I'll be in town long enough to take her up on her offer, but I don't want to sound rude.

"It's a deal," I tell her.

I could see how a person might miss the office of W. Blackmoor, Barrister. The letters stenciled on the plain frame door were as unobtrusive as they come. With Sheena's directions, however, I spot it immediately and make my way up the stuffy stairs, where I'm met with another door. A deep, sonorous voice calls for me to come in when I knock.

"Mr. Blackmoor?" I ask the white-haired man sitting at the desk facing me as I step inside the office. He looks like a less-craggy version of Clint Eastwood, a little rounder in the face and body, but with the same piercing blue eyes and shrewd look. The sunlight streaming through the lead-paned windows illuminate his white hair into a halo around his head. "I'm Audrey Eames. We spoke on the phone a few days ago."

"Audrey, very pleased to meet you. Call me Bill." Once the introductions are out of the way and I'm seated across from him, he pulls a manila folder out of a drawer and sets it in front of him. "Now, as I said, Roslyn left you the inn and its assets, barring a few personal effects. She and I drafted her last will and testament shortly after she received her diagnosis. She also asked me to act as her estate's executor." I nod. "I have a copy of her will here for you to review."

I scan the single sheet he hands over to me. Her share in the house they owned, along with her personal assets, she had left to Cora, who was also the sole beneficiary of a healthy life insurance policy. Then next paragraph:

To my niece, Audrey Isobel Eames, I leave my business, the Soberly Inn and Public House, as well as its contents and assets, excepting those listed below. It is my wish that my niece take over the management and day-to-day operations of the Inn.

Below is a short list of a few items Roz says she wants returned to Cora, including a clock Cora gave her and a few photographs, then signatures and the notary's mark. Nothing that explains her reasoning at all. I look up at Bill doubtfully.

"This is pretty short on details," I say. "Did Roz tell you why she wanted me to move halfway across the country, give up my career, and become an innkeeper?"

"No, she didn't, but she was adamant that you do," he replies.

"Was she..." I pinch the bridge of my nose between my finger and thumb. There's no delicate way to put my question. "Was she competent when she made this will? I know with some types of tumors a person's mental faculties can be affected. I mean, Roz never mentioned anything about this to me, and she didn't try and get in touch before she...passed. It's taken me completely by surprise."

"I believe she was, and her doctors were in agreement as well," he says. "I questioned her about this choice since Cora is so involved in the operations of the inn. I was surprised to learn they didn't own it jointly, to be honest. She didn't tell me why she was leaving the inn to you, but I suspect this might answer some of your questions." He pulls a sealed envelope out of the folder and hands it to me. *For Audrey,* it says. It feels thick, promising several pages inside. I tear it open with shaking hands. As expected, inside are five or six folded sheets, and I recognize the handwriting from the occasional Christmas cards that managed to find their way to me over the years. The first page only has a few lines.

Before you read the rest of this letter, I want you to go back to the inn. Go up to my office on the second floor, sit out on the balcony, then finish it.

I know you're impatient, and probably even a little pissed at me for bringing you here, but I mean it. This is important. Please do this one thing for me.

Love,

Roz

For a second I'm tempted to flip the page and keep reading. Roz is right—I am a little pissed at her for dragging me all this way, only to be sent on a treasure hunt all over town. I close my eyes, letting my mind wrestle with my heart for a moment.

"Go on, Audrey," Bill says, interrupting my mental war. He must be in on the plan. "I'll be here when you're finished."

A wry sniff escapes me. "All right then. See you soon." I fold up the letter, stuff it into my back pocket, and make my way back into the street. Suddenly I hate everything about Soberly, from its stupid quaint tourist-bait shops to the fact that there isn't a single Starbucks within ten miles. More than anything, I hate the dumb fucking Soberly Inn and Public House. I hate it for existing, for trapping my aunt here with its tacky coastal charms when she should have done bigger things with her life. I kick an empty soda cup into the street with a fury it didn't deserve. *Maybe if she'd lived somewhere that had modern amenities, her cancer might have been discovered before it was too late.* Fuming at the injustice of her early demise and my own predicament resulting from it, I make my way back to the inn. Cora peers at me over her half-moon glasses as I wrench the door open so hard the glass panes rattle.

"That was quick," she says.

"We didn't even get started." I throw the page down in front of her. Cora reads it over with a raised brow.

"Roz always had a flair for the dramatic. Her office is right up this way. I'll show you." She leads me through the same door she first appeared through, into a more utilitarian office, dominated by filing cabinets and cork boards with everything from staff schedules to tidal charts tacked to them.

"She's trying to persuade me to stay," I say as Cora unlocks a door and makes her way up the wooden staircase, each tread creaking under her weight.

"I know," she replies. "The view from her balcony was her favorite. It was what persuaded her to buy the inn years ago—the prospect of getting to see it every day. She always said you couldn't call what she did work when you got to spend your time looking out over the ocean from a spot like that."

"She should have picked Hawaii," I grumble. "Then I might consider it." Cora offers me a snort that might be her idea of laughter.

At the top of the stairs is a room that's part study,

part sitting room, with bookshelves along one wall, a sturdy-looking oak desk, couch, and a small kitchenette in one corner.

"Was this a guest room once?" I ask. Cora shakes her head.

"The previous owner's living quarters. It has quick access to the entry, for latecomers or any guests who required assistance after hours. Neither of us liked the idea of being woken up in the middle of the night, so we hired a night desk person, and Roz turned the space into her personal office." She nods in the direction of a set of double French doors. "Out there."

"Thanks." Cora's already halfway down the stairs. I could see how it had pained her to be in this room from the way she'd stayed close to the door, keeping her gaze away from the personal effects scattered about. A gourmet magazine had been left open on the couch. A dirty coffee mug, complete with lipstick stain, sitting on the desk. For all I knew, it was the first time she'd been up here since Roz's death.

I stubbornly avoid looking out at the sea as I settle into one of the Adirondack chairs. The sun is still high enough in the sky that I'm protected from its glare, but the sunsets must be spectacular from this vantage point. *Shit.* I'd been looking without meaning to.

Roz was right: the view was amazing. I can see for a couple miles in each direction. It's a perfect day for the beach, with the sunlight dancing like Fourth of July sparklers on the waves as they roll in toward the sand. Over the dunes toward the north, I can barely see a lighthouse perched on a rocky outcropping. Yep, as far as ocean views go, this one was pretty much perfect.

Dammit, Roz.

I've half-crumpled the letter in my too-tight fist, and there are faint marks left behind from my sweat. I take a moment to smooth the pages out on my lap and take a couple of deep breaths before focusing on the hand-written words.

Dear Aud,

It only takes two words for my eyes to well up. In my early school years, I'd always been taunted by kids calling me Odd, Oddball, or from one particularly creative jackass, Odd-pee, which was always followed by a *psss* sound, or a lunge for my crotch. To Roz, being called odd was never a slur. Odd was a badge you wore with pride, and when she affectionately shortened my name, it didn't feel like an insult.

"Shit, shit, shit," I say to the gulls circling lazily above, as the tears roll down my cheeks. It's the first time the impact Roz had on my childhood, mixed with the finality of her death, has really hit me, and suddenly I'm not mad at her anymore. With a couple of shaky breaths, I turn back to the letter.

Dear Aud,

Let me start by saying, it wasn't supposed to turn out this way. I never thought I'd die so young, and especially not when everything started coming together. No one does, right? This place—the town, the inn, the people—all of it is something I never knew I was looking for until I found it. It's so, so perfect, except for one thing missing. That was you.

I know I told you when you were young that

I'd come back for you, and we'd go on adventures together. I remember using those exact words. I wasn't just paying lip service—I meant it, but you know how it goes. Shit gets in the way, and you lose track of time. I always figured time was something I had plenty of. For years, I didn't really have anything of value to offer. I know you've always taken care of yourself—God, with your mother dead drunk half the time, and my brother's zealotry, what other choice did you have? I don't think you've found your way yet, despite your success with your career and the life you've made for yourself. You're me, ten years ago, searching for something you know you need, but can't identify.

The plan was supposed to be that once I'd turned the inn around and paid off my debts, I'd lure you here for a visit. In the stories I've created in my head, you'd fall in love with the place instantly. But the reality is I know you'd need some convincing. Probably a lot. I had all sorts of schemes. For starters, the history of the Oregon coast, and Soberly in particular, is fascinating and more than a bit mysterious. You could spend the rest of your career documenting the stories of the pirates, smugglers, native tribes, and early settlers. What I wanted was for us to run this inn together, as partners and co-owners. To give you the roots, the family, that you've never really had.

You see, things are going fine here, well, even. The inn is holding its own amongst all the other places like it along the coast. I could say the same about myself. I'm happy with the life I've made. Most days, I find it hard to understand how I got so lucky.

But. (there's always a 'but,' isn't there?)

I'm a bit selfish. Well isn't enough. Happy isn't enough. You—your passion for the past, your ability to find those interesting details that make history come alive (I've read every article and paper of yours I can get my hands on, you know) could make the inn one of a kind, something authentic, a testament to bygone days. You could fill the part of me that's missing my family, wanting to finally fulfill the promise I made eighteen years ago. As much as I think this place is what you need, having you here is what I need too.

Of course, that's all gone to shit. Suddenly I'm out of time and have to come up with some half-assed Plan B instead. So, here you go, Aud. The keys to the rest of your life, if you'll take them. I really, really hope you do. I'm not going to try and make bargains or set time limits. I'm not even going to pull the Dying Woman's Last Wish card. If I'm right, I won't need to, and this place will weave its way into your heart the way it did mine. If I'm wrong, know that I still love you, and always have. You're the closest thing to a little sister I've ever had, and if there's any sort of afterlife, I'm looking out for you. The decision is entirely yours to make, Aud. You know yourself best.

Seriously though, this view. Doesn't it make you feel like you could step over the side and fly like one of the gulls?

Love,

Roz

"That's *exactly* what it feels like," I say to the sky. I'm not sure at what point of the letter I started crying again, but the tears are flowing freely. "I don't know, Roz, I just don't know. It's so much to ask."

I can't think of anyone who could offer me advice, or even lend an ear so I could talk it out and process the position I'm in. I don't have even a Christmas card relationship with my parents anymore, no siblings, no close friends to speak of, not even an ex I'm still on good terms with. That lack weighs heavily on me now, and with a strangled half-laugh, half-sob, I realize Roz is probably who I would have called if anyone else had dropped this all on me. The difficult part is, I already know exactly what her advice would be.

She'd tell me to jump off the edge and soar.

REGRESS

His heart was racing, although the last tendrils of the dream were already receding from his mind, which was groggy from waking so soon after nodding off. Something about being pursued? He was uncertain, only that who—or what—ever had been chasing him in his sleep had frightened him so badly he'd sat up in bed, choking back a cry.

He was no stranger to nightmares. His dreams had always been full of terrors. He was a worrier, his subconscious filtering through his fears, transforming them into narratives that often left him as he was tonight, soaked with sweat, full of adrenaline, and afraid to close his eyes again. Sometimes the breathing exercises and calming words his doctor had taught him were enough to settle his mind, but tonight he knew he'd need the sleep tonic if he was going to get any more rest.

Gritting his teeth against the shock of leaving the warm covers, he slid out of bed, hoping not to disturb Lilith's slumber. They'd both stayed up too late, unable to tear themselves away from the radio and the terrible news from Pearl Harbor. Maybe the thought that America was under attack had triggered tonight's dream, he reflected as he padded down the hall, navigating by memory in the dark.

Lilith insisted he keep the sleep tonic in the kitchen, at the back of the highest cupboard where it would be out of reach from the children. Behind the cooking sherry and his single malt scotch, which he considered far more of a threat. The medicine cabinet in the washroom ought to have been safe enough—they kept a bottle of aspirin in there after all, for God's sake—but she was adamant.

"If—God forbid—one of them drank the whole bottle, they'd never wake up again," she'd said when he brought it home from the pharmacy. Lilith was asleep within five minutes of laying her head on the pillow, no matter what the circumstances, and didn't wake again until the alarm clock on her night table jangled the next morning. Even when the Japanese were invading. But it was easier not to argue.

He paused at the top of the stairs, hearing a small cough from behind the boys' closed door. Had he failed to muffle his scream and wakened one of them? Charlie was a restless sleeper, and, even at five, seldom slept through the night. Perhaps he'd come out of his room with his hair sticking out in every direction, rubbing his eyes, and asking if it was morning yet. They could sit at the table with mugs of warm milk and have a man-to-man talk before heading back upstairs. He smiled at the thought, hoping the boy would be up, but the door stayed closed. After a moment, surrounded by a stillness so complete he knew he was the only one awake, he stepped off the landing.

His foot landed solidly on a toy car—how had he missed it coming up to bed earlier?—and he felt himself falling backward as it skidded out from under him. Instinctively, he pinwheeled his arms forward, grabbing at empty air in an effort to remain upright.

This was a mistake. Rather than suffering a hard landing on his backside at the top of the stairs, he pitched head-first down them, tumbling over and over.

Still, he might have survived with only a broken collarbone, which snapped in half on the third step, if the newel post hadn't had such sharp corners at its base. His temple smashed into it with all the momentum of his body behind it, caving in his skull and killing him almost instantly.

His mind, still groggy and trying to process what had even caused such a calamity, was completely blank at the moment of death. He passed without even realizing these moments would be his last.

5

"Are things any clearer now?" Bill asks, releasing my hand from in between both of his own.

"Clear as mud, as a former professor used to say to me." Roz's letter is once again stuffed into my back pocket, and I feel it crinkle as I sink into the chair across from the lawyer's desk. Doubt shadowed me on the short walk over, eating away at the hope that had built on Roz's balcony. "I appreciate Roz's effort to try and help me, but this isn't right for me. The inn should be Cora's. I told her I wanted to work something out with her. This is her home, not mine. I'm sorry."

"No need to apologize, Audrey," Bill says. "Roslyn knew there was a chance you would want to continue with your life as you've made it. Transferring ownership to Cora is the most logical choice, and I know your aunt would be happy the inn isn't going to a stranger." The file folder is still on Bill's desk, and he pulls out a sheaf of papers. "However," he continues, "before a sale can be made to Cora, the inn has to be transferred to you, and that will take a bit of time. The will has to be filed with the court, and the title to the inn has to be made out in your name. Estate taxes will have to be paid, and after all that, the inn's financials will have to be reviewed. All debts and assets will have to be established so an accurate value can be determined, and then an offer of sale can be made. I expect it to take at least three weeks, possibly four if you intend on returning out east and we have to mail documents back and forth. If you can stay in Soberly, however, it's possible we could have everything finalized in eight or nine business days, with one more day for the sale to Cora, provided neither of you place any conditions on the sale that will require time to meet. Do you have a pressing need to get back home?"

"Not really," I say. "Although I haven't arranged to stay here either."

"One of the benefits of owning a hotel is that you always have a bed to sleep in," Bill says with a chuckle.

"Not tonight," I reply and tell him what Kellen said about the inn being full until the end of the weekend. I wonder to myself how comfortable the couch in Roz's office is. It might be my only option if I want to stay in town.

"Well, it's good to hear the business is doing well," he says. "Let's get to it, then," and starts handing me papers to sign. "I also need two pieces of government-issued identification from you. Your identity needs to be verified, and copies need to be filed with the county."

"Two? I have a driver's license." I start rummaging

through my wallet. "What about my old student ID, or my health insurance?"

"Both need to be issued by the government, unfortunately. A passport would be an acceptable second piece, or a birth certificate or social security card."

"I don't have any of those with me," I tell him, starting to panic. "My passport expired years ago, and the other ones are probably at the bottom of a box somewhere back home. I have my social security number memorized, so I never need the actual card. I'm me. I mean, I am who I say I am, I'm not an imposter."

"I believe you, Audrey," Bill says, his voice soothing. "It's a matter of the law, that's all. I do happen to know that you can apply for a new birth certificate online and have it mailed out to you. If you put a rush on it, you can get one in a week or two, depending on the state you were born in."

"We can get everything else squared away in the meantime, right?"

"A couple things, yes. The transfer of the property can't begin until your identity is confirmed and filed."

"Seriously?" I pinch the bridge of my nose between my finger and thumb. If I'm not careful, this habit of mine is going to leave bruises by the time this process is finished.

"We can fill out the application form right now on my laptop. Don't worry, Audrey. Think of it this way, you can have a relaxing week on the beach, eat the freshest seafood in the country, maybe read a couple good books, and before you know it, this will all be settled. There isn't a man or woman alive who doesn't need a good vacation, and the forecast this week is clear skies and sunshine."

His blue eyes twinkle. I frown in reply.

"Okay," I say, resigned to the inevitable. "Let's get me a new birth certificate."

It's not uncommon for me to see the moment of a person's death in a past life. It is, after all, a momentous event—maybe, after birth, the most important moment anyone experiences. The fact that we were meeting to discuss a shared acquaintance's passing might have triggered his spirit's recollection of that particular time. It was one I definitely planned on logging in my notebook and possibly pursuing further—finding an American man who died from an accidental fall on the day Pearl Harbor was bombed, especially when I knew the first name of his wife and one of his children, would not be all that hard. Then, if I could learn when Bill Blackmoor was born, I'd have a definite answer to the amount of time between his death in a former life, and his birth in this one. I'd only managed to unravel that time frame on a couple of other occasions, and I was excited to add to the data pool. Judging by his appearance, he ought to have been born right around the time of World War II.

My interest is purely personal. I have no intention of sharing my findings, whatever they might be, with Bill or anyone else. I'm curious about how the cycle of reincarnation—if that's what it even is—works: the frequency, the time lapse between lives, the method that draws the same people together, over and over again. I'm a researcher at heart, and it's a mystery that with enough sleuthing, I can solve, or at least fill in most of the blanks. It's questionable whether I'll ever get to the "why" of it all. I'm less interested in the "why"—that's one I'll leave up to the philosophers. I'm a "when" and "how" person.

Once the birth certificate application is filled out and sent off to the state office, I wander back to the inn. A young woman, Jana according to her name tag, is at the front desk now. She tells me Cora has gone home for the day, but I'm welcome to stay with her until the paperwork is completed, and hands me a piece of paper with an address on it. *Well, that's one problem solved.* I step into the pub. The same kid in the headphones is waiting at the host's station, but this time he pushes them down around his neck when he sees my face. With them off his head, I notice for the first time that the black hair on one side of his head is cropped close to his skull, and he has an intricate linear design shaved into it.

"You're back," he says. He half-hides his smile self-consciously with the back of his hand, but I catch a glimpse of crooked teeth that don't match the rest of his sleek urban style. "I'm Drew Segura, server-slash-busboy-slash-dishwasher-slash-host at the Public House." He does a little bow, and I grin.

"Nice to meet you, Drew. Audrey Eames. You wear a lot of hats around here." I offer him my hand, and we shake. The brief vision of Drew's past tells me that at some point, he was an amateur entomologist, and particularly enjoyed studying butterflies, spending hours poring over them with a magnifying glass and pinning their delicate bodies to canvas. I wonder what he collects in this lifetime.

"Your hand feels cold," he remarks. "But I don't see a pint in it yet."

"Poor circulation," I tell him. "They've always been that way, even on days like this."

"Mine too," he says. I'd noticed, but assumed it was from serving the drinks.

"Have you worked here long?" Drew looks like he might not have hit his twenties yet, but if he's serving in the pub, he has to be at least twenty-one.

"A couple years," he says. "Your aunt sort of rescued me, in a way." He lowers his voice, and his face turns serious. "I'd been hitchhiking down the coast, camping on beaches and sort of wandering wherever my feet and my thumb took me. I thought I was on some sort of adventure like I would find my purpose in life, or at least have enough interesting things happen to me so I could write a book about it. I thought I'd be the next Kerouac." The corner of his mouth lifts briefly. "The only incident of note was when a dude in a pickup truck beat the shit out of me, took all my stuff, and left me half-dead by the side of the road in the middle of the night a couple miles south of here." He begins fidgeting with the stack of menus, straightening them compulsively. "No one would help me when I made it into town. No one but Roz. She was at the night desk when I stumbled in, covered in blood and swearing loud enough to wake the entire inn. Did I mention I'd smoked a pipe before the guy in the truck made me his personal punching bag? Yeah. Anyway. There I was, tripping balls, bleeding all over the carpet, ranting away, and she looks at me and says, 'You look like you need a hot shower and some coffee.' I'd expected her to call the cops, or at least kick me out, but she showed me into an empty room, held a cool cloth on the back of my neck while I puked, and called the doctor in to stitch me up and tape my ribs. All before she even knew my name.

"After a couple days, once I was feeling a bit better and could move around, I decided to bail. I didn't have any money to pay for the room, or the doctor, and figured the best thing to do was get lost before anyone handed me a bill. There was Roz, right outside my door, waiting for me. She knew what I'd been thinking, and did she ever give me shit. Not because I wasn't going to pay, but because as far as she could see, I didn't have anywhere better to be, she thought we were friends, and who the hell was I to leave without saying goodbye.

"I remember feeling so surprised she didn't want me out of her hair. I thought I was a burden and a deadbeat one at that. When I told her that I didn't have any money to pay her, she said there was plenty of handy-work that needed doing when I was up to it, and she was happy to offer me room and board, as long as I stayed sober.

"I figured I'd stay for a week, maybe two, until I'd worked off my debt and had a bit of cash in my pocket to head out onto the road again. A couple weeks turned into a month, then two, then Roz told me one day that Kellen was moving behind the bar and there was a server position open, and coincidentally Carrie McMahon had her upstairs apartment for rent if I was interested. I've been here ever since."

"Wow," I say because there aren't any other words. It was what I had thought Roz might do for me one day, although probably with fewer drugs involved—to reach out to me at a point when my life was aimless and give me purpose. It was what she was trying to do now, I could see, but she was ten years too late. "Are you going to stay, now that she's—now that she's gone?" I ask, just for something to say.

"I guess that's your call." Now he's lining up the pens on the host's station, arranging them in perfect order, refusing to meet my eye.

"Oh, no, I'm not..." I falter. "It'll be up to Cora. I'm not staying." There, I'd said it out loud. I had expected it to feel freeing, but the words fall like lead from my mouth. "I can't," I continue. "I have..." A short-term lease on a shitty apartment? A contract that just ended? What exactly do I have? "I have stuff. It's complicated. I'm sure Cora will keep you on though. I mean, you must know the place inside-out."

"I'm surprised she hasn't given me the boot already." The corner of his mouth twists downward into an ugly sneer. "Cora's not on Team Drew, you might say. My bags are already packed. I'm waiting for the word to come down."

"Do you want me to talk to her? Maybe if she knew..."

"It's fine," Drew interrupts. "Without Roz, there isn't really anything keeping me here anyway." His voice has lost all its warmth. He grabs a plastic tub from under the counter and moves to clear some empty pint glasses from a recently vacated table. "How long are you in Soberly for then?" I give him a brief rundown of the property transfer process, along with the delay while I wait for my birth certificate to arrive. "I hate that legal bullshit," he says with unexpected vehemence. I wait for more, but that's all he has to share. "Are you staying to eat?" he asks. I shrug. It's been a few hours since the massive plate of fish and chips Naomi fed me, but I'm not all that hungry. However, working my way through some food, and maybe a cold pint or two, will kill time before I have to make my way to the house Roz and Cora shared, a scenario I'm dreading, so I sit down at a table.

"That one's reserved," Kellen calls over from behind the bar.

"Sorry, I didn't know. There wasn't a sign." I shift one over.

"So's that one." I raise my eyebrows and point at one vacant table after another. He shakes his head at each one. Apparently, there's quite a supper rush on weekends.

"All right, can I order some takeout, then?" I can eat it on one of the benches overlooking the beach, I guess.

"We don't do takeout."

"I just saw—" Not two minutes earlier, while Drew and I had been talking, a man had picked up a bag full of Styrofoam containers, paid, and left.

Kellen shrugs. "There is one seat free at the bar," he says with a poorly concealed grin, and I realize he's teasing me.

"Jerk." I smack his arm with a menu but take the bar stool he pointed out. Just to provoke him, I pull my earbud headphones out of my pocket and slip them in while his back is turned.

"Hey, hey, hey," he says, and tugs one out. "I don't care if you do own the place, you have to follow the dress code like everyone else. Headphones are strictly forbidden."

"Does Drew know?" The man in question has his firmly in place again—head bobbing as he busses tables.

"His are regulation. These are not. If I see them again, I'm going to confiscate them." I'm biting back a laugh by now, remembering the stern-but-kind mannerism of the school teacher I saw in the vision of his past. Conceding, I push them back into my pocket. As I'm about to ask him for a pint of the local microbrew, he slides a large wine glass full of ice in front of me and starts pouring something ruby-hued from a pitcher into it.

"I was going to—" I start, pointing at the taps, but he shuts me down with a scorching look that dries up my words. Even my thoughts are lost in his gaze, which is two parts exasperation and three parts lust. What does this guy want from me? Whatever it is, I'm half-tempted to give it to him, as imprudent as that would be.

"You are the most contrary, argumentative, difficult woman I've ever met," he says. He's leaning forward over the bar, and it wouldn't take much for me to meet him in the middle. "Just this once, stop trying to get the best of me and trust me. Okay?" I purse my lips and raise an eyebrow, but I don't reach for the glass. Even though it looks delicious. Even though I feel like the icy drink is the only thing that will keep me from spontaneously combusting on the spot. "It's sangria," he tells me in a more conciliatory tone. "Special of the day. I've been brewing it all afternoon, just for you, as a welcome-to-town."

"No, you haven't." The words come out before I have time to think, and his stare intensifies. One eyebrow arches above the other. Wordlessly, he points at the chalkboard over his shoulder, where the specials are scrawled. Underneath the catch of the day, it reads "The Apple of Audrey's Eye: a cabernet sangria infused with three types of Oregon-grown apples, fresh California citrus, and a slug of gin."

"Yes, I have. Now taste it and tell me how it is. I wanted you to be the first, so I've been telling everyone else it isn't ready yet."

The sincerity behind the gesture evaporates my playful defiance and brings me perilously close to tears. I'm not used to being treated so kindly by a near stranger, even a too-flirty-for-his-own-good one.

"Well?" he asks after I down a healthy mouthful, rolling it over my tongue and allowing it to cool my heated cheeks.

"Dangerously good," I tell him, and I mean it. "This could become a serious addiction for me. You need to tell me how to make it."

"Absolutely not," he says with mock outrage. "A good bartender never shares his recipes, but there will always be a bottomless pitcher here, waiting for you. That's a promise."

"Bottomless pitcher, you say." I've already drained my glass, and I'm starting to feel lightheaded.

"You just tell me when to stop." That look again. I'm burning up inside. What else to do, but keep on drinking?

6

"I have made a critical error in judgment," I mutter to myself as I stand outside the door of Cora's house. My knuckles are poised an inch from the wood, painted a cheery yellow. The sun slipped down below the horizon as I left the pub, and I am none too sober. Dangerously good indeed, Kellen's sangria and the pitcher was bottomless, as promised.

I'd thought Cora's offer for me to stay with her was generous at the time, but now that I'm here, I wish I'd snuck up to the office for a quick rest and a chance to sober up a bit. I'm not sure which is worse—showing up drunk or showing up in the wee hours of the morning. At least my bloodshot eyes I can pass off to grief, but there's no way of explaining the smell of wine on my breath, or that I'm a bit unsteady on my feet. If any of the neighbors had noticed me weaving up the sidewalk on my way here, the local gossip mill would be in full swing tomorrow.

With a sigh, I rap three times on the door and step back, hoping the fact that I'm a good six or seven inches taller than Cora will work in my favor. My plan is to collapse into bed immediately anyway. I'd barely slept on the night bus from New Mexico. That said, if Cora wants to talk, especially about Roz, I'm all ears. There was so much I didn't know about my aunt, and who better to tell me than her life partner? Maybe we could chat over tea, and she could tell me about how Roz came about owning the inn, how they'd met, and all the things I'd missed out on over the past eighteen years. I could tell her about what Roz was like when I knew her as a child, her dreams for her life, the way she'd taken me under her wing in a way. Maybe we could find common ground there, and start working together to—

Cora opens the door, a terry bathrobe wrapped tightly around her frame and an irritated look on her face. Immediately I feel like a child caught out past curfew, even though it's only a few minutes before 10 p.m. She's been waiting up for me.

"I hope I haven't kept you up," I say as I step into the modest bungalow. "I grabbed some food in the pub and got caught up talking to a few people. I didn't notice how late it had gotten until I saw the sun starting to set and Naomi said I'd best be getting home—I mean over here." *This is not your home,* I tell myself sternly. *None of it is.*

"Well, come on in then." Cora snaps the deadbolt home with a crack and heads down the hall. Shouldering my duffel, I slip my shoes off and follow her. We pass the living room, illuminated by a single lamp in the corner, and I spot a paperback on the couch. The lamp throws just enough light into the adjoining room for me to identify it as the kitchen. Cora turns a corner and flips a light switch in the first room on the left.

"The bathroom is across the hall. I'm an early riser—I need to be at the front desk by 6 a.m. You can fix yourself breakfast when you're up."

I mentally smack myself in the forehead. If she needs to be at the inn at 6 a.m., then she likely goes to bed a good hour earlier than I've kept her up.

"Umm, thank you," I say as she heads to her own room at the end of the hall. "I really appreciate you welcoming me into your home."

"You're welcome." This, followed by a faint sniff, is her only reply before she shuts her door. I vow to be as silent as possible while I'm getting ready for bed and set my duffel gently on the carpeted floor. Two white stripes from the straps stand out in stark detail on my shoulder next to the angry red covering my arms and chest, and I wince at the pain. I'd forgotten to get some aloe gel. Now that I don't have anything to distract me, I can feel the blood throbbing right under the surface of my skin, adding another layer of misery to my situation.

Cora had left a set of towels folded neatly on the bed for me, a bit frayed at the edges but clean and tidy. I pluck up the washcloth and tiptoe across the hall into the bathroom, noting that the light is already off in Cora's room. The cool cloth provides momentary relief, but as soon as I lift it the burning sensation resumes, and after a couple minutes, I give it up as a bad job, brush my teeth, and return to my room. My phone's been dead for hours, something that would normally be a crisis for me, but today I'd barely made note of it. I plug it in and set an alarm so Cora can't add laziness to the list of faults I'm sure she's compiling and turn down the quilt. As I slip between the cool cotton sheets, I can already feel sleep overtake me, despite the sunburn, everything on my mind, and the way my head is spinning from the sangria. I slip away into unconsciousness.

Cora is at the desk in the front office, looking back and forth between a stack of papers and the laptop's screen when I walk in at half-past eight. She glances over her glasses at me and back down to her paperwork.

"Good morning," I greet her, and extend the travel mug I'd brought with me. "I made some tea when I woke up and thought I'd bring you some." The label on the cream Earl Grey in the cupboard was from an upscale shop in Seattle, one I recognized from my time there. "I didn't know how you take it, so, umm, sorry for that. Anyway, here you go," I stammered, my words falling out of my mouth. She's looking at me with an unreadable expression until her eyes fill with tears. A litany of curse words runs through my mind. What had I done now? It was supposed to be a peace offering. Now I'm not sure if I should set it down on the desk like nothing's wrong, or if I should leave the office, the town of Soberly, and the state of Oregon, never to return. Instead, I stand frozen, my arm half-extended, and what's supposed to be a warm smile, but feels like a grimace, plastered on my face.

"I'm sorry, Audrey," she says, swiping at her eyes. "Roz brought me tea every morning too. I was always the first one up, you see, and she'd come by later with a mug for me and a mug for her, she'd pull up a chair, and we'd go over the day's business."

Is there anything *I can do right around this woman?* I withdraw the mug and begin spewing a torrent of apologies, assuring her I had no idea, but she holds up her hand to silence me and gestures for the mug with a weak smile.

"It's actually the nicest thing anyone's done for me since...since she's been gone. Thank you." She flips the top of the lid up, inhales the aroma of the tea, and her smile widens slightly. The thudding in my chest begins to slow.

"I was wondering if there was anything I could do to help out around here over the next few days," I ask her. "Mr. Blackmoor says the transfer of ownership and everything will take a bit of time—Roz's will must be probated, and I need a second form of photo ID. I'll be here for a week or so. I'll do anything. Cleaning, painting, filing, whatever you need done. Nobody will let me pay for my food in the pub," I add. The annoyance I'd felt last night when I'd attempted to settle my bill with Kellen returns. He'd been unrepentant that no one there would take my money, nor would they at any point in the future. The last thing I want to look like to Cora is a freeloader.

"Ran up a bit of a tab last night?" The corner of Cora's mouth twitches. *Busted.* "Well..." She hesitates long enough for me to wonder if she's trying to find some particularly tedious or unpleasant task. "Do you have any experience with bookkeeping?"

"Some. I was the treasurer for my university's

historical association for several years and do all my own bookkeeping and taxes as a contractor. I'm not an expert, but I know how to tell the difference between a payable and a receivable."

"Perfect. We use an accountant, of course, but there's half a year's worth of invoices, expenses, receipts, and payments to sort through and organize before it gets sent off to her. Roz was perpetually behind on that stuff, and I don't have a head for it at all. I was about to hire someone to take care of it for us, but if you're willing to tackle it, that would be a tremendous help."

I follow her up the staircase to Roz's office, resolving to stay far away from the balcony with the view. I hadn't thought about where I'd be working when I'd accepted Cora's offer. She seems a bit more at ease in the room today, moving briskly into the office, travel mug in hand. I'm so glad I brought her the tea—we had started on the wrong foot with each other, but maybe things would warm up between us now.

Cora drops a heavy cardboard file box onto the table in the middle of the room. Inside is an unsorted pile of papers eight inches deep.

"Roz's filing system," she says, "was to throw it in here and worry about it later."

Awesome. This should be nice and boring, the perfect thing to make me dread everything about the Soberly Inn and Public House. By the time I'm done sorting through this box, I'm never going to want to see the place again, much less own it.

Cora sets me up on Roz's laptop, and I spend a few minutes picking through her files until I find the spreadsheets I need. "Don't kill yourself over these," she tells me. "If you make any headway at all, I'll be grateful. Soberly is a nice little town. Don't keep yourself cooped up in here all day." With that, she leaves me to the box of papers. I resolutely move the chair so my back is to the window, keeping Roz's prized view out of sight, and dive in.

A knock at the door makes me realize I've been at it for almost five hours. Piles of papers now surround me—one for each month. Cora's estimate of half a year's worth had been off by two months. Just getting it all organized chronologically has taken me the entire morning.

"Come in," I call out. Cora wouldn't knock, and no one else knows I'm even up here.

"It's locked," someone replies. It sounds like Drew. I open the door, but an empty staircase greets me.

"Drew?" I call out, confused.

"Other door," he replies. There is indeed a second door going to the main hallway where the guest rooms are located. I hadn't noticed earlier, half-hidden by the frame of a bookcase. I open it to find Drew carrying a cardboard takeout container in one hand, and a large glass of what looks like sweet tea in the other.

"Cora asked me to bring this up to you," he tells me. I shift a pile of papers to the side to make room for it on the table. "What's all this?"

"Bookkeeping. It was one of Roz's jobs, and I asked Cora to keep me busy. This is what she found for me."

"What are you doing? Organizing it?"

"Right now, yeah. Eventually, I'll enter it all into some spreadsheets. Mr. Blackmoor, the lawyer—do you know him?" A nod from Drew. "He says all this has to be done and checked over by an accountant before I can sell the inn to Cora. I'd like that to happen sooner rather than later. Not that I don't like this place," I add, stammering. "I have a life to get back to."

"Oh, totally, of course. Yeah, I mean, that's a lot of responsibility, I don't blame you." He sets down the glass, some of the tea sloshes onto the Mastercard statement on top of the March pile. "Shit, sorry," he says, blotting at it with his T-shirt.

"Don't worry about it." The ink looks a bit smeared, but it's still legible. "I'm sure I can reprint it if I need to anyway. Credit card statements are archived for years online."

"That's true. Well, sorry anyway."

"Thanks for bringing me lunch," I say as he backs out of the room. The aroma of grease has been filling the room since he came in, and my stomach has been audibly calling out to the contents of the cardboard container. I peek inside with near reverence, wondering if whatever's inside can possibly be as good as it smells. A mound of diced hash browns, covered in pieces of bacon, sautéed onions, melted cheese, and on top of it all, two soft poached eggs and hollandaise sauce. My mouth fills with saliva in anticipation. It's all my favorite things in one dish, and I attack it with relish.

"No problem," Drew replies with a salute, and disappears back out the same door he entered.

☙

By the end of my self-imposed work day, my head is pounding, but I finally have an organizational system that will work to quickly input the data into the spreadsheets. I'm sure the accountant will still check over every statement and bill line by line, but this should make that work easier.

Satisfied, I close the laptop and put it back in its drawer, and then put each month's pile of papers in a folder, label them, and stack them neatly back in their cardboard box. The historian in me knows never to assume one-of-a-kind items will be safe, unprotected, and exposed, and while it's true they could all be reprinted, it would involve a tremendous amount of work to do so. Even one of the balcony doors blowing open in the night and scattering the papers around could mean an entire day's labor lost.

"Do you have a safe place to store this until tomorrow?" I ask Cora as I emerge from the staircase behind her at the front desk. She and the girl from yesterday evening look like they're changing off.

"I suppose I could bring it home with me," she says with little enthusiasm. Cora's probably never lost a week's worth of research and a set of priceless hand-drawn maps to a sprinkler malfunction.

"What about the safe?" Jana says. "It'll be a tight squeeze, but it should fit."

"That's a much better idea, thank you, Jana." Cora takes the box from me and disappears around the corner, returning in a few minutes empty-handed.

"You haven't eaten supper yet, have you," she asks, and I shake my head in reply. "Why don't you take a key, then, so you can let yourself in as you please. I should have left one for you last night."

The sun beat down on the young girl's back as she

meandered down the beach, harvesting mussels and spiny urchins for their tender meat. She avoided her reflection in the still pools of water, not wanting to see the freckles that were no doubt appearing on her nose and cheeks. Trinh and Kim-Ly, her two best friends from school, didn't have a single freckle between them. You'd never see them gathering food for the family pot. Their fathers didn't labor all day in the rice paddies.

"You're a lucky girl, Hao," her mother told her every time she complained. "Lucky to go to school at all. I never got to go to school, and neither did your father." And so on until Hao wanted to scream at her to be quiet. Her mother's list of grievances was long, but she didn't seem to understand how difficult it was to go to school with people above your station. Trinh and Kim-Ly took pity upon her, she knew, calling her their pet, their little doll, telling her how quaint she was. Their fathers were merchants. Trinh's father owned three ships that sailed up and down the coast, carrying goods back and forth.

Hao held up her net bag, decided it was full enough, and turned to go back, grateful that the sun would at least be behind her for the journey home. She tilted the hat her mother had woven back so it protected her neck and trudged onward.

"Thanks. I think I'm going to take a walk down the beach. I'm still stuffed from lunch," I tell her. "Maybe I'll catch the sunset over the water."

"Funny, I was going to suggest you do the same thing. You've been up in that room all day. I meant it when I said I didn't want you to spend all your time up there.

That paperwork has sat around for all these months with no harm done. It'll get done in good time."

"There wasn't a logical time to stop sorting it all out until now, but it'll be easier to work at it in shorter stretches now that it's organized. Anyway, I'll be quiet as a mouse when I come in, I promise." It feels like being back in high school, staying with Cora. "Oh, is there any place I can get a slushie before my walk?" I ask as we both step out the door. I definitely don't have room for supper right now, but a cold treat would be nice. Cora tells me the cafe does frappes and Italian ice and points me to the south. Her house is several blocks north, so we part ways.

Twenty minutes later, with every bit of exposed skin liberally slathered with sunscreen from the drugstore and carrying a mango Italian ice, I'm picking my way north up the coast toward the lighthouse. The smell of salt and seaweed drying in the sun is one I've always loved, and one I miss when I'm not living near the coast. Without the burden of my duffle bag like my last walk, I'm free to venture onto the slippery rocks cropped up near the tideline to explore tidal pools for signs of life. The sight of starfish, anemones, and tiny crabs scuttling away from my shadow fills me with endless delight for some reason. I scoop up a hermit crab whose spiral shell is no bigger than my thumbnail and let it wander over my palm for a few minutes, talking to it like a pet before depositing it back in the same pool I found it in.

An hour and a half later, my pocket full of shells and bits of sea glass, I settle into the sand with an enormous driftwood log behind my back to watch the sun dip below the horizon. The lighthouse appears as far away as when I started. It must be a good ten miles from Soberly instead of the two or three I'd estimated. There aren't too many people on the beach this far from the town with me, but I'm not alone by any means. Most people are doing the same as I am, pausing to take in the fire-red sky, although a couple of kids are too busy trying to whip each other with long strands of seaweed to pay any attention. When the last sliver of the sun's orb has slipped below the horizon, I haul myself up to head back the way I came, quicker now so I won't end up walking in complete darkness.

When I reach the town, the lights in all the main street windows are out. Most businesses close by six or seven, other than the cafe, which is open until eight for supper, and the inn's pub, where last call is 11 p.m. on weekdays. I'm torn about stopping in at the latter, even though it will likely mean waking up tomorrow morning with another hangover. My pace slows as I walk past, and one foot hangs off the curb, ready to cross the empty street. The cold voice of reason, the one that governs my decision to never settle in one place too long, butts in.

Don't let these people like you too much. It'll be all the harder when you leave.

It's a familiar caution, but for the first time in memory, I find myself resenting it.

It'll be all the harder for you too, Audrey. The one person who might have made this place home for you is gone.

My heart squeezes tight inside my chest, and I

square my shoulders with a deep breath, pushing all the feelings back down inside before they can take root too deeply. Reversing course back onto the sidewalk, I quicken my pace, eyes resolutely ahead.

7

The next morning, I head straight for the inn, travel mug of tea for Cora in hand. It's more than a gesture to stay on her good side; I'd seen from her expression yesterday how much that small reminder of Roz's love for her meant. As soon as I hand it over, however, she shoos me back out the door, admonishing me again not to spend my entire day cooped up with Roz's papers. I decide to stop in at the little antique store I'd briefly examined two days ago.

Sheena is behind the counter again and greets me with a friendly hello.

"I was hoping you'd be back soon," she says. "How are things over at the inn?"

"All right, all things considered," I tell her. "There's a lot of paperwork and stuff."

"Hey, you were right about that inkwell," she tells

me, pulling it out from a glass display under the counter. A new price tag on it reads $189. "It's late eighteenth century, according to a couple reliable Internet sources. I've got it up on eBay right now. Hopefully, it'll sell soon."

"You said someone found it when they pulled up their old porch?" Soberly would have been nothing but grassy dunes back then.

"Yeah, along with the usual under-the-porch detritus. A few milk bottles, mason jars, a wooden pipe. I confess after researching the first few things a little more rigorously, I assumed this was from the same time frame. Corb Maxwell's house is only around a hundred years old."

"It's a reasonable assumption." I find myself unusually eager to browse Sheena's shelves, not because I expect to find more under-priced treasures, but because this is my area of expertise. After spending months researching and dating the same style of sturdy, functional, but utterly bland pottery crocks, mixing bowls, and simple vases, I'm itching to dive into a good jumble of items from all kinds of different eras and see what catches my eye. Call it exercise for my brain.

"So, you're a historian, I hear," she says as I peer into the display case. I snort in reply.

"There's nothing like a small town for word to get around. You must know a thing or two yourself, to be in this business."

"I grew up in this store—it was my mama's before she retired to Florida and handed it over to me. I used to write my high school papers on things like how to date a glass buoy, and the influence of smugglers on the town's architecture, stuff like that." Sheena laughs at the memory, and I'm intrigued.

"Architecture? What do you mean?"

"Oh, almost every building more than eighty years old has a secret basement, a false wall, or something to hide contraband in. They stopped being used after Prohibition times, but for a while, this was a pretty popular place for the rum runners to put into shore from Canada. The one in my house is small, just a space about this big." She mimes a box the size of a dishwasher with her hands. "Behind one of my kitchen cabinets. It's big enough for a couple cases of liquor, but about fifteen years ago, TJ Wachowski almost broke his leg when he stepped through a rotting board in his own backyard. It was overgrown with grass, but when they pulled up the wood, there was a small cellar underneath that still had some liquor in it. It made the paper in Portland and everything. He hasn't shut up about it since," she adds with a roll of her eyes.

"That's pretty cool," I say. "Is there one at the inn?"

Sheena raises her eyebrows knowingly. "The inn was the center of activity. It hasn't been dry for a single day since it opened in 1916. Everyone for miles around knew you could always get a drink at the Soberly Inn and Public House. I haven't been down there myself, but there has to be a secret room in the basement, or was, once. It's been so long, maybe it's just a regular storage room or something now."

I've forgotten all about the bits of history in Sheena's shop as I mull over the story she's spinning. An idea is starting to form in the back of my mind, but it will require some fleshing out, and a lot of time spent wherever the town's records are kept. Still, I file the information away for later. Once I'm finished with Roz's bookkeeping, it could turn out to be a nice little project to keep me occupied, if I still have time to kill in Soberly. Roz's letter, where she'd told me the history of the area could keep me occupied for a lifetime, pops up in my mind. *Looks like she wasn't wrong.* I smile ruefully. If I wanted to—and could find someone to pay me for it—I could find plenty to study and investigate here.

A family wanders through the door, the father already admonishing the three children not to touch anything, "or else." The mother's eyes are darting in all directions in delight, but I see her hold herself back, her attention half on the children who don't seem inclined to mind their father's warning. Sheena's on it, however.

"Come on kids, we've got a corner over here where you can play with some real, old-fashioned toys, like your grandma or grandpa might have had," she says, beckoning to them.

"Or you?" The middle child, a boy around six or seven, pipes up, and I bite the inside of my cheek hard to keep from laughing. Sheena catches me and her glare shoots lasers in my direction. I wave goodbye and step out the door, mouthing *I'll come back tomorrow* to her.

Other than Sheena's antique shop, there isn't much else for me to explore on Soberly's four blocks of main street. I've been to the pharmacy, the cafe, the small supermarket, and Rooster's, the general store, and they don't look like they have anything out of the ordinary to catch my attention. There's an office offering whale watching tours, a souvenir shop, and a clothing boutique. I might have browsed the bookstore at the end of the street, but the hours posted indicate it's closed on

Mondays, so I turn back to the inn.

Cora retrieves the box of papers from the safe for me, and I lug it back up the stairs, ready to get into the meat of the work. With one month's worth of papers spread out across the table, I get down to entering them into my spreadsheet by date and type.

It's unbelievably boring work, and I find myself often staring off into space, usually out the French doors to take in Roz's favorite view, or pausing to browse her bookshelves, which are overstuffed and in no system of organization I can comprehend. Roz's interests were extremely varied if her library was any indication. I find contemporary Hispanic literary fiction alongside a recipe book on pit barbecuing, which is next to an anthology of Norse mythology. I wonder if she sourced all these titles from the Soberly bookstore, collected them during her travels, or if they'd all appeared on her doorstep in an Amazon box like most of my books.

I'm startled out of my musings by a rapid, sustained knocking on the door leading out into the hall, which doesn't stop until I open it. It's Kellen.

"You'd better get your butt downstairs for lunch." He's pointing his finger at me in mock aggression, and his smile softens his tone. "My mama's starting to wonder if you don't like her cooking."

"What? No, of course, I do. I'm just—" I sweep my arm around, indicating the table and its contents. "Busy."

"Busy people eat. Have you even had breakfast?"

"Of course, I have." It's not a complete fabrication. Ever since I've started drinking it, I've considered coffee a breakfast staple, and most days it's all I need until lunch. Kellen, however, isn't convinced.

"There's your tell," he says, breaking into a grin that shows off his perfect teeth. "You're a terrible liar, Audrey."

"Oh yeah? What is it?" I know as soon as I ask that he's never going to tell me.

"Yeah right. Come on—food's waiting."

I pop the lock in the doorknob and pull the door shut behind me, giving it a jostle for good measure.

"What do you have up here anyway?" Kellen asks as he leads me down the hall past the guest rooms. I can't help but appreciate his ass in his low-slung jeans as I follow him and feel my face reddening.

"Just bookkeeping. Stuff that has to be done before the transfer of ownership can go into effect." We pass through a door marked Employees Only and down another staircase. Now we're behind the pub in what looks like a staff room, with a comfy, but worn leather couch, a double row of lockers, a small kitchenette, and a battered Formica table surrounded by mismatched chairs. To my right is a door, and the window set into it gives me a view of the kitchen, where Naomi flits from one stove to another.

"That going to take a while? Don't answer yet. I'll be back in a second with lunch." The promised second is more like five minutes, but when he pushes back through the door, he's carrying a tray laden with more food than I can eat in a day, never mind a single meal. I shake my head in disbelief—about to tell him I couldn't possibly eat so much when my stomach betrays me with a growl so loud they probably heard it in the kitchen. One side of Kellen's face twitches as he tries to suppress a smile.

"You'd better not touch my fries," he says, and I clue in that he's carrying food for both of us.

"They look so good though." I snag one before he can swat my hand away and pop it into my mouth. I fully intend on poaching as many as I can, since my lunch, a bowl of thick chowder and a plate of fried clams, didn't come with any.

I explain about Roz's unfinished bookkeeping between mouthfuls, a subject which doesn't take more than a couple minutes to cover before I steer the conversation to what I learned about the town's past from Sheena earlier that day.

"You love that sort of stuff, don't you?" My enthusiasm must have shown on my face. He's also managed to steal two fried clams from my plate while I was retelling the story, so caught up in telling him what I'd learned this morning that I let my guard down.

"I do," I admit. "It's the fun side of history, the type of story people are interested in, even if it's a bit unsavory. Or maybe because it is," I add, holding up the three fries I've liberated tauntingly. It's been an all-out war ever since Kellen sat down across from me, despite my effort to use my soup bowl as a shield against him. "Anything else you've ever heard about it?"

"Nah, I mean, I've heard TJ's story because that man will take any excuse to tell it, but I think most everybody has this vague notion that a long time ago smugglers used to hide their booze here. I don't even know if there's anything in the cellar here from those times. I've never heard anyone talking about hidden rooms or anything, and I've been down there and haven't seen anything. Mama and I only moved here fifteen years ago though, so I'm probably not the best person to ask about it. Check in with some of the old-timers—they might have heard stories from their daddies or granddaddies. Bill Blackmoor might be one guy to talk to or Alice Jordan. Alice might even be old enough to have been alive during Prohibition, although if she was, she would have been a baby."

I make a mental note to ask Bill Blackmoor when I stop in to see him tomorrow to see how the paperwork is progressing. We had sent off my birth certificate application, but it hadn't arrived at the inn yet. Even with the rush request, it was still at the mercy of the postal service once it left wherever birth certificates came from.

"All right, that was a good idea," I concede as I push my empty bowl away from me. I have a feeling that as soon as I get back upstairs where no one will see me, I'm going to be popping the button of my jeans open.

"Supper is at six, and you can place your order now so it's ready," Kellen tells me.

"You expect me to think about supper now? I'm so stuffed I might not eat again until tomorrow."

"Your choices are Dungeness crab with garlic butter and a side of mash," Kellen begins as though I haven't spoken, ticking off each item with his fingers. "The Soberly Pub burger, which is topped with a fried egg and comes with fries and slaw; fish and chips—which I believe you've already had—or Monday's special, cedar-planked salmon with roasted potatoes and local vegetables." I open my mouth to reply, but he continues. "As for dessert, we have a selection of pies, baked fresh daily by the Crumbs Cafe and Bakery down the street, or six flavors of ice cream, served in one, two or three scoops—"

"*Stop*," I cry, unable to hold in my laughter. "Fine. The burger. No dessert."

"Have you tried Crumbs' marionberry pie yet? These are local marionberries, Audrey. Probably picked by Jenny Crumb herself, before the first light of dawn, all so she can craft the most delectable of pies. Do you know the sheer hardship of picking marionberries? The brambles? The thorns?" He shakes his head in mock disappointment and sighs. "All those scratches, Audrey. For you. So, you can have pie." He stares at me, a mock look of deep disappointment on his face, silently daring me to turn down the pie twice.

"Oh my God. Fine, a *sliver* of pie." I hold my finger and thumb an inch apart to show him how much pie I want.

"A scoop of vanilla on top?" He's grinning again.

"A good piece of pie doesn't need to be propped up with ice cream," I say with a sniff.

"Savage." Now he's laughing. "Well, have it your way, I suppose."

"If any of this was actually my way I—"

"Well, back to work for you, Audrey, enjoy your afternoon," he says before I can complete my protest. He lands a lightning-quick peck on my cheek before I know it's coming, shoots me one last triumphant grin, and disappears into the kitchen, leaving me alone in the staff room. He reappears half a minute later, a sheepish look on his face.

"Forgot the dishes," he says, stacking them back onto the tray and heading back through the door. "Mama about had my hide. See you at six."

♔

At the appointed hour, not a minute earlier, I step into the pub, abandoning attempts to smooth down my hair after a breezy stroll down the beach. It's absolutely packed, more so than on the weekend, and the din is almost disorienting after the peaceful hour I've had with only the waves, and the gulls as my soundtrack. Cora is here too, sitting at a table with six or seven others. She sees me, nods, and says something to the woman beside her. The entire table turns to look at me. I give her a weak wave in return and make a point of looking elsewhere in the pub so she doesn't feel obliged to offer me a seat I don't want to take. Drew and another server are both shouldering trays laden with drinks, moving from table to table and swapping full glasses for empties.

There's a strange undercurrent to the mood in the room. It doesn't feel like just a busy restaurant. Whether it's the low voices everyone seems to be speaking in, or the fact that nearly everyone is wearing a somber expression, I get the feeling something's up in Soberly. I hope that something isn't me, as there are more than a few people giving me curious glances now. Suddenly I'm uncomfortable to the point of panic, and about to duck into the washroom to take a breather when Kellen looks up from the beer taps and points to an empty seat at the bar, front and center.

Great. What an inconspicuous spot to sit and have everyone watch him flirt with me. The sight of one friendly face among strangers is enough to unfreeze my paralysis, however, and I weave my way through the tables to the bar. His usual wiseass smile is missing, and there's tightness in his jaw I haven't seen before.

"What's going on?" I ask in the same low tone, leaning over the bar so he can hear me.

"Bill Blackmoor's dead," he replies as he pulls another tray of beers. "Rudy Jamison found him a couple hours ago."

The entire town had already heard about it, from the look of things. I mentally chastise myself for the uncharitable thought. Soberly was a close-knit town, and the death of one of its longtime—maybe lifetime—residents would be a severe blow to the community.

Kellen is too busy to talk at length about Blackmoor's death, with the drink orders coming in as fast as he can make them. I request a red ale from a Portland microbrewery and don't mention supper. My entrance was only a momentary distraction for the pub's patrons, who have all returned to their previous conversations. Nevertheless, there's still a band of tenseness across my shoulders, and my chief thought is how Blackmoor's death is going to delay the sale of the inn to Cora even further, which makes me feel even more uncharitable for thinking about his death as an inconvenience rather than the sad misfortune it is. I'm not mired in my own self-flagellating thoughts for long, because Sheena shoulders her way in between me and the person on the stool to my right.

"Audrey, hey," she says. "Rob, Shawn, move down one. I need this seat here." The two men grumble a bit, but they do as she requests and she slides in beside me, setting her pint down on an abandoned coaster. "Thought I'd come keep you company. Hope you don't mind. You heard the news?" I nod, mid-sip. "Everyone's absolutely shocked," she says. "Rudy stopped 'round his office to ask him about a round of golf on the weekend and found him at the bottom of the stairs, dead as a doorknob. Doc Porter says looks like he fell and hit his head. Some people are saying his hip might've given out on him— he'd been complaining about it giving him trouble lately. The awful part is, Rudy says he was wearing yesterday's suit, which means he'd been laying there all night and this morning too." She took a long drink from her pint, her head bowed.

A fall down some stairs. It was the same way he'd died in the vision he'd given me when we'd first met two days ago. Had it really only been two days?

While people often held onto the same personality traits and habits from one life to the next, specific events like the way they died virtually never matched up. To be fair, I didn't have a lot of data to say this with certainty, but I couldn't think of an instance where a person had suffered the same sort of unusual accident more than once over their lifetimes. I once met someone during one of my research stints who had twice died in childbirth in the past, which up until the last century or so was a fairly common occurrence for women. Because he was male in this lifetime, there was no chance of that happening this time around, and I'd chalked it up to random chance. That was likely what this was as well, but it still struck me as strange.

"To Bill!" someone cries from across the pub. The crowd repeats the toast, glasses raised, foam sloshing over the edges. I lift my own pint silently in acknowledgment.

"To Bill," Sheena says a moment later, so quiet

I barely hear her. She sighs, and there's a great deal of sadness in her eyes, which are rimmed red from crying. "I should go. I need to call my mama and tell her the news. She'll be devastated. She and Bill grew up together, you see. He's a good few years older than her, but they were neighbors over on Meadowlark Street when she was a girl, and he always looked out for her, almost like an older brother. When Lilian died—Bill's wife—I always wondered if maybe they hadn't started quietly seeing each other, since my daddy's been dead since I was two and they became real close again. Mama never said anything about it to me specifically, but they were always doing stuff together, scrambling all over the dunes with binoculars looking at birds, taking watercolor classes, that sort of thing. They must have quarreled or something because all of a sudden Mama was determined to leave the only place she'd ever lived and move to Florida to live in one of those retirement parks. She's never been back once in almost eight years. Still, even if things did end badly between them, she'll want to know he's passed." She gulps down the last two mouthfuls of her beer, slides the empty glass toward Kellen, and leaves me with an apology for her somber mood and an invitation to stop into her shop again soon.

I have the urge to hug her, but at the last moment hold back. I tell myself it's because it would be awkward to swivel off my stool and stand up without bumping into the person on my left at the tightly packed bar. The reality is I don't feel like I have the mental fortitude to take on any visions. The grief she's feeling will most certainly leak into whatever snippet of her past she gives me, and the atmosphere of the pub is already grim enough. Instead, I squeeze her arm, sleeved in a light-green plaid flannel, and tell her I'll definitely see her soon.

Despite my wish to avoid any direct contact, it comes anyway, in the form of Naomi, who swoops into the spot vacated by Sheena with a plate bearing the food I'd ordered via Kellen earlier. She sets it down in front of me and gives me a long look.

"Our sorrow is yours too, isn't it, dear girl," she says. "I can tell you're feeling it, poor child."

I don't know how to reply to this assertion. It's true, but I don't quite feel like I have a right to it, not to the degree these people do. Yet as soon as she says it, I'm aware of the heaviness in my heart that's been present ever since Kellen told me about Blackmoor's death. It's a sharp, unwelcome ache.

"Eat what you can," Naomi tells me. "I always say, when in doubt, eat something made with love." She leans forward and presses a gentle kiss on my forehead before bustling back into the kitchen.

REGRESS

Yulia willed her body to still, suppressing the shivers threatening to wrack her thin frame. She didn't want her children to see how she suffered, not since she'd wrapped her warm woolen shawl around her youngest daughter. Although it was not yet dark, she considered telling them all to get ready for bed so they could share their warmth under the quilts. Perhaps she could spend the waning hours of the day making up fairy tales for them until one by one, they drifted off. They had long abandoned separate beds, preferring now to all sleep huddled together on Yulia's large mattress with all their blankets piled atop it. For Yulia, it had often been the only time she felt warm over this devastating winter; colder and longer than any she could remember. The meager fire burning at the hearth did little to heat her small cottage, but at least they had stones warming at the edge of the flames that she would wrap in flannel and tuck into the foot of the bed. As she did every night, she contemplated dragging the mattress closer to the hearth, but she was so worried a spark would set the bed ablaze and burn them in their sleep, she couldn't quite bring herself to do it.

"Mama, I'm still hungry," three-year-old Oksana said, tugging at her skirt. The other two were old enough to know not to complain, but Yulia was forever having to placate her youngest. Weariness washed over Yulia, and she fought back the urge to snap at her daughter. Of course, she was still hungry. She'd had less to eat all day than a child her age ought to have in a single meal.

"I'm sorry, my sweet girl. There is nothing left to eat today. We will have to wait until tomorrow when I go get our rations again." She kept her voice calm and steady, even though inside she felt like screaming. The rations were getting smaller, even though the council kept assuring the villagers that there would be enough to last through the winter. Last night, as she watched her son, twelve-year-old Dragan, remove his shirt, she saw his ribs sticking out of his already thin frame, and was shocked at how his shoulder blades jutted out of his back. She knew he was slipping Oksana an extra bite or two of potato or a morsel of bread almost every meal, and he always refused Yulia when she tried to give over her own small portion.

"I'm the man of the house now," he told Yulia when she'd confronted him in private. "When Papa left, he said to watch over his girls until he returned."

"*You cannot watch over us if you're too weak from lack of food.*" She'd smiled as she said it, proud of her boy for taking the role so seriously. "*I know Oksana's cries are hard to bear, but I cannot let you sacrifice yourself. We need you.*"

"*Ahh, Mama,*" he'd said, wagging his finger at her. "*Do you not think I could say the same to you? We need you as well. Who knows what will become of us if you—*" He couldn't finish his sentence and buried his head into her chest, a rare show of affection from her boy who wanted so badly to be a man.

"*Oh, my son,*" she'd whispered into his hair. "*I'm your mother. A mother would do anything for her children. Anything at all.*" Nevertheless, she'd resolved not to give over so much of her own ration to the children. Dragan was right. Without her to advocate for them and Zoran gone, would the village council look the other way and let them starve as well? Would anyone take pity upon them and take them in? As mature and willing as Dragan was, she didn't know how long he could head the household in the face of so much hardship.

"*But Mama, I'm hungry!*" Oksana shrieked, bringing her back to the present. She punctuated each word with a hard tug at Yulia's skirt. "*I—want—more—potatoes! I—want—meat!*" She dissolved into angry tears, and Yulia slid her hands under Oksana's arms and lifted her up to her hip.

"*Come now, why don't we wash our faces and hands, climb into bed, and I'll tell you a story. There will be a princess, a castle, and a dreadful troll. Doesn't that sound nice?*" Oksana howled, arching back away from Yulia, and the room before her eyes closed in, darkness overtaking her sight. With her last conscious thought, she set Oksana down before toppling forward.

The next thing she knew, she felt herself on the hard floor of the cottage.

"Mama, wake up," her ten-year-old daughter Elena was shouting. She could feel her small fingers digging into her shoulders, shaking her. With a great deal of effort, Yulia pried her eyes open to see Elena and Dragan bent over her.

"I'm fine, I'm fine," she said, although she wasn't sure if she had the strength to sit up. Her head was spinning, and Oksana's screams were making her head pound. "Help me to the bed, Dragan. I think I'd like to lie down now. Come, children, it's time for bed. Elena, get your sister washed up and changed into her nightclothes, please."

Dragan pulled her up, and although it was ten steps to the bed, she felt faint again before she was even halfway there. Collapsing onto the straw mattress, she allowed Dragan to remove her sturdy black shoes and cover her with the quilts.

"Be quiet, Oksana," he commanded. Oksana was resisting all efforts for her sister to wash her face and was still shrieking wordlessly. Thankfully, the toddler's cries subsided to whimpers, and she allowed Elena to get her ready for bed without further protest.

Yulia lay quietly throughout all this, trying to steady the spinning in her head. It was like the time she had had too much wine the night of her wedding to Zoran, but without any of the giddiness that accompanied it.

Soon they were all curled up in the bed together, and the warmth of her children surrounding her revived Yulia somewhat.

"Story, Mama," Oksana demanded. "I want a story."

"Not tonight, Oksana. Mama's tired," Dragan started, but Yulia hushed him gently.

"It's fine, I can tell you a story," Yulia said. "Would you like one about a princess and a troll?"

"Tell us a story about papa," Elena said. "Tell us about the adventures he's having and all the brave things he's done since he's been away."

Yulia was careful to keep her face neutral upon hearing her daughter's request. In the first days since her husband, Zoran, had left to attempt to traverse the pass, so deep with snow it had cut them off from the rest of the world, she had amused the children during the long days with imagined tales of his adventures. As the days turned into weeks—six in total—with no sign of him, she was fast losing hope he would return to them.

"All right then," she began, drawing them even closer. Oksana popped her thumb into her mouth and began to suck. "Four days after your father left, he lost his way and soon found himself deep in the forest instead of on the path he was meant to follow to town. Darkness was falling, and he decided to make camp for the night and try to retrace his steps in the morning. However, no sooner had he settled himself down beside his small fire when who should appear from behind an ancient tree, but a trickster..."

8

The vision Naomi gives me has enough in common with the one from Cora that I'm nearly certain they're from the same place and time. The problem is, neither has enough details for me to do further research. Based on the apparel and furnishings, I'm positive it's from earlier than the twentieth century, and the names all seem to be Russian, but beyond that, I have little to go on. At some point in the past, a village of unknown size was cut off due to a snowstorm or extended period of poor weather and had been forced to pool and ration what supplies they had. With grief and worry so near the surface of their current lives, the spirits of Cora and Naomi were revisiting those past hardships.

What I do know is that through their lifetimes, Cora's consciousness and Naomi's have been linked more than once. They are kindred in some way, and I wonder in the present time as well as the past, not only how they're connected, but how closely.

I'm surprised to see my meal has disappeared untasted, so preoccupied have I been in examining the details of Naomi's vision and comparing it to Cora's. The pub is still crowded, and with no reason to stay, I crumple my napkin onto my plate and head for the exit. I'm loathed to interrupt Cora, who's still sitting at the same table, so I make sure my path doesn't take me directly past her group, and a moment later the door swings shut behind me. Although the somber atmosphere hasn't disappeared, I feel some of the tension begin to release from my neck and shoulders as the din of the pub is replaced by the faint sound of the ocean, and the smell of ale and fried food with salt spray and seaweed.

Now what? I'm overcome with a crushing sense of loneliness, a foreign emotion for me. I'm used to solitude, and have always been comfortable in my own company, but at this moment, I wish I had the sort of community around me that the people of Soberly—and the residents of some unknown Russian village—do. I want to stomp my feet like three-year-old Oksana and scream for companionship the way she screamed for food. I want to bundle up under a pile of blankets with someone warm and safe. It's ironic that I'm full of food and starved for company, while she had been the opposite. Somehow, I feel like I'm the one who's worse off.

You're being ridiculous. What I need to do is make a plan for how to move forward without Bill Blackmoor, and the first step is to find the next closest lawyer who can continue to oversee Roz's will and the transfer of ownership first from her estate to me, then to Cora. That means a date with my laptop and Google. Resolutely I head for Cora's house, determined to at least have some names and leave some voicemails before I go to sleep.

Cora agrees to loan me her car, and the next morning I travel sixty miles inland to Eugene to meet with another lawyer. Greta Pickler was the first to return my call and happens to be the closest. She is an imposing, power-suited woman with a steely gaze framed by layers of thick mascara, and a puckered mouth that never so much as hints at a smile. I dislike her instinctively, but since she's willing to take on the work left unfinished by Bill Blackmoor's death, I'm willing to overlook the feeling. As expected, she tells me it will take some time to transfer the executorship of the will to her, further delaying my escape from Soberly. Her fees are also nearly twice as high as Blackmoor's, and, she informs me, she won't be available at the drop of a hat "like those small-town people are." I keep myself from rolling my eyes and thank her for being able to fit me in. We agree to communicate mainly via email and phone before I make my way back to the coast.

Cora pinches the bridge of her nose between her forefinger and thumb when I tell her the news. I can't tell if she's annoyed with me for being the bearer of bad tidings, Greta Pickler for not being able to instantaneously execute the will and complete the sale of the inn, Bill Blackmoor for dying, or Roz for getting us all into this mess in the first place. Maybe all of the above. In fact, probably all of the above. That would reflect my own feelings, anyway.

"I'm sorry," I offer, not knowing what else to say.

"It's not your fault," she replies, but I can see the tightness around her eyes and the effort it takes to say it. This isn't a good day to be hanging around the inn.

"I'm going to do my laundry this afternoon. Maybe call my parents." *Where did that come from?* I haven't spoken to either of my parents in years. Cora, unaware of our fractured relationship, nods, and I escape the lobby.

Forty-five minutes later, everything I've worn since I came to Soberly is in the dryer. I'd spent those minutes eating a sandwich, wiping up invisible spots on the table, sweeping the crumbless kitchen floor, and texting my former college roommate about my situation. She didn't reply, and now I'm at a loss for what to do. Cora's postage stamp-sized lawn has recently been trimmed, and the sprinklers come on every morning, so that's out. I have no interest in afternoon TV programs.

Bill Blackmoor's words come back to me. *"You can have a relaxing week on the beach. Maybe read a couple good books."* It *is* a beautiful day, maybe the nicest since I've arrived—not too hot, but sunny with a light breeze. Maybe an afternoon on the beach isn't a bad idea.

On the way back to the public beach access point, which is adjacent to the inn, I grab a paperback from the drugstore. Marnie, the pharmacist, is behind the counter as usual, and she waves hello.

"How's the burn?" she asks as I pay for my detective thriller.

"Peeling and itchy as hell." I pat my beach bag, where along with a towel, is the extra-large bottle of sunscreen I bought from her earlier. "Don't worry, I'm already coated."

"Every ninety minutes," she reminds me. Marnie is motherly without being overbearing, and I like her.

"Any suggestion on the best spot on the beach?"

"For reading or swimming? I'm not much of a swimmer, but if you want to relax I'd try and grab one of the lounge chairs in front of the inn. The surf is usually pretty calm around there too if you do want to go in."

I thank her, flip my sunglasses back down, and am soon settled into one of the cedar chaises she mentioned. I assume they belong to the inn, and since more than half are vacant, I don't feel any guilt in occupying one. If actual paying customers come around, I'll give it up.

Engrossed as I am in my book, I barely notice when someone drops into the chaise beside me a short time later. I definitely do notice, however, when they spring up again and push their chaise over so it's a hand-span from mine.

"Beautiful day, isn't it?" Kellen says, tossing my bag over my stomach to the other side so he can inch closer. I stare at him wordlessly as he stretches his lean body out again, fingers laced behind his head. He closes his eyes and smiles beatifically, brown skin radiant in the sunlight. He doesn't appear to have an inch of fat on his body, and, I note, his swim trunks sit dangerously low on his hips.

"How did you know I was here?" I ask, regaining my voice. Of course, it cracks.

"Hmm? I always sit here from"—he checks his watch—"quarter after one until three. How did *you* know *I'd* be here?"

"What? I—I didn't—" He's laughing. He's always laughing at me.

"You walked past my house half an hour ago. Cover-up, flip flops, beach bag. There literally could not have been any other place you were going, so I decided to join you." His eyes are still closed, so I give myself license to admire his abs a moment longer and come to the conclusion that I'm going to have to fuck this man and get it over with. Then maybe I can find my equilibrium again.

"Be my guest," I say, and turn back to my book. Only now, the story that had gripped me from the first page can't hold my attention at all, and I've reread the same paragraph four times without getting any further into the plot. That thin line of hair disappearing into Kellen's waistband is driving me to distraction.

"You and Cora are neighbors?" I blurt out, giving up on the book.

"For now," he says, turning to face me. "I'm your stereotypical millennial living in his parents' basement. Not for long, though. I'm aiming to buy Margot Oxford's house in a few months' time when she moves over to a retirement home in Newport. It's a little place, needs some fixing up, but it'll suit me pretty well. I'm looking forward to knocking down some walls and jackhammering concrete." He pounds his chest in a display of manliness, eliciting a snort from me. "Seriously though. Margot's taste in wallpaper runs toward dusty-rose floral with metallic accents. Straight outta the sixties. And the carpet. You have to see it to believe it. Now, your place, I imagine, is all clean lines, white on white, a pop of color here and there. Sleek. Minimalist, but trendy. High-rise condo?"

I shake my head. "Wrong on all counts. Third-floor

walk-up, various shades of beige, as chosen by my landlord. Thrift store furniture. Cardboard boxes I've never bothered unpacking shoved into corners. Mattress on the floor because I haven't had the time to find a frame for it." My description is grim, but I shrug it off. "It's just a place to stay. I do have a plant." *I never made arrangements for someone to water my plant.* I smack myself in the forehead with my book. It'll be dead long before I make it back to New Mexico. "Actually, I take that back. I had a plant. Ugh, I'm the worst." I frown at the thought of the little African violet slowly dying of thirst on my windowsill. The truth is, I kill every plant I adopt.

Cranky now, I turn back to my book, silently beating myself up. I had liked that violet and its lavender blooms. It was the only spot of color in my dreary galley kitchen.

"It's just a plant, Audrey," Kellen says.

"It's not *just a plant*. It's...it's a pattern of neglect. I'm careless about the living. All I ever focus on is the past." My words surprise me, both what they signify, and that I'd said them aloud.

"You're thinking about Roslyn." How could he know? I'm close to tears.

"What was she like? I never even knew her as an adult, not really. I haven't seen her since I was twelve. We kept in touch here and there, but even though she's my only family member I like, I still didn't make much of an effort to connect with her. I didn't even know she owned this place."

"Want to hear something funny? She didn't mention you to me often, but every time she did, she told me I'd like you, because of how well she and I got on. Said you had the same type of humor, and she's right. Sarcasm for days, you Eames women." He shakes his head. "Roz would never let me have the last word either and was stubborn as hell." He's smiling at the memory.

"You miss her."

"I do. She was someone I looked up to. Roz had room in her heart for everyone. There's a big hole in this town now that she's gone. I think the thing I admired the most about her is how determined she was. If she put her mind to something, it happened, no matter how many people told her otherwise."

He tells me the story of how she came to own the inn—she'd first arrived as a guest in her twenties, and kept returning over the years, slowly falling in love with the place, as she told it, and started taking courses in hotel management at the college in Eugene. Finally, one year she asked the owners if they'd ever consider selling, and since they were getting on in age, they jumped at the opportunity. With that and a hefty bank loan, Roz was an innkeeper. That was ten years ago. Naomi was already in charge of the pub's kitchen by then, the Greene family having moved to Soberly five years prior. Kellen's father commuted to Eugene, returning on weekends, but Naomi had wanted to live on the coast. "Then, as soon as it was legal, basically, Roz put me to work too, first washing dishes, then bussing, and eventually bartending."

He tells me the story of how Roz and Cora met and fell in love, too. "It was almost painful, how awkward those two were," he says, laughing at the memory. "Cora came on an internship from the same program Roz took. It was a second career for her. The two of them, with a serious case of whatever the lady equivalent of a hard-on is for each other, and neither of them doing a damn thing about it except the odd attempt at innuendo and a lot of blushing. Completely ridiculous. I bet it was Roz who made the first move, though. Cora stayed on after the internship was over. Roz was in over her head, trying to run everything by herself. Cora...I don't know. Roz changed something in her. Healed her, I think. She and my mama are pretty tight, and although Mama's never said anything specific about Cora's past, she's implied it wasn't all that great before she came here. That's what Roz does. Did. She saved people." He exhales deeply and rolls back onto his back. I've been laugh-crying through most of his stories, and I take a minute to blot my face with my towel so he can compose himself.

"Anyway," he says, his voice a bit unsteady. "I'm sure you've already heard most of that from Cora herself."

"Not at all," I say, shaking my head. "I don't think—" Drew's words from the day we met come to mind. "I don't think she's on Team Audrey. She's mostly been polite, but I can tell she wants me out of here as fast as possible. She hardly talks to me at all, unless it's about the inn specifically." I describe her reaction earlier when I told her how Bill Blackmoor's death would delay the sale of the inn even further.

"So, you're definitely going through with the sale?"

"Yep." I pretend to pick grains of sand out from under my nails.

"We're not growing on you even a little bit?" I can see through my lashes he's flashing the megawatt smile at me. The only things brighter than the sun today are his damn teeth.

"Growing on me or not, I have no experience running

a hotel, and it's not my place to come in here and sweep all Cora's hard work out from under her. I doubt she'd stay on if I didn't sell."

"We *are* growing on you." Impossibly, his smile gets wider.

"I didn't say that." To avoid further conversation, I flip over onto my tummy and rest my head on my arms, pulling my sunglasses back down onto my face.

"You need sunscreen on your back, young lady. Pass it over."

"I can do it myself." I rummage around in my bag. "And I'm older than you."

"You sure about that?"

"One hundred percent."

"You know it's my job to be able to peg a person's age, right?"

"You must be pretty shitty at your job then." I've been smearing sunscreen on my back the whole while, awkwardly reaching to get it distributed all over. The back of my bikini top keeps getting in the way, and I'm sure I've coated the black crochet material in thick white lotion.

"Will you tell me your age if I ask you?" An arched eyebrow is the only answer he gets. I'd never give him the satisfaction. "Didn't think so. Well then, I leave it to your sense of honesty to admit you're wrong. I turned twenty-eight in April."

"I am, indeed, older than you." Because age has little to do with maturity, I stick out my tongue.

"You're lying."

I push myself up onto my elbows, take my sunglasses off, and look him dead in the eye. "I'm older than you,

Kellen," I say, deadpan. "Now, since you claim to know my tell, you should know I'm not lying." With a satisfied smile, I lay my head back down and start to work with the sunscreen on my shoulders, where the worst of the burn from the day I arrived is.

"Well, shit, you aren't lying. What, were you born in March? Are we talking like, a couple weeks?"

"Less than…" I pretend to consider for a moment. "Ten years older." In truth, it's a little less than two. I turned thirty in June.

"Miserable Eames women," I hear him mutter. "Would you give me that? You're making a mess, and you missed a whole area in the middle." He makes a lunge for the bottle of lotion and because my arm is twisted up behind me, I can't fend him off. "Can I please help you?"

"Oh-my-God fine." I don't really have a choice since he's holding the bottle, but I'm also interested in knowing what his hands feel like on my bare skin.

They feel amazing. Warm, steady, and firm. I get one quick flash of the schoolteacher, a past life I've already encountered, as she sits studying for her entrance exam to college. Then, because he's sitting up on his chaise with one of his knees resting against my side, our skin never breaks contact until he's done. I'm glad because I don't want visions of the past to interrupt the present.

Kellen goes over my entire back with the sunscreen, rubbing it in with long, deep strokes, so it half feels like a massage. When he starts to push his thumbs in a circular motion over my shoulders, it becomes entirely a massage, and I groan reflexively as he digs deep at a knot.

"You're all wound up," he says, and there's no

laughter in his voice now.

"No shit." It hasn't exactly been an easy week.

"Better?" he asks after a minute. I roll my shoulders experimentally. They do feel looser.

"Much. Thank you."

"My pleasure." There's more than a simple acknowledgment of thanks in his tone. His hand lingers on the back of my neck for a moment, and he sweeps his thumb along my jawline once before withdrawing back to his chaise. I consider what he'd do if I rolled over and straddled his abs, pull loose the knot holding my top on, and demand he do my front as well. The idea appeals to me and I get the sense he wouldn't refuse, but there are children present, and if there's gossip about me in Soberly now, that would probably make the town explode. He'd have to hear about it until the end of his days, so I restrain myself and let my imagination run wild instead.

Sometime later, when we've moved well past sunscreen massages and bathing suits in my mind, Kellen sits up and stretches.

"Gotta go," he says. "Work beckons. Supper's at six again, and I'll make sure it gets out to you on time."

"Just a salad. I could barely button my jeans this morning. I need to find a gym around here or start running again." After only a few days, Naomi's home-style cooking is starting to show.

"Sounds like you accidentally bought the wrong size jeans," he says. "You look amazing, Audrey. Thick in all the right places." With that, he shoulders his backpack and leaves me.

9

Shortly before six, Drew greets me with a fist bump when I walk into the pub.

A young boy, maybe ten or eleven, sat on the curb, surrounded by sandstone row houses. Dust coated his shoes and the bare strip of skin between them and the hem of his patched trousers as he kicked at the pebbles littering the gutter. A group of kids shrieked and tumbled in front of him, all vying for control of the leather-covered ball. He watched them from the sidelines, waiting for an opportunity. It came a few minutes later when an out-of-control kick brought the ball almost into his lap.

"Can I..." he started to ask William. He and the younger boy have been neighbors their whole lives.

"We're even numbers on each side, Jamie," William

interrupted before he could finish his sentence. "It wouldn't be fair, you understand."

"Right, of course," Jamie replied. "Maybe when someone quits then."

"Yeah, sure." There was no enthusiasm in the other boy's voice. Will took the ball back and Jamie sat back down, waiting patiently. Then George's mother called him inside to scrub the kitchen floor, which elicited uproarious laughter from his playmates, and the game dissolved. All the boys scattered off to their own homes, leaving Jamie alone in the street. With a violent kick, he sent a stone sailing across the cobblestones.

Drew jerks his head over toward the bar, at what I'm starting to think of as "my" seat, as the vision fades. His headphones, as usual, arc over his head like a red rainbow.

"What is this?" I ask Kellen as he sets an enormous plate down in front of me.

"It's a salad, Audrey," he replies in a know-it-all tone. It's true, there are a few leaves of lettuce and some carrot shavings on the side of what can only be described as a platter, but there's also a mound of crab legs and claws, a dish of melted butter, and a scoop of creamy mashed potatoes. Damn, does it look good. My mouth fills with saliva at the rich, garlicky scent of the butter.

"I can just wear leggings for the rest of my life," I mumble as I scoop the first chunk of crab meat out of a claw and dunk it in the butter. Thankfully, I'd chosen a loose A-line sundress to change into after I was done at the beach. There is no way I can make it through this meal and still keep my jeans buttoned.

"Atta girl. Now I'd recommend you pair the blonde ale with this...salad." A pint appears in front of me, expertly poured with a half-inch of thick foam. I can't talk because I have a mouthful of the sweetest crab I've ever tasted, so I give him a thumbs up.

I absolutely demolish my plate, and two pints besides. I finish even the little afterthought of a salad. When I'm done, I ball up my napkin and burp discreetly into my fist. There's a small butter stain on the pale blue eyelet right above my heart.

"Where's your mom?" I ask Kellen when he clears my plate. "I want to ask her to adopt me so she can feed me forever."

"That would be kind of weird," he says.

"We could get bunk beds. It'll be fun."

"Even weirder." I can see him fighting back a smile.

"You can be on top." I lift my glass to my lips and add a wink over the rim for good measure and he cracks.

"Jesus, Audrey." I think he's blushing, and he can't meet my eyes as he polishes an already-spotless glass. I've won this round.

"What're your plans for the rest of the night?" he asks eventually. I've been reveling in his obvious discomfort at the lengthening silence between us, pretending to be engrossed in my phone while he opens and closes his mouth several times, at a loss for what to say.

"Bookkeeping. I haven't touched it today."

"Why don't you bring it down here to work on? Must be lonely in that room all by yourself for hours."

"Sometimes." I could bring the laptop down and set myself up in one of the quiet corners. The idea hadn't occurred to me before, mostly because the pub's always been so crowded, but tonight there are half a dozen empty tables. I wouldn't need to lug down the entire file box of papers, just a small folder. "Okay, don't let anyone take that table." I point to the one I want and dart out to grab what I need. Jana supplies me with my box from the safe, and ten minutes later I've set up my remote office. It reminds me a bit of my college days, writing papers in coffee shops and all-night diners. Kellen makes sure my pint is never empty, but otherwise leaves me to my work.

Sometime later, the lights come up slightly and Kellen announces it's last call. I check the time in the corner of my screen, surprised it's almost eleven. I've been poring over the credit card statements, trying to categorize each purchase based on the one-line description, many of which are cryptic and require some Google sleuthing. In the four hours or so I've been working, I haven't even made it through one month.

There are still a few stragglers in the pub, but Drew takes their payment efficiently, ushers them out, and starts wiping down tables. As soon as they've left, Kellen cranks the music up a few notches and changes it to a mellow electronica playlist.

"You're fine," he says as I start to pack up my things. He and Drew continue their end-of-day tasks while I puzzle over a few lines from the statement. I can't figure out what they are for the life of me.

"See you tomorrow," Drew says, and slips out the door. Kellen is sliding the last of the clean wine glasses upside-down onto their racks as I pass him my empty glass with an apology.

"I'll leave it for later," he says. "I've got more

important things to do right now." He comes around to my side of the bar. "C'mere, you." He slides his hands around my waist and draws me close, swaying along to M83. He smells like nutmeg, pine, and, inevitably, beer. I want to bury my face in his chest and inhale. Instead, I lace my fingers behind his neck—he's the perfect height to rest my forearms on—and close the last gap between us so our hips brush. That small move is all the encouragement he needs, and one hand moves to the small of my waist to press our bodies together in a slow grind while the other one slides up my back until it rests on the nape of my neck. It's not raunchy, but there's a clear intent behind the way we are moving together. The vision he gives me—just a flash—is very, very X-rated. Not everyone from the Victorian era was a prude. Two or three songs go by like that, the rhythmic, heavy bass of the music echoing in my pulse.

"Finally." His mouth is so close to my ear I can feel his breath. "Right where I've wanted you since the first time you sat down in front of me." It's the first thing he's said since we started dancing. His lips graze my earlobe, and I crane my neck upward, wanting more. I want to tell him how every time he smiles, my stomach twists in knots, and how if he doesn't get his hands up under my dress soon, I might die. Instead, all that comes out is a half-sigh, half-gasp. I feel his lips pull apart in a smile against my skin.

"There's a couch upstairs," I manage to say. Kellen stops dead and bursts out laughing.

"Let me kiss you first, sweet woman," he says, and does exactly that, slowly and thoroughly. It's the type of kiss that promises more than kissing is coming. I pull myself up onto a tall stool before my knees give out from under me, and he steps forward into the gap between my legs. Our lips break contact momentarily. I've got a fistful of his shirt in my hand, but he resists my playful tug forward for another kiss.

"You said something about a couch?" His hand, which had been in the vicinity of my waist a moment ago, has slid upward and his thumb is stroking the underside of my breast through my dress.

"The office," I reply. *My* hand is working its way down his chest, lingers for a moment on the waistband of his jeans, and moves lower still. He's definitely ready for the couch.

"Oh, that's a pull-out bed," he says, startling me out of my explorations. I give him a long, hard look, evading his mouth when it moves in toward mine. Why is he so familiar with my aunt's couch? Is sneaking women upstairs a regular occurrence for him? *I* didn't even know it was a pull-out, and I've been spending a considerable amount of time sitting on it for the past two days.

"No, no, no," he cries, horrified understanding blossoming on his face as he reads my skeptical expression. "I've never—I've never *used* it. I've just seen it a couple times. Roz used to crash on it when she'd do an overnight at the desk. I swear, Audrey. Shit, you gotta believe me." There's a hint of panic in his voice that convinces me of his sincerity, and I flash him a smile.

"All right, pull-out it is then." The unintentional *double entendre* hits us both at the same time, and we have to cover our mouths to keep the noise of our laughter from carrying. Then his mouth is on mine again, this time with more urgency, and his thumb traces slow circles around my nipple.

True fact: sex is usually fair to middling for me. I can almost never get myself relaxed enough with whoever's bare skin is pressed up against mine to surrender fully to the experience, and more often than not, end up feeling like I never quite got all the way there. In this moment, however, I feel like I'm so close to all the way there already that I'm going to embarrass myself and give him something to crow about until the end of time.

Thankfully, he breaks free, laces his fingers through mine, and pulls me toward the kitchen. We tiptoe through it and the staff room, up the back stairs, and down the hall to the office door.

"We need to be quiet," I hiss. I turn the key in the knob, and the pop of the lock disengaging sounds as loud as a gunshot. Jana's at the bottom of the back stairs, available for any late-night guest needs.

"No promises." Kellen's grinding into my back while I try to open the door, usher us both inside and close it again without any further noises. The moon is nearly full tonight, allowing us to make our way around the furniture without crashing into it. "There's the couch I have absolutely no experience with," he says, and pulls me down to sit beside him. I choke back laughter and try to lean back, hoping he'll follow my lead and stretch his body over mine, but he resists. "Slow down," he says into my ear, followed by a nip on my lobe. His hands are driving me mad—skirting all the places I want them most. Instead of pushing back further, I lunge forward, swing my leg over him so I'm straddling his hips, and grind into him the same way we'd begun when we were dancing in the pub.

"Fuck," he mutters and pulls my mouth toward his. Taking this as a sign of encouragement, I begin to unbutton the short-sleeve shirt with the inn's logo on the pocket he wears when he's working. "Audrey, we have lots of time," he says, but doesn't try to stop me.

We don't, we don't, I want to shout, to grab him by the shoulders, and shake him. *We might only have a couple weeks.* Instead, I push his shirt off his shoulders. I want as much of this as I can get.

"I need you to make me come. Right now." It's not a request. Never have I been so bare about my needs with another person.

"Kiss me." My urgency is apparent and there isn't so much as a hint of playfulness in him now. One hand clutches my hair while his mouth takes over mine, and the other slips up the inside of my thigh and under the band of my boy shorts, tracing the strip of lace there for a moment with his thumb. "I'm going to need a better look at these in a minute," he tells me, and the next thing I know, he's giving me what I need, finally. I grit my teeth and press my lips together to keep from crying out, pushing my forehead hard into his chest.

"Better?" he asks when my legs have stopped trembling and my breath is a little less ragged. I nod. "I was actually hoping you'd say no because I'm only getting started," he adds, pulling my dress up and over my head in one fluid movement. He gapes in surprise when he realizes I didn't bother with a bra tonight. When I packed to come to Soberly, meeting someone like Kellen had been the furthest thing from my mind. I didn't bring any nice matching sets.

He half-lifts me to fish his wallet out of his back

pocket and throws a strip of foil packets on the cushion beside him.

"You're not supposed to carry condoms around like that," I say. I don't care, but I want to tease him a bit. My franticness has abated, while his seems to have increased.

"I bought them yesterday." I laugh quietly at this. I'd done the same thing when I'd bought my beach supplies. Hopefully, Marnie the pharmacist has more discretion than some of the other townspeople, at least when it comes to people's purchases at the drugstore, because it wouldn't take too much mental energy to add two and two together.

Kellen's trying to maneuver himself out of his jeans with me still in his lap, with little success, so I raise myself up on my knees to help. However, this brings my chest up to eye level on him and distracts him entirely. His lips fix themselves around my nipple, drawing it into his mouth, where his tongue swirls and teases me until my breath is coming in short pants. I'm vaguely aware of the sound of foil ripping, then his hands peeling my underwear down to my knees. He grasps me by the hips to lower me down onto him and lets out a deep groan of relief as we move in rhythm together, the heat of our bodies combined, making us both slick with sweat. Although Kellen is silent, the way he touches me, moves beneath me, tells me more than words ever could.

"Audrey, I—" he buries his face into my neck, breathing hard. "Not yet." he's muttering into my skin. I grin and squeeze down on him. His body jerks convulsively under me, and the moment is my undoing as well. "What—the—fuck—" he says, half-laughing a moment later. "I wasn't ready yet, woman."

"Were you saying *golf?*" I ask him, smothering my own laughter.

"It's what I think about when I want to...not do that," he tells me. "Or, say, when I'm rubbing down a hot, half-naked woman with sunscreen, and trying to ignore her squirming every time my hands come anywhere near her ass."

"I was *not* squirming," I retort.

"I could see you clenching those same muscles you just used on me over and over. It was obvious as hell. Luckily, golf is the most boring thing I can imagine. Didn't do a damn thing this time, though."

"Sorry not sorry," I say.

"You're going to be so much trouble." I can see his mock frown in the moonlight streaming through the balcony doors as he looks up toward the ceiling.

"If you don't think you can handle me..." I start to pull myself off his lap, tugging at my underwear, hoping to provoke him. He doesn't disappoint. Before I know what's happening, he's got me flipped onto my back on the couch, one strong hand pinning both of mine above my head.

"Let me show you how I'm going to handle you," he says as his mouth travels down between my breasts, stopping for a moment to circumnavigate my navel before moving lower. His gaze never breaks from mine. "Then we're pulling this bed out, and I'm going to continue the demonstration until we're both exhausted. I don't care if we bring the whole damn inn down around us." I arch my hips up to meet him and close my eyes as his tongue hits

home. I'm going to enjoy this demonstration very much.

10

Some hours later, we are indeed exhausted. Kellen tugs the sheet up to cover my shoulders and wraps his arms around me when I shiver from the slight breeze coming in from the balcony. He kisses my damp temple and rests his chin on the top of my head, and I'm filled with a deep sense of peace and contentment. For the time being, none of my problems matter, and the past hasn't intruded once since our mouths first came together. There is only the present, a rare moment for me, and one I don't want to give up. Sleep creeps up on me, and I stretch my legs out, twining them in between Kellen's. Then, remembering, I groan and start to sit up.

"What are you doing," he mumbles, tugging my arm.

"I left all my papers and laptop down in the pub," I say. "I have to go get them."

"Leave them, you can grab them in the morning. The

pub doesn't open until noon. I've already set an alarm."

"I can't. They're too important." I'm pretty sure my dress is somewhere under the bed's folding frame and will be awkward to retrieve, but I still haven't even made it off the mattress yet because Kellen's still hanging onto me.

"I'll get them then." He heaves himself up, grabs his jeans from the floor and pulls them up over his slender hips. When I begin to protest, he leans over the bed and kisses me. "I don't want you using the excuse that you're dressed anyway to leave," he says. I frown. It's pretty much standard operating procedure for me to not spend the night, but up until I'd remembered the mess I'd left scattered across the table downstairs, I'd planned on staying exactly where I was, curled up into his side, at least for a while. "Don't move, I'll be right back," he says and gives me a peck on the nose. "Please," he adds when he sees my displeasure. "I'm at my best first thing in the morning, you know." Now that is definitely something to look forward to, but my discomfort at his insistence that I stay lingers. I'd been right that we'd have amazing sex, but that doesn't mean our relationship was anything more than physical. If he'd gotten any sort of impression otherwise, I'd have to set him straight right away.

Before I can decide definitively if I should get dressed anyway and tell him I'd prefer to sleep at Cora's, Kellen is back. He dumps my stuff onto the table, shucks his jeans, and slides back into bed, resuming his original position, but this time I can't relax my body into his. I barely register whatever moment from his past he gave me, it being only a few seconds long and inconsequential compared to the words I'm trying to put together.

"Look, I wasn't—" I still haven't figured out exactly what I want to say.

"I know," he says. "It's fine, Audrey. I overstepped, I'm sorry." He lays, still and silent behind me, waiting for me to speak or move. From the tension in his own body, I'm sure he expects me to get up and leave. Finally, not sure whether it's because I enjoy proving him wrong so much, or because I genuinely want to, I roll over to face him, rest my head on his bicep, and close my eyes.

Kellen is unable to prove his claims of morning prowess because when his alarm goes off and I see the time, I almost shriek. Sunrise was more than half an hour ago, and I had wanted to be gone before dawn.

"We have to get out of here!" I hiss, trying to both deflect his roaming hands and shove him out of bed. I'm not having any success at either. Cora will already be at the desk downstairs, and the thought that she could walk through the door and discover us at any moment, should she choose to wish me a good morning, has me in a panic.

Kellen is less worried. "We're grown-ups, Audrey," he tells me, rolling his eyes and grinning. "It's nobody's business that we're together up here."

"Everything seems to be everyone's business in this town," I mutter. My dress, I see, is in a heap beside the couch's armrest, and I slip it over my head impatiently. Kellen is still lolling in bed, watching me dress. My underwear is nowhere in sight. I'm sure Kellen knows where it is, since he was the one who divested me of it last night, but when I ask him, he shrugs.

"Come back to bed and climb on top. I'll be real quiet, I promise. Not sure you will, though," he adds after a moment's reflection and a smirk. His hands are laced behind his head, and the thin sheet does nothing to conceal the fact that he's ready for me. God, do I ever want to, but I wave him off with a frustrated groan.

"Get up and put the bed away," I tell him. I've decided since I have to make my walk of shame to Cora's in broad daylight anyway, I might as well do it commando.

My underwear proves to be under the bed, revealed when Kellen pushes the frame back into the couch. I shimmy into it and shove my feet into my wedges. Cora will know I hadn't returned to her house to sleep, so there's no sense in pretending. Once Kellen is safely out, I can pop downstairs and casually say good morning. I want to ask her about the line items on the credit card statements I can't categorize anyway. They can be my excuse for why I was up so late. I hope she doesn't notice my freshly-fucked glow.

"Do you hear that?" Kellen says, pausing with a couch cushion in his hands, his head turned toward the balcony. "Sirens. Sounds like they're out on the highway. Must've been an accident." Route 101 runs all along the coast in Oregon and Soberly is just an off-ramp away from it. Unfortunately, the balcony in the office faces away from the highway, and there's no way of knowing for sure from here.

"Hope everyone's okay," I reply. I feel awkward and unsure of myself now that we're both dressed and about to part ways. My usual "I had a really great time" line is supposed to convey a finality I'm not sure I want. Then again, if Kellen and I keep sleeping together, there's bound to be more heartache for both of us when I leave Soberly than if this ends now as a one-night stand. I can't decide which is worse.

Failing to stifle a huge yawn, I rummage around in my tote for a hairbrush I know isn't in there as an excuse to avoid meeting his eye. His arm slides around my waist from behind, pulling me into a loose embrace.

"Tired?" There's amusement in his tone.

"Didn't get much sleep," I say, keeping my voice light. "I had a late night."

"Sorry not sorry," he mimics my words from before. "Now, who leaves first?"

"You. Go out the back door or something. Cora will know I spent the night here."

"My mama will know I didn't come home either. I'm sure she's already figured it all out."

"Well tell your mama to keep quiet about this, then. People stare at me enough as it is here. I feel like I'm all anyone is talking about. You don't know what it's like, being the outsider."

"The only black guy in town doesn't know about being an outsider? Other than my brother and dad, I guess, but now Marcus is in college, they're hardly ever here." He rolls his eyes but waves off my wince at my insensitivity with a grin. "Everyone here wants to know how you're going to fit in, what sort of person you are."

"I don't fit in at all." I frown. Although I do feel like I'm under a microscope in Soberly, apart from Cora, everyone's been perfectly friendly and welcoming toward me. If I was being perfectly fair, my insistence that I was being treated like an outsider was off base.

"You could, you know. You could fit in just fine.

See you tonight." I open my mouth to protest his presumptuousness, and he grins. "For supper. Although feel free to cash in that morning lovin' IOU anytime. Doesn't have to be morning, either." He winks and slips out the door, closing it soundlessly behind him.

Cora's eyes are raised well above the rims of her glasses when I step through the door behind the front desk a few minutes later and wish her a good morning.

"Rough night?" Given I don't have a comb or toothbrush with me, I can see why she asks. I make matters worse by immediately blushing scarlet. Impossibly, her brows lift even higher.

"I can't figure out this darn statement," I say. To my ears, it sounds both lame and insincere. I show her the papers I'm clutching, and the lines I've flagged. After a moment's perusal, she shrugs.

"Just put them under Miscellaneous," she suggests. "I don't have a clue."

"There are seven or eight of them on each statement," I tell her. "On their own, they don't look like much, but added up it's a fairly significant sum, and I can't even figure out what the charge is for. If you don't know what they are, you should dispute them with the card company. At least they'll be able to tell you the originating company so you'll know if they're legit or not."

"Audrey, I'm sure it's a perfectly normal expense. This was Roz's personal business card. If there were fraudulent charges, I'm sure she would have noticed long ago." She's impatient and keeps glancing toward the door. It feels dismissive until I follow her gaze through the glass. I can see up the street to the highway where two police cars and an ambulance are parked at the intersection, lights flashing. Four or five men and women are gathered around the shallow storm pond there. There are also several townspeople walking up the street toward them, and an officer coming down to meet them, his hand held out, indicating they shouldn't come any closer.

"Was there an accident?"

"I'm not sure. I can't see any cars pulled over." More residents are starting to gather outside, clustered in groups of three or four. My stomach is sinking. Instinct tells me something terrible has happened.

"I'll stay here if you want to check." Cora hesitates for a moment, then gives me a grateful look.

"There are only three guests checked in right now. Do the best you can if anyone needs you until I'm back. I want to talk to TJ and Joanne for a moment." The bell over the door jangles as she leaves, and I sit down behind the desk, feeling painfully out of place. My phone is upstairs, and the laptop in front of me is password-protected, so I have nothing to do but examine the room until she returns ten long minutes later.

"There's a body in the storm pond," she says. "Somebody driving past called it in. No one from town seems to know who died because the police won't let anyone come near, but the word going around is that it could have been a hitchhiker. I can't think of anyone else who would have been walking up along the highway this early, anyway." The frown lines between Cora's eyes have disappeared now that she's convinced herself it isn't one of Soberly's own. This town has seen enough mourning in the past couple weeks already.

"A hit and run, maybe?" Cora only shrugs in reply.

Something is bothering me, something about the manner of death, but I can't quite get my mind to zero in on it.

"Well I'm going to go over and have a shower," I say after a moment's awkward silence. "That couch sure is uncomfortable. Don't think I'll be sleeping on it again."

"Didn't you notice? It's a hide-a-bed."

"Oh, is it? Good to know." I'm praying Cora isn't as astute a lie detector as Kellen is, but she's still distracted by the scene outside and doesn't seem to notice how false I sound.

Three blocks away from the inn, just as I'm about to round the corner onto Cora's street, a teenage girl races by me at a full sprint, heading into the main part of town. *Must be running to catch her bus to school,* I tell myself. *Or maybe she wants to check out the commotion about the hitchhiker.* The uneasiness I've been feeling gets worse, and I turn back to look at the girl, who's still running like her life depends on it. She's not carrying a backpack. I turn around and retrace my steps, breaking into a jog when I see the scattered groups of people all cluster together into one. I've lost sight of the girl.

When I reach the inn, Cora is standing on the step outside, shading her eyes with her hand. Everyone is looking up the road at the storm pond, where a state trooper is trying to hold back the girl, who flails and fights against his grip, trying to get past him.

"Who is that?" I whisper to Cora, aghast.

"Marnie and Gord Decker's daughter, Kenzie," she replies. Her face is pale. Kenzie, the girl Sheena had told me was found passed out in a trough a couple months ago.

"Has anyone seen Gord this morning? Or Marnie?"

someone in the cluster of townspeople asks, loud enough for the dozen or so people to hear.

"Gord's up in Seattle on business until the end of the week," a female voice pipes up.

"What about Marnie?" Heads swivel from side to side, waiting for someone to confirm that someone had laid eyes on the pharmacist this morning.

"I'm calling her," one person says.

"Someone check the drugstore," another calls out. A few people break away to do exactly that, while another small group goes back up the road to interrogate the troopers. Me, I know it's hopeless. I'm positive Marnie is dead.

The little girl in a smocked dress, barely out of toddlerhood, spotted the mahogany-colored colt at the edge of the pasture, nibbling at some grass. It was only a week old, and she thought it was the most beautiful creature in the world, with its dark mane and tail, and the white star emblazoned between its eyes. The sun's rays made it look like it was cast from pure bronze. She believed the pony must be magic, to be so perfect. She knew she wasn't allowed to leave the yard by herself, but she wanted to see the pony so badly she forgot the rules and climbed over the stile into the pasture, clutching a handful of wildflowers as an offering. Every time she approached the pony, however, it shied a few steps away, until it bounded off entirely, over to the watering hole where its mother drank. Still, the girl persisted, walking slowly to show she meant no harm.

"I jutht want to be friendth," she called out in her

childish lisp. She had the idea that if she could tame the pony, it would let her ride it. In her fantasies, perched upon this colt's back, she was a queen, but she could never tame it if it kept running away from her.

When she reached the pond's edge the colt pressed close into its mother's side, alarmed, and the mare snorted a warning at the girl. She wisely sat down on the opposite side, dipping her bare feet into the cool water.

"Don't you like my flowerth?" she asked. Looking down at them, she saw how they were half-crushed from her climb over the stile and already starting to wilt. It was then she spotted the water lilies floating in the middle of the pond, their yellow and white spiky petals creating bright dots of color against the murky background of the water. That would be a much more suitable offering for the pony, she decided, and waded in. The pond was much deeper than she expected, however, and the water was up over her knees after a few steps in, with the lilies still out of reach. The hem of her dress trailed in the water as she inched a bit deeper, pulling herself forward with her toes an inch at a time in the squelchy mud. The pretty flowers were so close. She could feel a smooth, flat stone in front of her, and thinking it safe, stepped forward onto it, arm outstretched to grab a bloom. As soon as her foot made contact with the stone, however, it slipped sideways on a thick layer of algae and the girl plunged forward, the momentum pushing her into the center of the pond, where the water was much deeper. The shock of the cold water hitting her face caused her to inhale sharply, filling her lungs, and she panicked, flailing her

*limbs in all directions, not knowing which way was up.
It was the first time her head had ever been submerged
under water. Her foot scraped the bottom of the pond
once, but she couldn't find any purchase, nor did she
have the sense to push herself up with it, and her head
never broke the surface again. Within seconds, her
vision went dark.*

That was the vision Marnie gave me the second time
we met, when I'd stopped into the pharmacy to grab a
book for the beach. With the whole town grieving Bill
Blackmoor, it hadn't been surprising she had death on
her mind, nor had her statement that she didn't much
enjoy swimming. It was so unusual that she'd been found
dead—assuming it really was her, and her daughter
hadn't jumped to the wrong conclusion somehow—in the
same type of manner as in the past, like Bill Blackmoor.
Once was strange enough, but the odds of two people
a couple of days apart seemed astronomically small,
especially when they were both such uncommon ways
to die.

"God, how terrible," I say to Cora now. She's
still watching the scene play out. "That poor girl." A
paramedic is tending to Marnie's daughter in the back
of the ambulance, accompanied by two troopers. The
consensus amongst the townspeople is that the troopers
would have sent Kenzie back down the road if the victim
was someone unknown to her, and most have given up
hope that the dead person could be anyone else.

The rest of the day passes achingly slow. After trying
in vain to focus on the inn's bookkeeping, I give it up

as a bad job and trudge over to Cora's house. I try to nap, but my dreams are full of people I know tumbling down a flight of stairs and landing in a pond, one after another. When it's Kellen's turn to step forward at the top of the stairs my eyes spring open and I spend the rest of the afternoon making notes in the journal I keep of my past-life encounters. My enthusiasm to find out the exact timing of Bill Blackmoor's death has vanished; I'm mainly focused on trying to recall if anyone else in Soberly ever offered me a vision of their passing from another lifetime. As far as I can recall, no one has.

Cora gets home shortly after six, with no new information about Marnie's death, other than the fact that her husband was back in Soberly, and the Deckers were being supported by their friends and family. No one has a clue what she might have been doing up by the off-ramp before daybreak.

I put together some spaghetti, and we eat together in stilted silence after my overtures at conversation are met with monosyllabic replies. After ten minutes, with half her food untouched, Cora puts her fork and knife together on her plate and pushes it away from her, saying she's ready to turn in. Inwardly I sigh, reminding myself that she's lost three people she knows in as many weeks, including her partner, and now has a complete stranger in her home to boot. Grief has little care for social niceties.

"Here, I'll take it," I say as she makes to carry it to the sink. As she passes the plate across the table, our fingers brush.

REGRESS

The villagers were gathered in the church, packed tightly into the pews, but this was not the usual Sunday service. Everyone was present, from Marta Smirnova, the oldest, to Polina Morozova's suckling babe, born more than a month after snow had blocked the pass. Konstantin Lvov, one of the village's elders, stood at the pulpit normally occupied by Father Lvov, his nephew, who sat in a plain wooden chair behind him. It was the Father and Konstantin who had argued for the mandatory pooling and equal redistribution of food when it became clear that without it not all were likely to survive the winter. Now, as the cold season stretched on and the rations became smaller, some townspeople were starting to grumble, and there was talk about taking the food back by force from the cellar underneath the church. The consensus amongst some was that it was better for a few people to starve than all of them. The cruelty with which they were willing to sacrifice their neighbors showed how desperate the situation was becoming.

Slava's plump thigh pressed into Kolya's thin one. Many of the villagers spoke to each other in hushed tones, but they remained silent, wanting to appear as model citizens awaiting the elder's speech. After the forced inspection of their home a week earlier, they could not afford to look even slightly unsupportive, lest it triggers new allegations and a more thorough search. For now, the council was still in favor of maintaining the ration system.

"My friends," Konstantin began over the chatter. "It is good to see everyone here." Kolya had ascertained no one in the village had died that week by scanning the pews for missing faces. "I know you are expecting an announcement that rations will be further reduced. I am pleased to tell you all this will not be the case." Several audible sighs of relief echoed throughout the church, and his sister Yulia, sitting in front of him, put her arm around her oldest child and gave him a squeeze.

"No, it is a different matter that brings us all together today," Konstantin continued. "That of heat. It has come to the attention of the council that some households are close to running out of wood to burn." Indeed, Zlata Dudnyk had been found frozen to death in her own home ten days earlier, under a mound of blankets beside a cold hearth. Her body lay now in a shed beside the church until the ground thawed enough for her to be interred. Nor was she the first. The village had lost some eighty residents, nearly a quarter in all, to the bite of winter, although most had been caught out during one of the many storms that swept down from the mountains.

Kolya paid close attention to what Konstantin was saying. It was true, he and Slava were struggling to stay warm, and had burned most of their furniture. He would dismantle the chicken coop next, the laying hens having long been eaten, but the thin boards wouldn't last long. He had come to fear the cold far more than the hunger.

"Surely you aren't suggesting we pool our firewood as well," someone cried. Many in the crowd grumbled in agreement. Kolya could feel Slava tense beside him, waiting for Konstantin to answer.

"No, good people, I do not ask this of you at all. What I am hoping, my friends, is that tomorrow all the able-bodied men will join me to cut down ten or twelve trees and chop them into firewood to the benefit of all."

There was an uproar amongst the men at this suggestion. Konstantin's eyebrows raised at the passion with which they opposed this idea.

"What about the energy we will expend doing all this chopping?" one man asked. "Will we receive extra food in compensation?" Many cheered at this statement.

"I still have plenty of firewood, why haven't others planned better?" shouted another. These were some of the same arguments presented at the meeting the village called when the need to ration and redistribute *food came up. Kolya, on his part, did not support these arguments. He and Slava needed the wood.*

"Friends, friends, please." Father Lvov had taken over from Konstantin at the pulpit and looked out at the crowd of over two hundred people. The Father was a man in his mid-thirties who had grown up in the village, left it to study theology as soon as he reached adulthood, and returned to serve as its priest ten years ago. He was a charismatic, persuasive speaker. Now his cheeks were as hollow from want of food as many of the others sitting before him. He held up his hands, and the angry men quieted down and took their seats again.

"My people, I know what we ask of you is a great sacrifice. Our bellies are nearly empty, and our muscles ache. We are tired, and the wind cuts sharply. It is much easier to stay inside, if not well-fed at least sheltered, and hope tomorrow brings better fortunes. It is easy to ignore our neighbor's suffering when ours is so great as well.

"It is my job to guide your eternal souls to heaven. Have you forgotten the words of John the Baptist? 'Whoever has two tunics is to share with him who has none, and whoever has food is to do likewise.' Our labors are needed to help those among us who cannot help themselves. Could you live with the death of Marta Smirnova on your conscience?" The Father indicated the village's eldest citizen. "What of Yulia Budanova, whose husband Zoran has sought help from neighboring villages at great personal risk? Would you see Zoran's children shiver in their homes because

you would not give two hours of your time in service to them?" Father Lvov held out his hands entreatingly to the crowd before him. Those who had protested looked ashamed. Kolya saw his sister dab at her eyes with the corner of her shawl. Slava did the same, but her eyes, he saw, were dry.

"We will gather at the edge of the woods midday tomorrow, as long as the weather is clear," Father Lvov said. "Anyone who is in need of wood may speak to me after the meeting."

There was little else to discuss. Father Lvov praised the man who had caught the hare last week and encouraged others to continue hunting for game, adding that he himself had set several snares that week.

As people filed out of the church, Kolya approached Father Lvov at the pulpit to express his need of firewood.

"Kolya, I knew I could count on you to join the party tomorrow," the Father said, slapping him on the back genially. Several people turned to look at him, as the priest had spoken quite loudly.

"Father, we have need of wood," he said, head bowed, purposely making his voice meek and drawing his shoulders in to appear smaller.

"All the more reason to lend a hand, eh?" The shrewd look he gave Kolya implied he was not easily fooled by Kolya's sudden timorousness. "I will see you tomorrow, and make sure you sharpen your ax tonight. Do not be late."

11

I carry Cora's plate to the dishwasher robotically, barely acknowledging her goodnight to me. As soon as I hear her bedroom door close, I race to my own room and jot down as many notes as I can remember from the vision. I'm struck once again not only by its length, but how vividly it plays out in my mind. Most visions drift through my thoughts like vapor, easy to ignore if I don't care to pay attention to them. This is like a virtual reality experience in comparison, almost immersing me into the scene. The time frame is familiar—I've seen it from Cora once before and Naomi as well, but neither of those moments took over all my senses like this one did. What makes it so different? I hate having so many unanswered questions.

The next day dawns gray and chilly. Dark storm clouds are moving in from the Pacific, giving the town a gloomy pall that surely reflects the mood of its residents. For the first time since arriving, I have no desire to leave my cozy bed, and I lay under the blankets, flipping through entertainment sites on my phone, hoping celebrity gossip will distract me. It doesn't, and I soon toss my phone aside and stagger to the shower.

Marnie's death is affecting me more than it ought to, given that I only met her two or three times, and we never did more than exchange superficial pleasantries. Maybe it's the thought of her daughter growing up without a mother, or the way Soberly will feel the loss of another key member of their community. Maybe it's because I saw an echo of her death in a past time.

As the water beats down on my head, I wonder what I should do if another person's past reveals an end-of-life scene. Should I try and warn them? How would I explain that they're, say, at an increased risk of cancer and should go for a screening immediately, or should avoid riding in a car for the next while, without looking like my mind is slipping? I can't. No one would ever believe me. If there is a pattern, and people in Soberly are suddenly experiencing their past deaths in this lifetime, I have no choice but to sit back and watch it happen. The thought makes me feel ill.

Before leaving for the inn, I make myself a sandwich and tuck it and an apple in my purse. I plan on holing up in Roz's office and working the entire day, both to appease Cora's impatience and to keep my mind off the town's matters. *They're none of your business, anyway. Leave these people to their grief. You don't need to make everything about you.*

With that chastisement planted firmly in my mind,

I walk into town, passing Sheena's antiques shop. The hours posted on the door say it's closed Tuesdays and Wednesdays, so I can't say hello to her as I'd planned. I hope she has friends to be with today. From the way she'd talked to me about Marnie the first time we met, they'd been at least somewhat close, despite the difference in age.

The pharmacy is closed as well, as I expected, and there are two or three bouquets of flowers resting against the door. I hurry past, wishing I'd thought to bring something to offer, and take a moment to wish Marnie's spirit peace in her next life. Had it already occupied a new body, and was gestating inside another woman somewhere in the world? I wonder if her heartbroken family would find solace in the knowledge that someday, they will meet again?

The inn is quiet when I enter, and the parking lot is mostly empty. Cora barely looks up from her laptop when I say hello. Her eyes are red-rimmed, and she's clutching a wad of tissues in one hand. If her body language hadn't made it so obvious she didn't want to talk to me, I would have offered her the condolence I've been rehearsing in my head on my walk, but she leaves to grab the box of receipts and statements from the safe almost as soon as I enter. When she returns, I make sure I'm not close enough for her to pass it directly to me, lest our hands brush.

The rain starts to fall as I spread April's paperwork out on the table, and the sound of the droplets hitting the panes on the balcony door provides a soothing background soundtrack as I lose myself in the work. At some point, it stops and the sky clears; steam rises from roofs and concrete as the sun burns off the moisture. I eat my sandwich and apple on the balcony, watching as at first a few people emerge onto the beach, looking warily at the sky for signs this is a temporary reprieve, and are soon joined by many more, eager to enjoy the last few hours of daylight.

No one disturbs me throughout the day, a fact for which I'm profoundly grateful, and I have most of April's income and expenses entered into my spreadsheet by early evening. Roz's credit card statement for the month has the same mystifying charges on it as the previous months, but even though it doesn't sit right with me, I do as Cora instructed and categorize them as 'miscellaneous.'

It's hard to get a picture of how the inn is doing from only a few months' worth of information, and low season months at that, but from what I've been able to put together so far, the business is not doing very well. Only one month of the three has been profitable—the rest posted small losses. Even now, in the middle of summer, which should be busier, Cora had said there were only three rooms occupied now that the weekend is over. At this time of year, the inn should be packed. Based on what Roz had written in her letter, I expected things to be in far better shape financially.

Curious, I do a quick search of lodgings along the highway close to Soberly to see what the inn's main competition is. There is no shortage of small hotels, inns, and bed-and-breakfasts along Highway 101. Airbnb is also a competitor. Many of them have no vacancies, even though it's the middle of the week. What's causing tourists to pass Soberly by, and how can the inn change that? I have some ideas, but I need to talk to Sheena.

A quiet knock interrupts my musings, and when I open the door Kellen's on the other side.

"I'm not hungry," I tell him before he has a chance to speak—sure he's here to berate the fact that I haven't shown up in the pub to be fed today. I still have half my sandwich, in fact. Some people eat their feelings—I've always starved mine.

"Me neither. Come for a walk down the beach with me."

I can't think of a reason not to, although I do try, since long walks on the beach are not the type of thing one does with their one-night stand, so I follow him out the door. This time he leads me down the hall, past the guest rooms, down a different flight of stairs, and out a door that opens onto a verandah at the back of the inn. Roz's balcony is directly overhead.

"Which way?" he asks. I shrug, not having a preference, and he chooses north, toward the lighthouse. We walk in silence, picking our way over the driftwood that marks the storm surge line until we reach the water's edge. I doff my shoes before the waves can catch me, grateful I chose capris instead of long pants this morning.

"Shouldn't you be working?" I say to make conversation. The silence between us doesn't feel as comfortable as it has in the past.

"My day off."

"Oh." The silence lengthens, and I spend a lot of time gazing out over the water.

"Did you know Marnie well?" For a while, Kellen doesn't say anything, and I wonder if I've spoken out of line. Maybe he asked me to walk with him because Marnie's the last thing he wants to talk about.

"Everyone did," he says when I'm about to point out some bird, or pretend to spy a shell to pick up, anything to break the painful dead air between us. "She made a point of knowing everyone, too. Not to be gossipy, or because she was nosy, but so she could take the best care of people that she could. She was the person you could tell the things you couldn't talk about with your own parents, and know your secret was always safe. When we first moved here, some people weren't all that nice to us, but she made a big point of welcoming us and introduced my parents to everyone. She was the one who persuaded me to try out for football when I was afraid I wouldn't fit in, coming to a new school where I didn't know any of the other kids. All Marnie ever wanted was to make sure we were all happy. That we knew, no matter what, we had someone on our side. It absolutely kills me to think that when she needed someone for her, she was alone. No one had her back."

"I'm sorry," I say, at a loss for anything else.

"Me too," he says. "I don't—what the hell is going on here lately?"

"It's just—it's bad luck is all. A horrible coincidence." I hope it's true. I have to believe it is, otherwise everything I thought I knew about the past and how it influences the present has been wrong.

We're far from the inn and have this part of the beach completely to ourselves. The sun has almost entirely slipped below the horizon now, and Kellen leads me up away from the water to a massive driftwood log to watch the last rays of light disappear. He puts his arm around my waist and I let myself lean against his shoulder as the dim purple of twilight descends around us, hoping he finds it a comfort. I'm not who Marnie was to him, but I'm glad he trusts me to talk about how he feels.

"There's no one around," he says after a careful glance up and down the beach. "Can I kiss you?" I tilt my face toward his in reply, and for a long time we sit there, taking the time we didn't the night before. There's a fleeting vision, tinged with sadness, but I let it go, preferring to focus on the present. This time I don't try to push things further, letting him take the lead if he chooses. It's almost fully dark when he pulls his mouth a fraction away from mine and tells me he needs me.

I climb into his lap again and the sex is slow and sweet, better than last time, better than any time. When we're done I rest against his chest with my face pressed into the hollow of his neck so I can listen to the beat of his heart gradually slow.

"We should head back," he says into my hair.

"Nuh-uh." I'm dozing off, perfectly happy to stay exactly in this spot for the foreseeable future. To my surprise, Kellen doesn't protest, and an unknown amount of time goes by before the distant sound of a ship's horn startles me out of my semi-slumber. The air has cooled off, and even with Kellen's warmth, I shiver as a sea breeze cuts through my T-shirt.

"Up you get," he says, depositing me on my feet and tugging his shorts up. "I'll give you my hoodie." I retrieve my capris and shake the sand out of them before putting them back on and wrapping myself in the proffered hoodie. It's many sizes too big, but it's warm and smells like Kellen, and I'm not sure I'll ever give it back to him.

With the lights of Soberly twinkling in the distance, guiding us back, and the glow of the rising moon illuminating the surf as it washes up onto the sand, neither of us feel the need to use the flashlight app on our phones. The roar of the tide coming in is the only sound between us, but this silence feels far more comfortable.

"Audrey, are you still..." Kellen hesitates. *Don't,* I want to say. *Don't ask.* "Are you still selling the inn? Are you still leaving?"

"Yes," I say, my voice so low I half-hope he can't hear me over the sound of the ocean.

"Then why are you—" The words explode out of him. I wince, hearing the anger and unhappiness in his voice.

"Why are *you?*" I interrupt before he can complete his sentence. "*I* didn't start this." Does he think he's the only one who's going to be hurting when the papers are signed, and my time in Soberly is done? Despite what I want it to be, this feels like it's verging into more than a friends-with-benefits arrangement, and I can't pull myself away. I sidestep away from him and pick up my pace, kicking up sand with every step. Is it just the wind in my face that's making my eyes smart, or something else? Without warning I stub my toe hard on an unseen rock jutting out of the sand and stumble, nearly falling to my knees. "Ow, fuck," I curse as I regain my balance. Kellen, who's only been a couple steps behind me, finds my arm to hold me steady, but I wrench it out of his grip. "I don't need your help," I say, my voice sharper than I intended.

"All right," he says. "All right. Just stop for a moment." His flashlight comes on, illuminating the beach in front of me so I can see where I'm going. I'm about to tell him I don't need his help for that either, but suddenly I don't have any fight left in me. When I don't start walking again, he flicks the light off, and I see the shape of his silhouette move in front of me. His hands find my waist and pull me toward him, and a moment later I feel the weight of his chin rest on top of my head.

"I'm sorry," he says. "I'll stop if you want me to. You only have to say the word, and it never happens again." I hesitate, the blood rushing in my ears, and shake my head. Wrapping his arms fully around me in a tight hug, he whispers, "Good." His hand finds mine and we start making our way back down the beach toward the town together.

The first thing I do the next morning is leave a voicemail for Greta Pickler, my new lawyer. I haven't heard a thing from her since we met in Eugene, which worries me. Today's the day my birth certificate is supposed to show up, which means we can start making some progress on the transfer of ownership from Roz's estate to my name.

Sheena's antique shop is open when I walk up the main street, and I pop in for a moment. The dark circles under her eyes and the slow way she moves to greet me tell me what kind of night she had. Hopefully, I can offer her a bit of distraction.

"Got plans for lunch?" I ask her. "I want to pick your brain about something."

"Well, this sounds curious," she replies. "What about?" I tell her she'll have to wait until then and promise to return a few hours later with food.

My birth certificate is indeed with the morning's

mail at the inn when I arrive, and when I tell Cora the good news she nods approvingly.

"That's one obstacle down," she says.

When lunchtime rolls around, I make my way over to Sheena, laden with two takeaway containers of fried clams, chips, and a six-pack of beer. Kellen is back behind the bar and pretends to grumble when I won't tell him where I'm taking my food, or who I'm eating it with.

"I'm scheming," is all I'll tell him. I distinctly hear him mutter something about Eames women before I'm out the door.

"Tell me more about smuggling in Soberly," I say without preamble as soon as Sheena flips the *Closed for Lunch, Back in 30 Minutes* sign on the door.

"I already told you pretty much everything I know," she replies around a mouthful of food. "There's probably some old newspaper articles on microfiche somewhere that might talk about specific cases or incidents. Like I said, there are a few people in town who would have stories passed down from their parents or grandparents you should talk to, if you want some firsthand experiences."

"Next question. Who has these hidden cellars and hiding spots in their homes or businesses?" I have a notepad and pen at hand to jot down the names Sheena gives me, amounting to more than half a dozen, including her own modest false cupboard.

"Did you find anything at the inn? Is that why you're asking?" she asks when she's finished her list.

"No, I haven't checked there yet, but I'm going to. Depending on what I discover, I have an idea I want to pitch to Cora."

"Oh my god you *have* to let me come with you," Sheena says with a squeal, and I see her shiver at the prospect. It's the first time she's looked interested in our discussion. "I'd give almost anything to get to dig around in the inn's basement looking for a secret room. It's straight out of a Nancy Drew mystery."

I laugh, but I agree and tell her she's more than welcome to join me. We make a plan to meet tonight to explore after she closes up her shop. I'm glad to have the company—the idea of doing it alone frightens me a bit, although I don't know why. I've done plenty of digging around in old buildings. Maybe it's the pall of death hanging over the town that has me on edge.

"Hypothetically, if I wanted to get into the basement here, how would I go about doing that?" I ask Kellen when I return to the pub, sliding up onto my usual stool. Other than a couple at a corner table and the same family of five I'd seen in Sheena's the other day the place is deserted. Kellen gives me a long side-eye as he slices lemons into wedges.

"Why do you want to know?"

"Reasons," I say, knowing my non-answer will both drive him up the wall and guarantee he won't tell me. When he raises his eyebrows and offers only silence in reply, I shrug noncommittally. "I can always ask your mom if you won't tell me," I add. "Or Jana. Or Drew."

"But not Cora," he says, noticing my omission. The side of his mouth twitches, and I pretend to frown a little.

"I'm sure she'd tell me too, I suppose," I say evasively. "Haven't seen her around today." If I confronted her directly, I know it would be odd for her to deny me the information, but there's a reason I don't want to mention it to her yet, and Kellen's picked up on it like I hoped.

"No? She tends to be in the same place every day." He jerks his head to the left, indicating the wall that separates the pub from the lobby.

"Fair point. See you around then." I start to slide off my stool.

"Fine," he says with a long sigh. "Tell me *why* you want to know, and I'll tell you how to get into the basement. I'll take you to the door itself, in fact."

I keep my voice mega-casual as I explain. "I want to see if there's anything in the basement that might link the inn to the rum runners. This building's been around long enough. I find it historically interesting," I add before he can ask me why I'm curious.

"Is that so? Who'd you have lunch with?" he asks.

"Hmm? Just someone I've been talking to a bit about stuff here in town. The past, that sort of thing."

"A friend?"

"I guess so, sort of." Far from being annoyed, like I'd expected, he surprises me by breaking out into the trademark megawatt smile. I'm both captivated and perplexed.

"That's awesome. I'm glad to hear it," he says.

"Why?" The question is out of my mouth before I can bite it back, betraying the fact that I'm not as nonchalant as I'm playing.

"Isn't it nice to have friends?" he says, still grinning. "You're puttin' down roots without even knowing it."

"I am not," I say, wrinkling my nose at him.

"It's a little root. There are a few of them, here and there. I can see them taking hold. This new friend, your"—he makes air quotes—"historical interest in the town."—he brings his face close to mine—"And me." With my elbow on the bar, I rest my chin on the back of my hand and shake my head at him, smiling."Whatever. Be ready right after the pub's closed." I get off my stool for real this time and leave without a backward glance. Damn him, he's right. Roz's plan is working.

12

Sheena meets me outside the pub a few minutes after eleven, and we walk in together. Drew's on his way out at the same time, and he fist bumps me—a gesture I've come to recognize is his usual method of greeting.

"Boss lady," he adds, lifting the headphones off his ears for a moment and shooting me a grin. I tell him I'm not his boss and wish him a good night in return before Sheena and I head inside.

"*This* is your new friend?" Kellen says when he sees us, a look of mock horror on his face. "Oh lord, are we in trouble."

"Shut up, Kellen Greene," Sheena says, but she's laughing.

"You know, I thought *she* was the biggest troublemaker in town until I met you," he says to me, pointing at Sheena. "If the two of you have joined forces, there's no hope for any of us. What's she got to do with any of this anyway?"

"I'm an expert on antiques," Sheena says with a roll of her eyes. "I also did a high school project on this smuggling stuff," she adds in a slightly lower voice. Kellen catches it anyway and bursts out laughing. "Which I got an A on." He only laughs harder.

"Half your life ago. You're both dressed for sleuthing too, look at you." I hadn't noticed when she walked up, but Sheena's in head-to-toe black, like I am. She even thought to bring a large flashlight. "There are electric lights down there, you know," he adds, and Sheena purses her lips and flushes slightly.

"You never know when there's going to be an outage," she mutters.

"Well, I'm glad you brought it. I don't want to be stuck down in a spooky basement in the dark," I say in her defense.

"Through the kitchen and down the main hall," Kellen says. "After you, I need to get the lights in here."

Kellen catches up to us, and his hand grazes my ass through my leggings, making me shiver. He feels it and gives me a squeeze. I elbow him in the ribs in return.

At the end of the hallway, he pushes through a *Staff Only* door into a utility room containing an industrial washer and dryer, a housekeeping cart, and various supplies. At the far end is another door, and it's this one he indicates.

"I could have found this myself," I mutter, but I'm glad he's here. A set of wooden steps descend into darkness, and when I flick the switch on the wall to my left, a single bulb illuminates the way down.

When we reach the bottom, I'm underwhelmed, to say the least. A vast space is spread out in front of me, about the same size as the aboveground footprint of the hotel. It's dimly lit by more hanging bulbs at regular intervals. They reveal a few stacks of chairs against a wall and some folding tables. That's it. There are no interior walls or partition, no ancient-looking crates marked with Xs, no earthenware, narrow-mouthed jugs. Sheena's crestfallen appearance no doubt matches my own because Kellen puts an arm around each of us and gives us a reassuring squeeze.

"Don't give up hope, ladies," he says. "Maybe there's a false wall, or a trapdoor or something. Let's have a good look around."

We split up. Sheena is tasked with examining the concrete floor, and Kellen and I take opposite sides of the perimeter to check for hidden doors, unusual cracks, or anything out of the ordinary in the walls. For a time, no one speaks, each of us concentrating on our respective job. I run my hands over the plaster in addition to examining it, paying special attention to the bottom three feet in case there's a crawlspace. It's slow work, and before I'm halfway down the east wall I'm coated in dust and an uncomfortable quantity of cobwebs.

Turning the corner onto the south wall, I immediately feel a difference in texture underneath my hands. All along the east side, there was brick under the plaster—a fact revealed by a few spots where it had fallen away— but this feels different, smoother. Still, maybe that's how the south wall was constructed at the time. Until I move a few feet to the right, and the rougher texture of brick resumes.

"This might be something here," I say. Sheena shines her flashlight over in my direction and immediately blinds me. I shade my eyes with one hand and wave her and Kellen over with the other. "Feel it," I say. "Here," I run my hand over the plastered brick, "and here. This spot is smoother. Maybe it's wood? Like a door?"

"Why would you plaster over the door to your secret room?" Sheena asks. "That doesn't make sense. You can't open it."

"I don't know," I reply. "I didn't say it was a door. I just said it felt different."

"What are you going to do?" Kellen asks. I shrug in reply. I feel all over the smoother area, trying to discover its exact outline. It is, indeed, about the size of a door, but I hesitate. Kellen solves my dilemma by taking Sheena's flashlight and hitting the plaster, hard, with the butt of it until a chunk of it falls away, revealing wooden slats.

"Looks like you were right," he says, grinning. He makes to hit the wall again, but I shout at him to stop.

"You can't just destroy the wall," I tell him, horrified.

"Don't you want to see what's behind it?"

"Yes, but—"

"This is *your* hotel, Audrey. If you want to break down this wall, then do it." His gaze challenges me, and Sheena is practically dancing she's so excited.

"Fine," I say, hoping I don't regret it. "Be careful. Don't damage anything more than you have to." He chips carefully away at the plaster until an area about one by two feet is revealed.

"There's a knothole," Sheena says, pointing at a spot right at the edge of one slat. "Good thing we have *a flashlight*," she emphasizes, plucking it back from Kellen and crouching to get the small hole at eye level. "There's definitely a space behind here," she says after a minute. "I can't see how big, but it's not nothing."

"Let's open it up," I say in a hushed whisper, and take the flashlight from her hand. Gone are my concerns about being cautious. I want to see what's behind this door.

I concentrate my plaster-busting efforts on the area close to the edge where the wooden slats meet brick, and soon the entire seam from floor to top is uncovered. Unfortunately, there is no door handle or any means of opening it that I can see. It seems like the opening was permanently boarded over. However, there are several more knotholes.

"Think if we each stuck a couple fingers through and pulled, we could swing it forward?" I ask. We each move into position and on the count of three pull at the boards. At first, it doesn't give at all, but after Sheena tells us all to put our backs into it, we're rewarded with the sound of plaster starting to crack.

"Harder," she says and with one last great heave, the one slat closest to the brick pulls away enough that Kellen can get his hands into the gap. In a shower of plaster, he yanks the entire door out of the brick frame and sets it to the side.

Sheena's flashlight reveals a small room, about ten by ten feet, lined on all sides by plank shelving. There is no electric wiring in here. The walls are earthen, rather than brick, and the floor is covered in thick wooden boards instead of the poured concrete of the rest of the basement, which must have been put in later. Large metal hooks hang from beams along the ceiling.

"This is a cold room," I say, swatting at a cobweb as I step inside. Sheena and Kellen follow. "Perishable goods would have been stored in here before refrigeration was available. Every old house has one of these." The shelves are empty now, and the room is bare of anything else of remark. I try to hide my disappointment at the thoroughly mundane discovery. I'd hoped to find more.

Sheena hasn't stopped shining her flashlight around the room since we entered it, no doubt looking for even the smallest relic, but I can see there's nothing noteworthy in here. I make to leave the cold room, intending to finish my examination of the rest of the wall, when she tells Kellen to move from where he's standing, adding a shove when he doesn't move quickly enough to satisfy her. She kneels, sets down the flashlight, and somehow a second later is holding an irregular-shaped section of the floor in her hands, revealing an opening below. There's a ladder leading down into it.

"Holy shit," I breathe. "How did you know that was there?"

"I saw the two holes." I can see now she has a finger in each hand stuck into two holes that look drilled from their evenness. "They looked like they lined up, so I pulled on them. I honestly didn't believe anything would happen." She shines the light down the hole, which looks about seven feet deep. "So? Who's going first?"

"You found it," I tell her since she's already got her head halfway in the opening, trying to cover everything with the flashlight beam at once. I can see she's dying to go down. "Is the ladder safe?" I add, mindful that it probably hasn't been used in seventy years or more.

"Looks sturdy enough to me," she says and tests her

weight on the first rung. "It's a short drop anyway, only about eight feet. Oh my *God,* this is so exciting." Tucking the flashlight into the waistband of her leggings, she disappears from view.

Kellen and I are momentarily left in near-pitch blackness, and he takes the opportunity to kiss me hungrily.

Miss Dean paused at the door of the small schoolhouse for a moment, her eyes darting eagerly from student to student, wondering which would be her favorite and which would give her a hard time. Her first day as a teacher was about to commence. The pupils, some twenty children from all over the parish, were playing in the yard outside. Their raucous shouts were full of glee as they enjoyed their last minutes of freedom on a sunny autumn day.

Checking the small gold watch she kept in her pocket for the twentieth time, she took a deep breath, seized the large brass bell, and pulled open the door.

"Come inside, children," she said, with what she hoped was a friendly smile. "The day is about to begin."

"Do secret rooms turn you on?" I whisper playfully.

"You turn me on," he replies, grabbing a fistful of my hair to pull my mouth to his again.

"Oh my god, Audrey you *have* to see this. Are you coming?" Sheena shouts from below, and I jump out of Kellen's arms. For a moment, he'd made me completely forget what we were doing here.

"Yep, I'm on my way. Wanted to give you enough time to get all the way down. I didn't think it would be safe to have two people on the ladder at once," I stammer, stepping onto the first rung.

"Holy shit," is all I can say when I'm at the bottom. "Wait, don't touch anything," I caution Sheena, who is examining some papers tacked up to the wall. This room is smaller, about twelve by eight feet, but unlike the cold room above us, it is far from empty. A small table and chair are pushed against the earthen wall in one corner, and crates are stacked three or four high all along the opposite one. An unlit oil lamp is suspended from the ceiling. I hear Kellen's feet land behind me, and although I'm expecting some sort of surprised expletive, he's completely silent. His hand reaches out and squeezes my forearm for a moment, and I rock back on my heels a bit to return the pressure.

"Amazing," I keep repeating. "This is *amazing*." The crates, unmarked on the outside, are filled with straw. When I touch a piece of it gingerly, it crumbles into dust in my hand.

"What are the papers?" I ask Sheena, who is poring over them.

"One of them is a tidal chart," she says, running the beam of the flashlight over it.

"Really?" I cover the lower half of my face with my hands, not believing our luck. "That means we can get a precise date on when this room was used."

"This one looks like names, but I'm not sure if they're people or ships. This last one is definitely people. I recognize a bunch of the names. They're all from town." She lists off a few, and even I recognize a couple family names from my short time here.

"Do you know how historically significant this is?" I

say, enthralled. I can't wait to dive into all the research and cataloging this is going to require. There are more papers in a manila folder, yellowed with age, on the table, but I won't touch them until I have a pair of latex gloves to protect them from the oils in my hands. The entire room will need to be photographed in detail before I disturb anything.

"Would've been nice to find a stash of eighty-year-old rum," Sheena says. "It's too bad all these crates are empty."

"This one isn't," Kellen says from the corner, where only a single crate sits on the floor. Sheena trains the light on it. He's right—there are three bottles full of amber liquid lying on their side amongst the straw. The necks and corks are covered in thick, dark wax.

"It's not rum at all," she says. "It's whiskey."

"That makes sense if it's coming from Canada," I say. "Rum came mainly from the Caribbean and the south." The bottles look well preserved, still full thanks to the wax preventing evaporation over time, and the labels, while yellowed with age, are still legible.

I start making a mental list of all the things I need to learn to get started building a history of what went on in this room, beginning with who owned the inn during the Prohibition era. Whoever it was, they had to have been complicit in the smuggling. If only there was a personal diary included in the room's contents, but that would be beyond the bounds of good fortune.

"Okay," I say finally, tearing my gaze away from the papers on the wall. I have a few snaps of them on my phone to study later. "Let's get out of here. We need to put everything back the way we found it. I don't want to tell anyone else about this room yet. Please?" Both Sheena and Kellen nod. I know I can trust Kellen, but I'm not sure about Sheena yet. She's definitely a part of the town's gossip train, but I hope she'll hold this information back until I can find out more. I particularly don't want Cora finding out about it from the rumor mill before I can show her in person.

Kellen is the first up the ladder, followed by Sheena, who shines the light down from above so I don't have to ascend in darkness. We replace the wooden trap door into the uneven hole in the cold room. There are scuffs in the thick dust from our feet that show the room has been occupied, but nothing to draw attention to the door in the floor specifically.

Kellen rests the plaster-covered door to the cold room back into its brick frame. It's much more apparent here that all is not what it seems, thanks to the piles of plaster dust on the floor and the exposed wood where we'd chipped the plaster away, but I'm hoping that since the inn's basement isn't used, no one will find it in the meantime. To be safe, I kick the plaster dust with my sneaker, scattering it in a thin layer over the concrete.

"I'll walk you home," I tell Sheena, and we bid goodnight to Kellen.

"That was better than I could have ever expected," she says as we walk down Lighthouse Street. "I feel like we're in a real mystery novel. A bootlegger's secret hideout." She's got a grin from ear to ear, and it's hard not to match her enthusiasm. In my work as a historian, I'd never made a discovery as significant as this. Right now, I feel like Indiana Jones discovering the secret passage in the library, and I didn't even have to deal with rats. "How come you want to keep it a secret?"

"Just for a few days. I want to find out more about who built it and who used it. Once the secret's out, everyone's going to want to come look and I want to have answers for their questions. I also need to find out if we're even authorized to investigate and catalog it. The state might have regulations about discoveries of historical significance. Please, please don't tell anyone yet, Sheena." I stop for a moment and catch her eye. "Not even your mom."

"Cross my heart and hope to die," Sheena says, making an X over her chest with one finger. "I *will* pester you endlessly about what you're learning, though," she adds, and I laugh. Then she changes the subject abruptly.

"So, you're fucking Kellen Greene." There's no judgment or approval in her voice, it's just a casual statement.

"I—you don't know that," I say, flustered. I'm glad it's dark so she can't see how red my face is. "I mean, I am, but how did you...did he tell you?"

"No, not a word. It's the way he looks at you. You have this...it's obvious."

"To everyone?"

"I don't know. It's obvious to me. Don't worry, Audrey, it's cool. He's a good guy if that's what you're worried about." We walk half a block in silence. I open my mouth several times to speak but close it again. I'm at a loss for words.

"You have mixed feelings about it," Sheena prompts. We're standing outside her front door. I shrug.

"I guess so. I'm selling the inn to Cora as soon as the paperwork goes through and leaving Soberly. He wants me to stay and keep it. He wants a relationship." It's a difficult thing to say out loud. Sheena's got a wide wooden swing on her porch, and she settles into it, motioning me to take the seat beside her.

"Why don't you?"

"Because—" I stop to compose my thoughts. It's harder to come up with an answer than it was a week ago. "Because I like my job. I like the types of projects I work on, I like seeing different parts of the country. I like knowing I can pick up and go anytime I want, that I'm not tied down by anything. I don't know anything about running a hotel, except that there's a maddening amount of bookkeeping. Roz and Cora both went to school to learn how to do this. I'd be flying by the seat of my pants. Alone. Because I'm positive if I do decide I want to stay and take it all on, Cora will leave, and I can't do it without her. She's indispensable. And she hates me."

"She doesn't hate you. She resents you."

"Same thing. She wants me out of town, out of her life. The longer I'm here, the more irritated she's getting. I should have never agreed to stay at her place."

"So, move out."

"That would make things even more tense. At least while I'm staying there, there's a sort of forced civility between us. Besides, where would I go? I can't stay at the inn indefinitely."

"Stay with me then." A sarcastic laugh bursts out of me before I can contain it.

"You'd do that? Offer up your house to someone you've known a week?"

"Why not? We get along well enough, and I hate

living by myself. Having a roommate would be nice, even if it was only for a few weeks." The way Sheena makes outrageous statements like they're the most logical, matter-of-fact things is one of the things I like the most about her, but it also surprises me every time she does it. I realize I've never made skin-to-skin contact with her and haven't had a single vision of her past. I know—and like—her purely on who she is in this lifetime. I'm not sure I've ever befriended someone on these terms before.

"I'll think about it," I say. "I want to keep Cora on my good side for now, but if things go south..." and I have a feeling they soon will, if she's not open to what I'm planning, "I hope the offer's still open."

"Absolutely. You're always welcome." She gets up and stretches with a loud yawn. It's well past midnight, and after thanking her again and wishing her goodnight, I make my way down the street toward Cora's.

A voice hisses my name when I turn the corner, making me jump. It's Kellen, sitting on the front step of what I presume is his house. He motions me over, rising to meet me.

"Want to see my bunk beds?" he murmurs into my ear. I stifle a laugh, which turns into a low groan as he palms my breast over my shirt. I nod my assent, and he takes my hand, leading me into the backyard and a set of stairs going down to the basement. It turns out he doesn't have bunk beds at all, but he gets to be on top anyway.

13

Sunlight streaming through a crack in the curtains wakes me, and I'm disoriented for a moment, unsure of where I am. I've finally gotten used to waking up at Cora's. Now I'm in a strange bed again. Kellen's warmth at my back, his body curled around mine, reminds me. His stillness and even breathing tell me he's still asleep. I consider easing out of bed, creeping up the stairs, and tip-toeing out of here, but there's no way I'll be able to separate our bodies without waking him. Besides that, I find I don't particularly want to. The clock radio on the bedside table says it's past seven, Kellen's bed is warm and comfortable, and I have nowhere pressing to be. Once again, beyond the point where I can pretend I came back to Cora's after she went to bed. Audrey Eames, queen of the one-night stand, is enjoying a cuddle. The idea almost makes me snort. Instead, I close my eyes again and let the rhythm of my breathing match his.

At half-past his alarm goes off, and his arm swings over my body to silence it. Then his hand slides down my side, pushing the covers away, and he hums in my ear.

"This is nice, waking up with you," he says and starts teasing me with his fingers. In no time at all he's brought me to the brink of climax, my breath coming in hard, ragged gasps. Then, right above our heads, the sound of footsteps, and I startle violently.

"Ignore that," he says, never breaking stride in the circular motion he's making, and although he takes me over the edge moments later, it's not nearly as fulfilling as it could have been, and I'm pretty sure he can tell, based on the fact that he doesn't move to take things any further.

"Why are you so secretive, Audrey? Are you ashamed of being with me?" he asks after a moment's awkward silence.

"*No,*" I say, appalled at the question. "No, of course not. I just don't like the idea of people here thinking I'm...that sort of woman."

"What sort of woman, exactly?" Kellen props himself up on his elbow and looks closely at me.

"The sort of woman who sleeps around." I can feel the heat rise in my cheeks.

"Are you sleeping with anyone else in town?" he says, eyebrows raised.

"Of course not. No, I mean I'm supposed to be grieving, not banging the hot bartender. I feel like it makes me look bad. Heartless."

"It doesn't. It makes you look like a normal human

being. No one cares, Audrey. Seriously. Stop thinking about what other people think so much. Look, I'll show you." He swings his legs off the bed and opens the door of his room, poking his head out. "Hey Ma," he shouts up into the house, ignoring my frantic waves to stop what he's doing immediately. "Can you make some extra breakfast? Audrey's here." An "of course" floats down from above, and after waiting a moment to see if Naomi would say anything further, Kellen nods in satisfaction and closes the door again. "Now, if there's one thing about my mama, it's that she does not suffer fools gladly. If she thought this was the wrong thing to be doing, I'd be getting an earful about it."

"She'd come down here and chew you out right now?" I can picture Naomi, alternately waving and pointing a wooden spoon, giving Kellen the type of lecture that leaves you shaking with fear afterward while we both clutch the sheets around us.

"No, she'd call me upstairs on the pretense of helping her with something, and do it in the kitchen," he says. "Besides, although she hasn't said anything to me, I'm pretty sure she's known for a couple days, and she's had plenty of chances to talk to me if she wanted to. Now, breakfast is usually ready around eight, which doesn't give us much time to shower." He makes sure I can hear the click of the lock on his door and holds his hand out toward me.

REGRESS

The search party struck out again at first light after having been forced back to the village by darkness the night before. It had been snowing for three days straight now, and the cold was so fierce, the men wrapped scarves around their faces so nothing but their eyes were visible. This time they roped themselves together so as not to become separated in the blizzard, Father Lvov in the lead. Each had a long walking stick, and the last man dragged a wooden sled behind him. None spoke of what it was for.

"We will make our way directly down the cart path in single file," he had instructed them before they left the small church. "Once we reach the forest, we can untie ourselves and search amongst the trees." Face set,

Father Lvov led them in a short prayer, asking God to let them find Alexandra safe and well.

Father Lvov refused to admit that the only outcome now was the recovery of Alexandra Rusova's body. He had to believe there was still a chance she was alive, had only lost the cart path when the snow began to fall. Perhaps she had made a shelter amongst the trees, where the snow did not fall so hard. Perhaps she had even decided to risk the mountain pass to the village below and was now safe and warm in front of some kind person's hearth, with no way of getting a message to her family. The pass had become untraversable within a day of the blizzard's commencement. This was not unusual, and Father Lvov's small village was used to interruptions in travel during the winter, sometimes being cut off from the rest of the world for a week at a time.

By her mother's account, twenty-year-old Alexandra had offered to check her uncle's snares in the woods while the man was tending to the family's livestock, preparing them for the incoming storm with extra feed and water. Everyone expected to have to hunker down for a few days, and an extra hare or two would be welcome. However, an hour after she left the cottage she shared with her mother and uncle, the winds came howling down from the mountains. Her uncle, who had a strong dislike for his brother's daughter, had insisted on waiting until morning before looking for her, telling his brother's widow, now his own wife, that she had assuredly found shelter with another villager. Come sunrise the next day, when that proved to not be the case, her mother raised the alarm.

Father Lvov could see the young woman's face in his mind as he pushed forward against the cutting wind—the soft brown curls that framed her face, the way the corners of her eyes crinkled when she smiled, which was often. Conversations between them were so easy. When he had begun calling on her in the fall, there had been no awkward silences or moments of agony, wondering what to say, and so their friendship grew into what Father Lvov felt, and could see that she felt too, was something more. His uncle Konstantin, his closest adviser and confidant, had agreed that the time had come for him to bring up the subject of marriage, a prospect that held no fear or dread for him like it did for some.

With these thoughts in his mind, Father Lvov pushed forward against the wind, head bowed even as his spirit remained unbent. Alexandra was smart. She had grown up in these mountains, in this village. She knew how to take care of herself.

By the time they reached the area of forest they were to search today, icicles caked his eyebrows and the area of his scarf in front of his mouth. He stomped his feet to quicken the blood in them and motioned the men to move into the woods. Once off the road, protected somewhat by the thick growth of evergreens, the sound of the wind abated and he unwound the scarf from his face to speak.

"We go in pairs," he told them. "Check your compasses often. We will call down the line to each other so we do not become separated. Look for anything that might give shelter—a fallen log, low-hanging boughs, a

hollow tree. She was well-dressed for the cold, so there's a good chance she's still alive."

No one contradicted him, but nor did anyone rally to echo his optimism. Instead, the men untied the ropes that bound them to each other, split off silently into twos, and began walking amongst the trees, calling Alexandra's name and poking their sticks into hollows.

It was slow going, for even in the forest floor was blanketed by over a foot of snow, unmarred by tracks of men or beast. Father Lvov called Alexandra's name every minute or so, straining for any reply. None ever came, but he did not give up hope, nor did he give up praying. He had been praying since the moment he heard she was missing in the storm.

To his right, three short blasts from a whistle pierced the air. It was the search party's agreed-upon signal that Alexandra had been found. Father Lvov plunged through the forest, forgetting entirely about his companion. The three blasts repeated, closer now. Could Alexandra still be alive?

"Where are you?" he called out, and a member of the party shouted in reply, so the Father could follow the sound of his voice. He nearly sprinted the remaining distance, gulping the icy air into his lungs so they felt they were being stabbed by thousands of frozen needles.

"Alexandra. You found her?" he gasped, nearly losing his footing at the last moment. Although there had been other search pairs between them, he was the first to arrive after the signal was raised, and so it was only the two men and himself. "Where is she?"

One man prodded the branches of an ancient

evergreen whose boughs were bent to the ground from the weight of the snow upon them. Underneath, Father Lvov knew, would be a small space, protected from wind and snowfall, smelling of spruce sap and rotting needles. He had played among such caves countless times as a child.

"Father, wait," one of the men said as he stepped toward the tree. "She's not—She didn't survive the storm. The Lord has taken Alexandra home."

Silence seemed to fall all around Father Lvov as all his senses, save his vision, deadened. Whatever the men were saying fell on deaf ears; the rawness of the cold no longer stung his aching skin; his brain cleared of all thoughts but one: he had to see her.

Slowly, he pushed aside a branch, crawling on his hands and knees to pass under it. Sure enough, there was a little pocket where no snow had entered. Here, curled up into a tight ball against the trunk of the tree, sat Alexandra Rusova, pale and still, clutching two hares on a string.

Father Lvov held his breath as he looked into her face, wondering how he could continue to enjoy the luxury of oxygen in a world where Alexandra would forever be denied it. Her skin was gray, lips tinged blue. Her dancing eyes were closed, the skin around them smooth. She looked as though she was sleeping.

"My love," he whispered. Hot tears burned scalding paths down his half-frozen cheeks. They were words he'd never had the chance to speak to her in person, and now never would. Regret and grief burned deep in his belly, warming him in a way nothing else in this

moment could, and he shoved his gloved fist into his mouth to keep from sobbing.

"Father," a voice said from outside. "Let's take her home." Father Lvov nodded, although no one could see him, and crawled backward out from under the tree.

14

"Good morning, Audrey," Naomi says to me with a warm smile when I follow Kellen upstairs. "It's good to have you. Now, have a seat, and help yourself." The table is set for three, laden with a stack of pancakes, a serving dish full of fluffy yellow scrambled eggs, and a plate of breakfast sausages. Kellen hands me a mug of coffee with the logo from the 1996 Atlanta Summer Olympics on it and passes me the eggs with a mischievous *isn't this so nice* smile.

Meanwhile, I have absolutely no idea how to behave. This is completely foreign territory for me, so I keep piling food onto my plate, despite the fact that I almost never eat breakfast. If cooking is how Naomi shows her approval, then I'll eat anything she puts in front of me with a smile and a thank you.

"Joanne told me the coroner finished the autopsy on

Marnie yesterday," Naomi says, adding for my benefit that Joanne worked as the dispatcher for the local police station. "They're saying it looks like foul play could be involved. She was hit in the head before she drowned. She might not have even been conscious when she went into the water. No one has a clue how she ended up in that pond. Kenzie told the police that right as she was getting ready for bed, her mom got a phone call and told her she'd be back soon—Kenzie assumed she was going to open up the pharmacy for someone like she sometimes does. No one knows what happened after that."

I wipe my face with my napkin, all traces of appetite now lost. "That's absolutely terrible," I say, looking at Kellen to see how he's taking the news. His head is bowed over his plate, and he looks sick.

"I thought you should hear it at home, instead of from someone else," Naomi says, resting her hand on her son's forearm. Kellen places his hand on top of hers and gives it a squeeze.

"Thanks, Ma," he says. "Thank you. What else did Joanne say?"

"The police are trying to figure out who called Marnie that night, to see what they have to say, I guess. That person might have had something to do with it, and they might not, but Marnie never did open up the pharmacy—the alarm wasn't disarmed. So far no one has come forward to say they were looking to meet up with her."

The food in my stomach sits heavily as my mind churns over this new development. Not only have two people in Soberly died in the same way they did in a past life, at least one of them looks to have been murdered.

"Do you think it's related to Mr. Blackmoor's death?" I say, more thinking out loud than anything. The look on both Naomi and Kellen's faces is one of confusion.

"Of course not," Kellen says with Naomi echoing his denial. "Bill took a fall down some stairs. He was getting on in years and had been having trouble with his hip lately. It might have given out on him at just the wrong moment. Why would you think otherwise?"

"I just..." There was no way I was going to explain to them both about the visions I had. Maybe Kellen, on his own later, but not his mother. "It seems so strange, two people dying unexpectedly so close together in a small place like Soberly. Maybe someone is..." I don't finish my sentence. Kellen's brows are furrowed deeply and Naomi's lips are pressed tightly together.

"Soberly's not like that," Kellen says firmly. His mother nods in agreement. "I know you've lived a lot of places, big cities where that sort of thing might happen all the time, but not here. There's no indication at all that Bill's death was anything other than an unfortunate accident." His expression changes to one of concern. "Saying otherwise definitely won't make you any friends in town, I promise you that. Please, put the idea out of your head, Audrey. For your own good, and for the sake of Bill's and Marnie's families. They don't need that kind of rumor going around."

"You're right," I mumble, prodding listlessly at my eggs with my fork. "I read too many mystery novels. Everything's always connected." Although I say it, I'm not quite sure I believe it. It would be easy to push someone down the stairs and have it look like an accident. If so, did that mean there was someone out there like me, who could see people's past lives through some means? The thought is both tantalizing and terrifying, and I feel a surge of excitement that doesn't quite line up with the seriousness of the situation. Being able to compare notes, so to speak, with someone else who had the same ability would be a once-in-a-lifetime opportunity: a chance to learn about how it manifested in them, if it was also via touch and whether they had discovered anything about it I hadn't. On the other hand, that person could very well be a serial killer who took pleasure in murdering people in the same manner as their past death. Was it a coincidence that we were both in Soberly at the same time? Were they able to recognize me as having the same gift? There were so many unknowns to pore over. I needed to spend some time sorting things out in my journal.

Then there was the matter of Kellen's vision. It seemed to take place early in the winter, during the initial onset of the blizzard that cut the village off from the rest of the world. The heartache his past-self felt at the loss of his would-be lover still dwelled deep in my chest. Although present-day Kellen had done a fine job distracting me in the shower, all the details of the vision were still sharp in my mind. I needed to transcribe them as well.

"Thank you for breakfast," I say to Naomi. I scrape my plate and load it into the dishwasher, waving off her insistence that I leave the dishes for her. "I have some work I want to get started on, so I'd better go." I also need to change out of yesterday's clothes, but I figure the less reference to the fact that I spent the night, the better. I still feel a bit awkward with the whole situation, even though she's been nothing but welcoming. Kellen rises to show me to the door—the front door. I suppress my sigh and hope the neighbors have better things to do than look out their window to see me leave. Cora's house is less than a block from here. Despite what Kellen says about the disinterest of the townspeople in my sex life, it's going to take some time to get used to being open about our—well, whatever we are.

Out of sight of the kitchen, where Naomi can be heard loudly clattering dishes about, Kellen bends to kiss me, pulling me close. The vision he gives me is a flash of a lifetime I haven't seen yet from him, but it's the sort of mundane scene that always fades from memory seconds after I see it.

"Thank you for staying," he says. "Come for supper tonight. I want you to tell me more about your plan for that little smuggling room we found. Oh yes—I know you've got plans," he says when he sees my shrewd expression. "You're cooking up something, I can tell. Maybe I can even help you out if you'll let me."

"All right," I reply. "See you at six."

I let myself into Cora's minutes later, without having met anyone on the street, peel out of my dusty clothes, and jump into a stretchy maxi skirt and tank top. I tuck my journal into my shoulder bag and head for the inn, bracing myself for a confrontation with Cora, in case she decides to ask me where I've been sleeping. She must either feel it's none of her business, or she already knows and has nothing to say about it, because she only offers me a tepid good morning when I walk in. She's already retrieved the box of paperwork from the safe and set it by the door, so I hoist it up onto my hip and head up to Roz's office. From the balcony doors, I can see it's shaping up to be a beautiful day, and I risk opening them to let in the fresh smell of the sea and the sounds of birds. The box of paperwork gets deposited on the table. I do plan on working on it at some point today, but my first priority is my journal.

Although I've avoided it up until now, the temptation of the balcony is too great, and I curl up in one of the chairs to transcribe my thoughts. The details of the vision Kellen gave me comes first, then my thoughts about how Marnie's and Bill's deaths could be connected. If someone is intentionally killing them the same way they died in a previous life, the most logical solution is that there's someone else who has the same ability as me. How can I find them? I wonder if it's something I'll recognize the first time our skin meets, a connection different from everyone else's. If that's the case, I'm certain it's not anyone I've already made physical contact with. Although there have been several intense visions, notably from the townspeople who have cast me back into that small village in the midst of famine, no one has felt different or "other."

I sigh and look over the pages I've written, then out at the ocean, electric-blue in the sunlight. If Roz were here, I would have confided in her. She would listen, I was sure of it. More than that, she would believe me, even though it seems like madness and is completely unprovable. For the first time, I wonder what sorts of visions she would give me, should our skin meet. Was she, too, a resident of that tragic Russian village? I flip through my notes, looking for anyone who seemed adventurous, a mentor to others, a nurturer, but no one springs to mind. That doesn't mean she wasn't there, however. I haven't met the full cast of characters by far.

Looking for personality traits similar to Roz's gives me an idea. If I use the knowledge that people tend to carry over their dominant behaviors from lifetime to lifetime, perhaps I can find the person who killed Marnie and Bill by connecting with their past lives and examining who they once were. It's not absolute proof, but if there's someone who exhibited traits like rage, sociopathy, or even someone who had been guilty of killing someone in the past, there's a chance they could be involved with the Soberly deaths. There's a certain amount of risk involved since I could out myself as another person with this type of ability. But, but if it can prevent another death, or bring a killer to justice, I've got to chance it. It's an easy enough plan to execute— make physical contact with as many people as I can, as often as possible, searching for any suspicious past-life mannerisms. Once I find someone I feel could be a suspect, I'll have to get the police to investigate. How—I have no idea. That's a problem for Future Audrey. Present-day Audrey is going to go into town and start shaking some hands.

By mid-day, I drag myself back to the inn, emotionally exhausted from the near-constant influx of foreign experiences. I need to pace myself. Walking into the cafe and introducing myself to nearly every person there on the pretense of ordering a chocolate sundae might have been overdoing it, and that was after I browsed my way through most of the shops on the main street. Shopping isn't going to be enough for me to reach the majority of the population of Soberly; I tally up the total number of townspeople I'd encountered at over a dozen, none of whom had provided me with any useful information.

I'm going to have to go to church.

The thought fills me with a sort of dread I thought I'd buried long ago. As the daughter of a fundamentalist minister, church had been my entire life growing up, but rather than it being something I found comfort and purpose in, my father used our faith as a weapon to break my mother and I to his will. We were never faithful enough, never virtuous enough. We were filthy sinners who would burn for all eternity. My mother escaped it by turning to drink. I'd turned my back on the church the day I left his home, and my father essentially turned his back on me, his only child. Needless to say, I have a lot of baggage around the faith community. Tomorrow's Sunday, though, so whatever I need to do to mentally prepare myself to enter that environment again, I need to do it fast. The ice cream I've finished starts to churn in my stomach, and for a moment I feel like I'm going to be sick. *Maybe I can sit in the back and wear headphones.* I discard the idea immediately. If the point is to mingle and meet people, I need to be right up there in the thick of the congregation.

It's hard to concentrate on the inn's paperwork over the afternoon. I keep returning to the thought of walking through the doors of the small, clapboard building my father preached in, the simultaneous sensations of fear at not being holy enough, and the dread of having to sit through the long, hate-filled sermon washing over me. The anger at what the forced isolation and social ostracization of being the preacher's daughter from "that weird church on the edge of town" meant for my childhood. The fact that my own parent nearly let his child die to prove faith could heal. Nausea in my stomach gets progressively worse, and several times I dart into the washroom, fearful that I'm going to throw up, but never managing more than a dry heave or two and a bit of bile.

Cora comes up the stairs at one of these moments, when I'm bent over the bowl, wishing my roiling stomach would get it over with and purge already.

"Audrey, what's wrong?" she cries, hurrying forward. There's genuine concern in her voice.

"I'm just—" I burst into tears, to my surprise and dismay. With my face pressed into the cool porcelain of the toilet, I sob noisily while she tucks my hair behind my ear and rubs between my shoulders. Whatever vision she might have given me is for once blocked out by my own mental cacophony, so I hope it isn't an important one. Once the crying fit starts to subside, she hands me a wad of tissues, and I push myself up so I'm sitting against the wall, knees tucked in front of me.

"I get nauseous when I'm upset too," she says. "I couldn't stomach food for days after Roz...left. My guess is you're pretty stressed about all this stuff with the inn." I nod. It's not why I'm sick, but she's not wrong. "And maybe...other things?" I meet her eye for the first time since she came in and nod again, then look away, feeling nothing less than abject misery now. Definitely other things.

"Well," she says after a moment. "There's nothing I can do about the latter, that's something you're going to have to figure out on your own. As for the former, maybe this has something to do with it." She hands me an envelope addressed to me from Greta Pickler, the lawyer I've retained to be the executor of my aunt's will. It's what must have brought her up to the office in the first place. I tear it open, wondering why the woman didn't just call. I've been leaving her messages for two days. Then when I read it, I understand. The cover page inside states she's filed the will with the court, and it does not need to be probated, thanks to the fact that Roz and Bill Blackmoor set the inn up in something called a living trust for me. All I have to do is sign the documents included and mail them back to her, and the ownership of the inn will be transferred to me. I breathe a sigh of relief and pass the letter to Cora to read. Finally, some progress. I still need to complete the bookkeeping before the inn can be properly valued for the sale to Cora, but at least we're getting somewhere now.

"There, you see?" she says, handing it back. "It'll all get sorted out, Audrey. If you want, we can send the whole lot off to an accountant today and let them figure it out."

"No, that'll cost a fortune," I tell her. I know from the work I've already done it is money the inn can ill afford. "I can finish it myself. Maybe we can sit down in a couple days and go over everything together?"

"Sure," she says. "Let's do that." I heave myself up onto my feet and toss the snotty mass of tissues into the garbage.

"Well then, back to it," I say, forcing a weak smile.

"Thanks." I hadn't expected sympathy from Cora after my outburst. Maybe there's still hope for us to build some sort of a relationship. Cora retreats to the desk downstairs, and I splash some water on my face, grimacing at the puffiness around my eyes.

Just over an hour later it's suppertime, but I feel less like eating than ever. My head is pounding after my ugly cry, so I stop into the pub to tell Kellen I'm heading to Cora's for an early night.

"You've been crying," he says as soon as I take my usual stool. He tosses the bar towel he has slung over his shoulder onto the bar and motions for Drew to take over for him, but I wave him off.

"I'm fine, it's nothing. I have a terrible headache. Too much staring at numbers all day. I just need some rest." He gives me a long stare. If he catches the lie, he doesn't call me on it in public.

"I'm going to come see you tomorrow morning, all right? After Cora's left."

"Tomorrow I thought I'd go to church, actually." I feel the bile rising in my throat again saying it out loud. "What's the church here like?"

"It's pretty progressive, very forward-thinking." He's hyper-focused on me now, his eyes searching my face closely. "For some reason, you don't really seem like the churchgoing type."

"My father's a minister," I say, my voice rising half an octave on the word *minister*. "I grew up going to church. Do you? Attend, that is?"

"Sometimes on the holidays." He shrugs. "You'll see my mama there though. She goes every week. Is this Cora's idea?"

"Cora's a member?"

"Yes, a pretty devoted one, I think. She's heavily involved in the ladies' group, and volunteers on a bunch of the committees."

Something untwists a bit deep inside me. If the Soberly church allows an openly gay woman to attend there, it couldn't be like the one I grew up in at all. My racing heart slows a bit, and I take a deep breath of relief.

"I had no idea. No, it was just something I wanted to do."

He lowers his voice and leans in, his hand finding mine. "You sure you're all right? Don't take this the wrong way, but you look pretty rough."

"I was sick this afternoon, and now I've got this headache. Like I said, a good sleep is all I need to get myself sorted out. I'll probably see you tomorrow." I'm still too shaken up to notice the brief vision his touch gives me.

As I slide off my stool and turn to leave the pub, I see a few heads look away from us quickly and return to whatever conversations they'd interrupted. *Whatever,* I think, ignoring the curious stares. *Two people can have a conversation.* If one of those two people was gently stroking the hand of the other while they talked, drawn to touch almost by instinct, their heads so close as to be almost resting against each other, that was no big deal either.

15

Services at the Soberly church don't begin until 10 a.m., so I get to sleep in a bit for the first time since I've arrived in town. I'd told Cora the night before that I was planning on attending this morning's service, eliciting a surprised smile from her.

"I have to leave early to set up for the ladies' group after the sermon, but I'll see you there, I'm sure," she'd told me before I turned in for the night.

True to my expectations, my headache is gone when I wake up, and although I'm still anxious, it's not nearly at yesterday's level. I put on my blue sundress, a cardigan, and wedges, and head on foot for the church spire. It's easy enough to find—the spire makes the church the tallest building in Soberly and is visible from every part of town. The church itself is a small building made of wood painted light gray, built in the shape of a cross, the same as countless small-town churches of the time. Four or five stained glass windows run along each of the long sides of the building. I judge it to be around the same age as the inn and many of the other buildings in town—about a century old. I make a mental note to ask Sheena if she ever found evidence the church was involved in the smuggling business.

Outside, a dozen or so people are milling by the door, enjoying a few extra minutes of sunshine before heading inside. I smile and nod at one family as I move toward the group, uncertain whether I should start making my hellos now, or wait until after the sermon. Then I hear a familiar voice.

"Audrey, it's good to see you." It's Naomi, and she motions me over to where she's standing with several other women, all around the same age as her. I shake hands dutifully, paying careful attention to the short visions each one gives me. Although the chances of a woman in her mid-sixties being a serial killer are slim, I can't rule anyone out. Everyone looks somber, and I understand why when the conversation resumes and Marnie's death is the subject.

Accordingly, three of the five visions I'd been given had involved death, either remembering the passing of a loved one, or their own last moments. I file it all away to record later. *This is good,* I tell myself as I wave at Jenny Crumb, who introduces me to her husband Mark. If everyone has dying on the mind, I can look for anyone who feels pleasure at the idea of death or suffering. If I'm really lucky, I'll find someone who might have committed a killing in a past life. The thought ratchets up my anxiety a bit again, and I discreetly take a few deep breaths to settle myself. People begin moving inside the building, and I follow suit, heart pounding. I swallow hard as I step over the threshold. Sweat pools under my arms and on my temples, and I swipe at the latter with the back of my sleeve, half-expecting to be struck down by a bolt of lightning. The familiar panic at being branded as unworthy has returned in full force. For a moment, I stand frozen in the narthex, unable to step into the nave to take a seat.

"Sit with us, Audrey," Naomi says from behind me, misinterpreting my hesitation as not knowing which pew to choose. "It's nice and cool inside, come on," she adds and pulls me by the elbow to a pew three or four from the front. She bustles me in and I plunk down onto the smooth wood, worn from untold thousands of people over the decades settling themselves in like I am now. No blast of light obliterates me from above, and just like that, I'm sitting in church.

The reverend, I see with shock, is a woman. *This is not my father's church,* I tell myself.

The reverend begins by enjoining everyone to pray for Marnie and her family and says a few words about her service to the town and her loved ones. Most people are dabbing at their eyes with tissues at the tribute.

The sermon itself is, like Kellen said, very progressive. By the end, my fear of having to sit in silence and listen to an angry diatribe is entirely dispelled. Not a single person was condemned to hellfire. In fact, hellfire wasn't even mentioned.

"Let me introduce you to Reverend Miller," Naomi says afterward and shoos me up the aisle to the altar, where a few people have gathered to chat. The woman in question looks to be in her mid-forties, with a broad, friendly face framed with loose blonde waves. I remember seeing her amongst the crowd when Marnie's body was first discovered in the storm pond.

"Audrey Eames," I introduce myself, extending my hand. She grasps it firmly.

Dirt from the explosion rained down on the men's helmets as they crouched in the narrow trench. Most hunched their shoulders instinctively against the harmless projectiles.

"That was a close one, Sargent," one of the men shouted. "They've fixed our location. What do we do?"

"Should we fall back?" a second man yelled. There were around thirty of them spread out along the trench. The Sargent knew he couldn't reach them all with his voice amongst the commotion of the shelling, so he motioned them to gather close to him.

"Hold the line!" he bellowed. "We do not fall back. Air support is on the way. We hold, and then we follow orders and take back this town."

"Air support, incoming three minutes!" the radioman shouted from his position at the machine. The Sargent saw everyone tense.

He looked at their frightened faces. Most were little more than boys, young farmers fresh from eight weeks of basic training on the Canadian prairies and shipped overseas, leaving behind parents, siblings, and sweethearts. It was his job to make sure they made it back home to their loved ones again. It was also his job to make sure they served their duty to help win the war. At some point, those two jobs were going to conflict with each other. That time was likely today. They were already under heavy fire, and as soon as their air support arrived, they would be leaving the relative safety of the trench to engage the enemy directly.

"Gentlemen," he began as another shell fell close enough to shower them with dirt. "Today is our moment to show the enemy what we are made of. Today is the day we make not only our friends and families, but our entire country proud. This is no small skirmish, men. This is the real thing. This is what you've been training for. This moment. This is why you enlisted. That feeling when you signed the papers to join the army—pride, bravery, belief that what we fight for is just and true. That's what I want you to carry forward with you now. Are you ready?"

The men roared in response at the same moment the bombs from above impacted at the other end of the pockmarked field, shaking the earthen walls around them.

"Advance!" he bellowed, heaving himself out of the trench to lead the way.

"Trish Miller," she replies with a broad smile. "It's very good to meet you, Audrey, and may I offer my condolences on the loss of your aunt. I've been meaning to get over to the inn and welcome you to the community, but it's been...well, a busy week, as I'm sure you understand."

"Of course," I reply. "I enjoyed your sermon today, Reverend."

"Oh, call me Trish," she admonishes. "Thank you. I'm

sure I'll see you around town." She turns to another of the congregants and greets her. Most of the worshipers have moved outside again to mingle on the lawn, and I join them. A few introduce themselves, guessing who I might be. Everyone is friendly, and by the time I leave, I feel more at ease with the people of Soberly than I have since I got here. They *are* good people, as both Kellen and Sheena have told me. Their past and present demeanors prove it. I haven't picked up on a single sinister note from anyone I've met.

Cora invites me to join the ladies' group afterward, but I beg off with the excuse that I want to take a nap. Once again, the large number of past-life memories in such a short amount of time has exhausted me emotionally. Before I leave, Trish seeks me out.

"If you ever want to talk about your aunt, I'm here for you, Audrey," she says. "Maybe we can have a cup of tea sometime."

"I'd like that, thank you," I reply as she squeezes my arm in a gesture of friendship.

REGRESS

Karina would go to the devil before she married Pavel Markov, she swore furiously to herself. She had finished delivering an impassioned speech avowing that very thing. There was nowhere to escape to with the temperatures outside fatal to any who braved them for long, so she fumed silently at the dinner table, ignoring the bowl of thin soup in front of her. Her hands were trembling far too much to lift the spoon to her lips, so she clenched them under the table. Her father, who had threatened to beat her if she spoke so much as another word against the match, considered the matter settled, but it was far from it. Even if they dragged her kicking and screaming down the aisle, they could not force her to say the words that would bind her to a bully, a man she knew was cruel and cold-hearted. A man who did not love her. A man her parents were desperate to make an alliance with, thanks to his power as one of the village's councilors and his family connections in the city far to the south. None of that mattered to Karina, however. She was appalled that her parents would sacrifice her future happiness this way, all to further their own shortsighted ambitions.

Pavel, who smiled oily at her from the opposite side of the table, spooned his soup into his mouth as though nothing had occurred. Only Father Lvov spoke up.

"Alexei," he said, his voice warm and subdued. As soon as Karina heard his tone, she shot him a look of thanks. He was on her side. "There are obviously still obstacles to overcome before this marriage can be made. Karina clearly is not in agreement—"

"It doesn't matter if Karina is in agreement or not," her father interrupted. "She will do as I command, or she is no longer my daughter." Although his voice was level, her father's face was reddening rapidly, and Karina knew when it reached a certain point, no one in the room was safe from his anger—or his fists.

"All I'm saying is if you want this marriage to succeed, perhaps more work needs to be done both on Pavel's part to convince Karina that he truly cares for her, and on your part to convince her it's the right choice to make."

They could talk themselves hoarse. Nothing would change her mind. She was certain Father Lvov knew it as well and was only trying to diffuse the situation and save her from a beating. Far from relieving the tension in the room, it ratcheted up as Alexei perceived the Father's words as criticism. Enraged, he pushed his chair back from the table and stood.

"You dare insult me in my own home." He shouted and grabbed for the Father's coarse woolen sweater. Father Lvov leaned back just in time. He rose and took a few steps back, holding his hands out in front of him, beseeching Alexei to calm himself. Karina watched in horror, while Pavel had a small smirk on his face. It was common knowledge he did not like the village priest and sought to undermine him and his ideas often. Karina's father was several inches taller, and at least thirty pounds heavier than Father Lvov.

"Alexei, sit down. You shame yourself," Father Lvov thundered, but the man ignored him and took a swing at his head as the Father danced backward out of his reach. Alexei swung again, and this time his fist connected, although Karina felt like it might have only been a light blow. The Father didn't even look dazed as he darted forward, faster than the bigger man, and hit him twice in succession, sending Alexei reeling into the table. The bowls clattered to the floor, spilling soup everywhere. For the first time, Karina's mother moved, leaping backward away from the mess. Alexei grabbed Karina by the hair and pulled her around to face

him.

"This is all your fault," he snarled as she shrieked and struggled to free herself. Blood was pouring from his nose, and fine droplets rained down on Karina's head. Then Father Lvov's fist made solid contact with his face, and he sank to his knees, his grip releasing from her hair as he fell backward, unconscious.

"Come with me, Karina," Father Lvov commanded, pulling her winter cloak off the hook beside the door. He was out of breath, brows drawn together until they almost touched as he glared at her father's prone form on the floor. "You can stay with my uncle Konstantin and his wife tonight, I think." Bracing herself against the cutting wind, she followed him out the door, leaving her home behind her.

16

Trish is a part of the same close-knit group of people in Soberly who are drawn to each other through lifetimes, I muse as I dawdle my way back toward Cora's house. It makes me happy to know she's found her kindred and is in the right place. I also have another entry for my journal, along with more insight into Father Lvov's personality, this time from an outside perspective. In Trish's vision, he demonstrated a strong sense of protectiveness toward the young Karina, and a desire to ensure she was treated with dignity. That itself was uncommon in a more patriarchal time, but his willingness to jump into a fight is what surprises me most. Is that an integral part of who he is, or was that how disagreements were settled in those days? I haven't known Kellen long enough to be able to tell.

Walking past Kellen's house, I'm about to stop and

knock—knowing his mom is still at church—when I remember he's probably at the inn, working. Weekends are particularly busy on the pub side, and this is lunchtime. The thought makes my stomach growl, and I almost change my destination. Now that I've survived my first church service in over a decade, my body is starting to remember how to be hungry again, and a big platter of the pub's food would hit the spot. On the other hand, I'm completely peopled out; the thought of spending even a short period of time in a room with a new bunch of folks gives my anxiety a spike. For now, solitude wins the day.

The only person I meet on the way is Drew, who is headed in the direction of the inn. He slides the headphones off his ears and we bump fists as usual. He gives me a brief vision of an adult woman knitting placidly in the evening in front of a fire. While the room she's seated in is finely decorated, she wears the clothing of a servant. Nevertheless, she appears content.

"Working?" I ask.

"Yep. You coming by?"

"Not today, I don't think. I've got other stuff to do. I'll be there all day tomorrow though."

"Awesome." He flashes me a smile and we part ways.

Once back at Cora's, I decide to spend the afternoon doing some general research on the smuggling trade on the Pacific Northwest coast during Prohibition. I also look up whether I have to notify the state about the discovery in the basement of the inn. I'm in the clear there—although it concerns criminal activity, it's decades outside the statute of limitations, and the fact that the room is on private property means I'm fit to do with it whatever I please.

I spend the rest of the day downloading journal articles from historical periodicals to sift through. All cover the subject of bootlegging in Oregon. The basic strategy was to have Canadian whiskey loaded onto small fishing vessels in British Columbia, then have them sail south under cover of darkness and put into port in various towns along the coast. That way, even if one ship was pursued or captured, the others could deliver their cargo safely. Then the liquor was transported inland. I find multiple references to this part of the state in my reading; mostly records of Coast Guard pursuits and arrests, but there are a few interviews with smugglers as well. Although nothing ever mentions Soberly specifically, one article talks about raids on towns close to here. Based on that omission, it seems likely the bootleggers here had managed to stay under the radar. I won't be sure until I can go through the town's records and look through the arrests for the time period.

The thought of diving into a project like this, with such a lurid history, fills me with an excitement I haven't felt on the job for a while. There's not much to get enthusiastic about when it comes to a potter's guild that mainly manufactured plain beige crocks, canisters, and platters, which was the contract I had completed when I found out Roz had died.

Cora doesn't return from her ladies' group until after supper, at which point I have a headache again, probably from hours spent staring at my laptop's screen. She tells me I look like I need to lie down, and I don't argue with her. Armed with an ice pack for the back of my neck, I prop myself up against the headboard with some pillows, flip to a new section of my journal, and begin writing down my big idea to draw more clientele to the inn. *It's just to help Cora out,* I tell myself. I want the inn to succeed because it was Roz's dream, and I loved her.

When I'm done my rough plan, I sit back and read it over for a long time, feeling lower than the day I arrived in Soberly and read Roz's letter, imploring me to consider making my life here. I'm not sure I want to hand this plan over to Cora, head back to an apartment in the Southwest devoid of personality, pack up, and move from town to town in a rented car every year. In one short week, everything I thought I knew about what I wanted in life has been turned on its head. Normally when I'm faced with big decisions, I make a list of pros and cons and pick a choice based on what's most logical. This time, my heart is overriding all my objections, and I don't how to factor it in. Closing my eyes, I try to imagine having this conversation with Roz where I tell her all my problems and ask her what to do. Her answer comes so easily; she doesn't even have to think before she replies.

I'm going to keep the inn.

I work doggedly on the inn's paperwork all the next day, even though the crash of the ocean and the seabirds are calling me to join them. I have the rest of my life to enjoy the surf if I want to; right now, I have to finish the task at hand.

Again, I struggle with properly itemizing the credit card statements. Multiple charges each month have no corresponding paper invoices, and Google is no help in deciphering what the cryptic line item descriptions could mean. Everything else is so easy to categorize, and my background as a historian and researcher makes it difficult to just call them "miscellaneous" like Cora has suggested. On the other hand, I know nothing about operating a hotel and pub—or any business for that matter—and this may be the norm when you're managing hundreds of transactions every month. Right now, I don't even know what I don't know. I'm going to need a crash course in running this place, and I know I might not be able to count on Cora's help.

So far, I've avoided thinking about that uncomfortable conversation, but now I spend a few minutes rehearsing several scenarios in my head. Hopefully, my appeal to her love for Roz and what she wanted for me and for the inn won't end in her throwing in the towel and telling me to go fuck myself like I initially envision.

What would be ideal—I muse—is if she would enter into a fifty-fifty partnership with me. As much as we have a superficial personal relationship right now, perhaps we could have a beneficial business one. That would be the best-case scenario for everyone—we both get to stay, the inn continues to benefit from her expertise, and I get to continue my historical studies of the smuggling culture in the area, hopefully implementing my tourist-drawing idea as well. That's something I suddenly want to fill Cora in on sooner rather than later so she can see I'm committed to helping make the inn succeed. Energized by the thought, I jot down some notes about how our partnership might work as a precursor to a more formal business plan proposal.

Before I know it, it's the appointed supper hour. Normally, I would head straight into the pub, but today

I stop by the front desk to talk to Cora.

"Have you been working upstairs all day?" she says and frowns slightly when I nod.

"I'm feeling a lot better today. I'm going to grab something to eat, do you want to join me?" I ask before I can second-guess myself. Other than the one awkward, near-silent meal we'd eaten together at her house, we've spent virtually no time together.

"Jana doesn't start until eight tonight," she replies. I'm half-disappointed, half-relieved we won't have to partake in an hour of chitchat.

"Oh, well that would work too if you don't mind sticking around for a little bit afterward? There's something I want to show you." This is a better plan. I'll take her right down to the basement and explain my idea there, in the full ambiance of the hidden room. Cora's eyebrows are raised above her glasses, but she nods in agreement. "It's really cool, I promise," I assure her with a grin as I head out the door.

The pub is full of low murmurs when I enter and is fuller than I expected for a Monday night. Nearly every seat is occupied. Heads are crowded together as faces that are starting to become familiar talk in hushed tones, but a few people look up and nod hello to me. Then the smell of fresh-fried fish hits me full on, and my mouth begins to water.

"You look as hungry as the first time I saw you," Kellen says as I slide onto my stool. He's already pouring me a glass of sangria. "Happier, though. What's up?"

"I've been doing some research, and I'm going to show Cora the hidden room tonight," I tell him.

"And?"

"I have this idea for what to do with it that I'm hoping she'll be into." I trace patterns into the condensation of my wine glass with my fingertip.

"Cool, I hope she likes it," is his reply, which surprises me. I was expecting him to ask what my idea was, and I was looking forward to telling him he'd have to wait until later to hear it. "I know you'll tell me when you're ready," he adds with a wink. I smile wryly at how he flipped the game.

"Busy tonight," I say, looking around.

"Oh, Irene Bell passed away last night. In her sleep," he adds pointedly. "She was in her eighties so I suppose it wasn't unexpected. Her home care nurse found her this afternoon."

"Irene Bell." The name sounds familiar. I'd met her yesterday, at church. She had been with her daughter, and Naomi had introduced me to both of them. I shook her hand.

The pain in her head, right behind her left eye, jolted her out of a deep sleep. She struggled to sit up, but her body did not seem to be responding to her commands properly. A weak cry escaped her lips, but there was no one in the house to hear it. She sank back into her pillow, no longer fighting. She knew what was coming and did not resist the inevitable. It was time to go home, to reunite with her beloved Muhammet again. Her parents and her brother would be waiting for her as well. It was them she thought of in her final moments, how happy she was to be able to see them again after so many years apart. She did not fear death, and as the darkness closed in and the pain faded, she was at peace.

"That's too bad," I murmur. I want more than anything to ask if it was from natural causes, but I'm sure Kellen would tell me if that wasn't the case.

"It is. She lived in Soberly her entire life, raised five kids here. She would have been a great person to talk to about your bootlegging project."

I nod, feeling the shine wear off my excitement as I contemplate yet another Soberly death that mirrored a past life. Dying in one's sleep was a common way to go. Surely, I could chalk this one up to coincidence— couldn't I? Somehow, I wasn't so sure, but all I could do was wait and see if the coroner found any irregularities.

Naomi emerges from the kitchen bearing a heaping plate of battered cod and chips for me a few minutes later, greeting me warmly.

"I heard you weren't feeling well yesterday," she says, examining my face. I shoot an irritated look at Kellen, who puts his hands up, palms toward me, pleading innocence. "It was Cora who told me, and about all the work you've taken on here to take your aunt's place," she says, her voice stern. "You're working yourself too hard. We're in no rush to run you out of town, child, and that includes Cora," she adds in a gentler tone. I open my mouth to tell her that may soon change but close it again without speaking, opting to remain positive that Cora will be receptive to my offer. "Now eat up," she orders me. "You're too pale. What you need for the next few days is some good food and more rest." She throws some definite side-eye at Kellen at her latter remark and shakes her head. "This isn't what Roz wanted for you, Audrey. You need to slow down. Now I know I'm not your mama, but I hope you see I like you well enough, and I'm looking out for you right now since yours ain't here herself."

"She wouldn't give a shit," I mutter under my breath, stabbing at the fish with my fork. Naomi's already turned away and doesn't catch it, but I can tell Kellen does from the way he presses his lips together.

"You got off easy. My guess is she's going to put me back on curfew," he jokes. "She's right though, Audrey. Cora knows the sale will go through eventually." He busies himself pouring a round of pints for an order Drew drops off. "You could even maybe try and draw it out a bit if you wanted. Stick around a little longer," he adds, avoiding making eye contact.

I almost tell him my plans right there and then, but hesitate, not wanting to get his hopes up before I talk to Cora.

"Don't worry, there's still tons left to do. I'm not going anywhere for another couple weeks, at least. You're going to be utterly sick of me long before then."

"Doubtful." He smiles out of the side of his mouth, and I know we're all right.

I meet Cora back in the lobby at eight after promising I'd come back to the pub to tell Kellen how it all went. The news of Irene Bell's death and Naomi's lecture had dampened my excitement a bit, but it's coming back on strong as I lead Cora down the hall and into the basement.

"As you know, I'm a historian," I tell her. "When I first came to Soberly, Sheena—"

"Sheena Underwood, who owns Out of the Attic Collectibles?" I nod. *How many Sheenas are there in Soberly?* I almost ask.

"Sheena told me about how the town has this history of bootlegging during Prohibition, how her house and few others have secret hiding places for smuggled whiskey, and that someone named JT even has a sort of cellar dug into his backyard. It got me thinking about the inn because it was around during those days and was a pub on top of it. A couple nights ago, I came down here to see if I could find anything, and—" I haul aside the wooden door to the root cellar, belatedly remembering I should have brought a flashlight. My phone will have to do.

"This is very interesting," Cora says as she surveys the room's barren shelves. "I admit, I had no idea this room was down here."

"No, this isn't it," I tell her with a grin, and, poking my fingers into the holes in the floorboard, pull up the trap door. "This is. Come down and see." I make my way down the ladder first, and when she meets me at the bottom, the shock and wonder on her face are genuine as I shine my phone's light all around the room for her to take it in. "Isn't this amazing?" I ask, barely able to bring my voice above a whisper. "It looks like everything's intact. There are dates, names, everything. There are even a few bottles of whiskey left behind." I show her the crate and its contents.

"It's like walking right into a museum," she says, studying the papers pinned up on the wall. "To think how many decades this has sat here, right below us, with none the wiser. You show up and unearth it in a matter of days." She shakes her head, and a small smile appears. So far, so good—she doesn't seem to mind that I've been poking around, or that I held back the discovery from her for a couple days.

"This whole thing gave me an idea that might help the inn and bring more tourists into Soberly—what do you think about running a bootlegging tour? Some of the other people in town who have false walls or hideouts like this would have to sign on—from what Sheena's said, this guy JT is really into it and would probably be on board for sure—but the idea would be that a guide would lead people through the town, visit a few of the sites, maybe go down to the beach to see where the boats pulled in, and give them an overview of what it was like to be a smuggler in the '20s and '30s. Tours could start and end at the pub, and maybe we could even include an old-fashioned whiskey drink with the tour price. A lot of places are doing ghost tours, but no one is doing anything like this. I think it would set us apart from the other towns along the coast—"

"Us?" Cora interrupts as I'm about to tell her I think we could get the tour up and running by fall for a couple months' test run before next spring. *Shit.* I'd been trying not to insert myself into the plans, but she'd caught my slip of the tongue. I swallow hard and begin the part of this conversation I've been rehearsing in my head for the last twenty-four hours.

"Yes. I've been thinking a lot the past couple days, about the inn, and Roz, and the town. And I think...I want...to stay." A heavy silence falls as Cora takes this information in. "What I'd really like though, is to do it together. A partnership. Fifty-fifty. Would you—is that something you'd consider doing? With me?"

"A partnership. The two of us." Cora's focus is entirely on me now, the surroundings that so recently held her full attention forgotten. Her voice is full of condescension, and if we weren't in such cramped quarters, I would have stepped back to give her some space.

"It's just—I keep going back to Roz's letter, and what her last wishes were for the inn, and for me, and she was right. I should have listened to her and given it some time like she wanted. I also know you've put so much of your heart into the inn as well and I don't want to take that from you, and I bet Roz didn't either—"

"Oh stop, Audrey," Cora snaps. "Enough with the 'Roz would want this, Roz would want that' bullshit. You don't know the first thing about her or who she was. Do you want to know something? All the things she said in her letter about wanting to be co-owners with you someday, about how it would make everything perfect in her life, she used to tell *me*. As soon as my student debt was paid off, as soon as I could get approved for a loan, we were going to do it. Your name never came up once until she found out she was dying, then all of a sudden everything was all about Audrey, the niece who'd never even bothered to visit and barely remembered to write. The inn had to go to you, and to hell with our plans with each other."

Each sharp sentence is like a slap in the face. Tears begin to prick at my eyes, and I swallow hard, willing them back. I will not cry again in front of this woman.

"Want to know the best part? I have half a dozen or more witnesses who can swear to the court that Roz had told them at various points in her life she wanted me to be co-owner. I could dispute her will, say the tumor that killed her made her incompetent when she wrote it, and

I'd win. She knew I was angry, so she made me make a promise. She made me promise I wouldn't try and undermine you. That I would even stay on as manager and *help* you. I, unlike you, keep my promises, which is the only reason why I'm still here."

"I'm sorry," I say, trying hard to keep my voice steady. "I shouldn't have been so hasty about saying I wanted to sell when I first got here. It was a mistake. What I want to focus on now is moving forward, and I still want to do that with you. Please. What do you say?"

"I think I already said my piece," Cora replies. "The inn is yours if that's what you want. I have no intention of entering into any sort of business partnership with you, but I will stay until you find a replacement." *That had better be soon,* is her unspoken implication. She steps around me to the ladder and begins to climb, jaw set. "I'm sure your bootlegging tour will be popular," she adds through clenched teeth. "Great idea." Her low heels clack away across the basement floor above me and up the stairs to the main level, leaving me alone in the dimly lit room.

17

An unknown amount of time later, I hear footsteps on the wooden planks above me again, this time sneakered. Probably Kellen. I've been sitting on the floor in the corner, alternately crying and running the conversation between Cora and myself over in my mind, wondering what I should have said or done differently. I contemplate pulling the wooden trap door back into place above me, but the amount of energy it would take to get to my feet and climb the ladder seems overwhelming right now.

"Audrey?" he calls from above, and I watch his legs drop down onto one of the rungs.

"Yeah, I'm down here," I say.

"You all right?"

"No."

"Didn't think so. Your conversation with Cora didn't

go well?" He settles down onto the ground beside me, hip to hip, shoulder to shoulder. Reconnecting physically with Kellen after such an emotionally draining ordeal feels like I've reached an oasis after crawling, parched, through the desert, yet my body remains rigid, unable to lean into his side and give in to the need to be supported. I'm glad the light from my phone is dim enough that he can't see how swollen my eyes are, or the part of my shirt where I wiped my nose.

"Not really, no."

"I'm sorry." We sit in silence for a minute or two. He seems like he's waiting for me to fill him in on the details, but when I don't offer anything further he doesn't push it. "Why don't you come on up out of this place," he says. "It's late. You should get to bed. Are you going back to Cora's tonight?"

Shit. I haven't even thought about my living situation. "No, and in fact, I think I'm homeless."

"Not when there's a hide-a-bed with your name on it upstairs," he says. I can hear the smile in his voice. "Come on. I'll tuck you in or stay if you rather. Not to— well, just to stay if you don't want to be alone."

"Okay," I say, and take his proffered hand to stand. Since he came down to join me, a dull numbness has set in. He could have offered to lead me into the ocean, Sylvia Plath-style, and I probably wouldn't have objected. Silently, we make our way out of the basement and up to Roz's office. My office now, although I'll probably always think of it as hers. I move mechanically, stowing the couch cushions in an organized pile while Kellen hauls out the mattress. I plunk down on it and stare at the bookshelf opposite without really seeing it at all. A deep well of emptiness is opening up inside me from Cora's rejection. Despite the fact that we were never friends and she is only family in the most superficial of ways, I feel myself grieving for what must surely be an irreparable schism in our relationship.

"You told her you were planning on staying."

"How did you know?"

"When you said you were going to church—the idea seemed to terrify you, but you were going to do it anyway. You don't need to tell me why right now, but sometime I'd like to hear about it." He drops a kiss on the top of my head and sits down beside me. Still, my body resists the inclination to lean on him for support. "I knew if you were willing to do something that bothered you so much as you start to get to know people here, you weren't thinking about Soberly as a temporary stop anymore. Mama said you made a point of introducing yourself to almost everybody there."

"I'm so naive to think she would want to work with me," I say, shaking my head. "What on earth would she gain from partnering up with me instead of owning the entire place herself? Of course, she turned me down. And I'm angry about it. Even though it makes perfect sense. I am so. Fucking. Angry." I punctuate each word by slamming my fist into a pillow. Kellen tries to rein me in, pulling my body toward him, but I shrug him off and push myself to my feet. "It wouldn't have killed her to pretend to be nice, you know? Instead, I've gotten the cold shoulder from the moment I got here, despite bending over backward to reach out to her. Some part of me even hoped that even though I'd lost one aunt, I could maybe gain another. At the very least, she should understand that I didn't ask for any of this. Roz, there's another one. What the fuck was she thinking?" I'm pacing back and forth in front of Kellen now, gesticulating broadly. Jana must be able to hear me downstairs, but I'm past the point of caring. "Throwing the two of us together, she must have known what would happen. She should have realized as much as she wanted us to take this on together—and even that's questionable, according to Cora—it would never work without her. On top of that, she thought I'd have no problem throwing away my entire career to move across the country on a whim and start all over again. I've got a master's degree from Columbia, but sure, I'll just drop everything and spend the rest of my life asking people if they've been happy with their stay." Tiny drops of saliva are flying from my lips. "Then that asshole Bill Blackmoor has to go and die too and make everything ten times more complicated. Great timing, Bill. And *you*." I stab my finger at Kellen, who's been remarkably calm as I rave. "You and your ridiculously white teeth. Smiling at me. Bringing me food all the time, and taking me for literal long walks on the beach like we're living some personals ad. And your stupid perfect dick. You're the worst of them all." I wad up a piece of scrap paper and toss it at him. He catches it easily and gives me an inscrutable look.

"So, you're mad at me because I fuck you too well, and I feed you?" The corner of his mouth twitches ever so slightly.

"Shut up. Yes." If he laughs at me, I don't know what I'll do. I feel like hurling furniture over the balcony, so this tirade is, in my opinion, me showing considerable restraint.

"You're angry because I make it harder for you to want to leave." I look at him for a long moment and exhale noisily, finally nodding before turning my back on him to face the bookshelf again.

"Not just you. Everything."

"But I'm the worst."

"Yes, all right? Congratulations. You win. You're the worst."

"I would have gone with you, you know. Back to wherever it was you were headed if you'd decided to sell." I turn around to see if he's serious, and from the sober expression on his face—no trace of a smirk now—he is. "I mean it, Audrey. You're not some casual fuck. I'm all in." Inexplicably, my eyes fill with tears, and I swipe at them furiously with the back of my hand. I can't even explain to myself why this makes me angrier, only that I can feel myself tipping over into a complete emotional overload. My head fills with an endless stream of wordless screams. I know what he's talking about, know exactly what he means, but if he says it out loud right now, I know I'll push back and walk out because that's all I know how to do. Not because I don't feel the same way, but because I've spent my entire adulthood carefully crafting a life that rejects any type of permanence, of the sort of intimacy that would bring me to rely on someone else for comfort. On the deep nourishment you can only receive from others. Roz had tried, and that's probably why I held her at arms' length and "forgot" to write and call her so often.

Kellen rises from the mattress and pulls me close into him, wrapping his arms around me in a tight embrace. Gradually, the rhythmic sound of his heart beating against my ear penetrates the screams, and they begin to still.

"Can we try it?" he asks, his voice muffled in my hair. I realize I'm holding my breath when I start to see bright spots in my eyes. I scrunch my face together and nod before I can think too much about what he's asking. This is already more than I've ever let anyone offer me.

"Okay. Good. Whew." I can hear the relief in his voice. He was holding his breath too. "Into bed," he says, and sitting me down, he unlaces my Chucks himself and slides my jeans down over my hips in a completely non-sexual manner. All this time tiny fragments of his past are buzzing in and out of my head like wasps, moments I should probably be paying attention to, but can't summon the mental clarity to give them their due. The fact that I'll never get them back nearly sets me to crying again, until I feel the cool pillow under my cheek, and with it, the unstoppable pull of sleep. Hazily, I sense the heat of his body envelop me from behind.

"Hey, Kellen?" I say before darkness overtakes me.

"What?" he replies, his mouth close to my ear.

"I'm thirty." He half snorts and gives me a squeeze. Then sleep drags me under.

After retrieving my belongings from Cora's the next morning and leaving her key in the dish by the front door with a note saying I'll be staying at the inn, Kellen and I drive to the closest big-box store for a few items to make the office suite more livable. As we unload the microwave, hot plate, and a few other small appliances I'd deemed essential, a man walks through the inn's parking lot, headed in the direction of the beach.

"Hey, Aaron," Kellen says, giving him a nod.

"Kellen." His voice is neutral, but he gives me what feels like a dirty look, despite the fact that I've never met him before. He's about my age, with a reddish-blond beard and a red MAGA hat. Nevertheless, I try to reserve my judgment.

"Hi, I'm Audrey Eames," I say, dropping one of my bags momentarily so I can extend my hand to him.

"I know who you are." His voice is cold, and he ignores my hand until I drop it awkwardly back to my side and stare at him, perplexed.

"Is there a problem?"

"Just heard the news this morning is all. Yeah, there's a bit of a problem." I stand there, waiting. Out of the side of my eye, I can see Kellen tense, and he, too, puts down his bags. "We figure you'll run the inn into the ground in six months, max. With no inn for people to stay at, there go half the other places in town. We all depend on tourism to survive here, and you've got no business threatening our livelihoods. You're in over your head. Everyone thinks so."

"That's way out of line, man," Kellen says, stepping forward at the same time I chime in saying he has no idea what I'm capable of. This Aaron has just voiced my worst fear since I decided to stay, but there's no way I'll let him see it.

"Why're you defending her when you'll be one of the first to lose your job? Are the two of you setting up house together?" He tilts his chin at the bags of appliances. "Take my advice, Audrey. Leave the inn to people who know what they're doing. Visit all you like. Enjoy our lovely town. Get laid if you want. If Kellen's not willing, I certainly am, and I bet you'd look great on your knees—"

Kellen's fist comes out of nowhere, leveling Aaron in one swing. The sickening crack of the punch echoes in my ears. "You fucking pig," he snarls as Aaron picks himself up, bleeding badly from a split lip and breathing so hard he's almost panting. I can see bits of gravel embedded in his palms, and that makes me wince more than the blood does. For a moment, I think Aaron is going to tackle Kellen and try to take him down, but instead, he spits a mouthful of frothy red saliva onto the pavement and looks murderously at us both.

"I won't forget that, Greene," he says, pointing his finger at Kellen before turning and resuming his original track to the beach, shoulders hunched inward. He spits again and wipes off his face with the tail of his shirt as he reaches the far edge of the parking lot.

"I fucking hope not. Maybe it'll remind you not to talk shit." Once Aaron is out of sight, Kellen leans against his car and cringes, cradling his hand against his chest. The bravado falls from his face. "Broke my fucking fist on his Neanderthal face," he says, examining his knuckles gingerly.

"You shouldn't have hit him. People have said far worse things to me, and I suppose I'm going to have to get used to it here if people really are as upset about me and the inn as he says." I reach out to examine him, but he pulls away reflexively.

"That's not why I did it. You don't know the guy. He doesn't stop at catcalling or groping girls in bars. He's been accused of drugging and raping women twice but got off both times because there wasn't enough evidence to convict him."

"Oh. Well, then I guess I'm glad you hit him." I try to catch his eye to give him a smile, and eventually, he relents and the corner of his mouth lifts. "Also, he's right, you know. I do look good on my knees, and I'll show you later if you let me have a look at your hand." He chokes back a laugh and holds it out to me after exacting a promise that I'll be gentle. With the lightest possible touch, I take his hand into my own.

Father Lvov knelt before Pavel, his hands soaked with blood, staring at the knife plunged in his chest. The knife he had put there. The hilt was the only part visible, and he could still feel the sensation of its weight in his hand the moment he struck. He reached out with a trembling hand to pull it back out, wishing he could somehow take back the wound he had inflicted, to reverse time, even. But he could not. Pavel's unstaring eyes looked toward the heavens, and he, Father Lvov, had sent him there.

18

"What is it?" Kellen asks. My shock at the vision he gave me must have shown on my face and given me away. The kind-hearted, progressive priest a murderer? It didn't fit in with everything I'd seen of him so far, both from Kellen himself and some of the other residents of Soberly. I shake my head to remind myself not to jump to conclusions, and focus on Kellen's hand, which is starting to swell.

"Nothing," I say. "Just thinking about how much this must hurt. I think you should go to the clinic. You might need a cast."

"Awesome," he says, frowning.

I drop him off since he can't shift gears himself and head back to the inn, finally hauling the shopping bags up to the office. I bypass the front desk, not wanting to confront Cora at the moment. There's a piece of mail waiting for me on the table from my lawyer, with a copy of the title of ownership for the inn showing that it's in my name now. Reading it gives me a strange thrill, fear warring with excitement. *It's actually real.* For better or worse, the Soberly Inn and Public House belong to me. Then the excitement loses ground and fear surges, making my heart pound and vision narrow. *I have no idea what I'm doing.* Aaron is right. I'm in way over my head. Surely Cora won't let things fall apart, especially since Roz extracted that promise to help me. Except Cora said she didn't want to stay on. Would she also let her work slide until I found a new manager?

I have my answer when she comes into the office a short while later.

"Payday is tomorrow," she says in a clipped voice. "You need to sign these checks." I nod and sign my name one by one, burning with shame that I haven't once thought about the people who work here, and whether or not Roz's death had interrupted their pay schedule. There are a few I haven't even met yet—the two housekeepers, a server, and one of the kitchen staff in the pub. These are the types of things I don't have a clue about. Meanwhile, I've been spending my time imagining up bootlegging tours instead of focusing on the basics of keeping operations going.

"Thank you," I say quietly as I hand the checks back to Cora. Mustering up my courage, fully expecting she'll turn me down again, I ask her if she'll sit down with me and go over the day-to-day operations of the inn, as well as things like inventory management and the schedule for payroll. "I know it's not something I can learn in a few hours or even a few months, but I'd like to start somewhere," I tell her.

"I think that's a good idea," she surprises me by saying. Her voice is still acidic, and she's looking somewhere over my shoulder instead of meeting my eyes, but at least she's agreed. "You can start by reading these," she adds, and pulls a couple books off one of Roz's bookshelves. I'd never noticed them before. She drops them on the table beside me with maybe more force than necessary, but I'm not intimidated by the thickness of the tomes at all. Research is what I *do*. I flip through the top one, noting how multiple passages are highlighted in bright yellow and sometimes accompanied by Roz's notes in the margins as well.

"Thank you," I say again, and Cora retreats back to the front desk, checks in hand. I grab the top book and a pad of paper for my own notes and questions and take them out to the deck to begin my crash course in hotel management.

Kellen texts an hour later to pick him up, and when he emerges from the clinic, he has a neon pink fiberglass cast on his right hand. "Three weeks," he says before I can ask him how long he has to wear it.

"Can you work?"

"I dunno yet. I'm going to try." His index and middle fingers aren't bound by the cast, but his ring and pinky ones are completely immobilized, as well as his hand and wrist. He won't be able to pick up or carry anything; something which I imagine is pretty critical for a bartender. Not only that, he'll have to work with his left hand.

We drive back to the inn without saying a word to each other. Kellen's face is set in a sort of semi-grimace, and I can't tell if it's from the pain in his hand, or because he's started to regret hitting Aaron. Myself, I can't think of anything to break the silence because I'm still thinking over the brief flash of a vision I received about the killing of Pavel. It had been so short I hadn't gotten any sense of context from him about the events leading up to it. Was it a calculated act, or did it happen in a sudden burst of anger? Was it an accident, or self-defense? I do know the priest was shocked when he realized what he'd done but was that on account of the possibility of being caught? It was impossible to know.

When we walk into the pub, more than one person nudges their neighbor to point out Kellen's pink cast.

"I think I figured out what happened to Aaron Glass's face," Drew says, eyes widening. He holds out his fist for our customary bump, but his eyes never leave Kellen's face.

"Was he back here?" Kellen asks, his voice lowering to a near-growl.

"No, I saw him about an hour ago when I was on my way in. Told him he should come in and have a round or two to numb the pain, and he said he was never setting foot in this place again. Said he'd do all his drinking over at the Mast and Mussel from now on." The Mast and Mussel, I knew, was a popular bar and restaurant in the next town over. "Why'd you beat on him?"

"Cause he's a shit-talking prick, that's why." This outburst causes Drew's eyes to widen further, but he doesn't press for specifics.

"All right, calm down. People are staring," I say out of the side of my mouth. His jaw clenches tighter, but he stalks through the tables to the bar, silently daring anyone to challenge him. No one does, thankfully, but I'm sure that won't last for long—Naomi hasn't seen him yet. I bite my lip and glance at the kitchen door, where she's sure to emerge at some point.

"It's her day off," Drew tells me, following my gaze. I breathe a sigh of relief. Given the speed of the gossip train in Soberly, it's likely she'll still hear about it before he gets home, but at least they can hash it out in private. "So, what happened?"

"He said some nasty stuff to me, is all. That no one in town wanted me to stay on at the inn. Then he made a crude remark. That was the last straw." I'm assuming that at this point, Drew knows Kellen and I have at least some sort of relationship. I look around the pub. Almost all the tables are vacant, and of those that are occupied, none of the faces around them look familiar. "Slow day?" I ask Drew. It's that time of the afternoon when people have already finished lunch, and it's too early for supper, but I'm used to seeing at least a few old-timers sitting around, shooting the shit over a pint to beat the heat.

"Little bit," Drew replies with a shrug, his face glum. I know the majority of Drew's income depends on tips, so a slow day at the pub means he earns less.

"Do you think it's because of me?"

He shrugs again. "Who knows. People will probably be a bit weird about it for a few days, then get used to the idea and things will go back to normal. Change is a part of life. Is it really true? You're not selling to Cora?"

"Yes, it's true. Roz wanted me to do this. It took some time to get on board, but I'm starting to understand why. I wish I could get Cora behind me too."

"I'd like to say maybe she'll come around, but..." he

trails off. "Anyway, I gotta get back to work. Don't want my boss to see me slacking off." One side of his mouth pulls up in a grin, and he heads to one of the tables to check on its occupants.

Kellen is still in a foul mood when the pub closes, and heads for home after a perfunctory kiss and a promise that he'll be in better spirits tomorrow. I'm glad for a night apart—the emotional rollercoaster of the past couple of days has finally caught up to me.

The next morning my reflection is a testament to the quality of sleep I had. The dark, puffy circles under my eyes are only superficially masked by concealer, and for unknown reasons, my skin is breaking out to the left of my mouth. It's at this point I realize I didn't buy a hair dryer yesterday and will have to let my hair air-dry, the result of which is always a lank, wavy mess. Awesome. I walk over to Sheena's shop; hopeful she'll be able to fill me in on the pulse of Soberly with respect to my decision to keep the inn. The sign on the door reminds me that it's closed today, however, so I walk a few blocks further to her house and knock on the door.

"You look like shit," she says without preamble when she answers. She, on the other hand, looks effortlessly casual, hair flat-ironed, makeup flawlessly understated, in a breezy white lace-trimmed sundress. I give her the finger and scowl. Maybe this wasn't such a good idea. She beckons me inside with an understanding smile and tells me she'll put on some tea.

"Heard the news about you deciding to keep the inn," she says as I sit down across from her at the table. Her kitchen is decorated cheerily with yellow walls and white cupboards, accented with all sorts of antique treasures she's no doubt rescued from her shop, along with fresh-cut flowers and spider plants hanging from pots. It's an eclectic mix, but somehow it works. "Cora's not taking it so well."

"Only Cora?" I ask with a pointed look at her.

"Maybe a few other people besides Cora," she acknowledges. I heave a big sigh and wonder if I should ask her who, exactly, is against me, before thinking better of it. "Don't worry about it too much, Audrey," she tells me. "It's true there are some people who aren't too thrilled with the idea. They felt the same way when Roz bought the inn from the McCuaigs, you know. There was a lot of talk back then about how no one would be able to run the place the way they did, that people would stop coming if there was a new owner. You know what? They were wrong then, and they'll be wrong now. You'll see."

"Except Roz had some actual training in hotel management," I point out. "All I have are a couple of her textbooks, and a manager who goes from wanting to help me, to wanting to see me crash and burn at the drop of a hat. Honestly, I'm not surprised people don't have confidence in me. *I* don't have confidence in me." It feels good to say it to someone so it isn't festering inside my head anymore. The kettle whistles and Sheena sets a few boxes of teabags on the table and fills my mug with boiling water. I select a peppermint herbal tea, hoping to settle my stomach, which hasn't stopped churning since my confrontation with Cora in the hidden cellar.

"She's leaving, then?" she asks. I nod.

"I don't want her to, but I think she's got her heart set on it. I don't know what she'll do after that. Leave Soberly altogether? She has friends here. This is where she made her home with Roz. It makes me sad."

"You're not responsible for her choices, Audrey," Sheena tells me. "If that's what she ends up doing, you're not to blame for it."

"I hope everyone else sees it that way." I stare into my mug glumly.

Sheena seems like she's about to reply when her phone buzzes on the counter. I motion for her to answer it if she wants, and after glancing at the display, she does, telling me it's Joanne the dispatcher at the police station.

"Oh my god, are you serious? Are they sure?" Sheena covers her mouth as she speaks, and her eyes widen. She listens for a long moment. "I can't believe it. I mean— oh my god. That's terrible. Just terrible. That poor, poor woman." They must be talking about Marnie, I conclude. Maybe the autopsy was complete, and there were more details about her death. Sheena is still listening, uttering the odd "mm-hmm" here and there before saying goodbye.

"Marnie?" I ask as she sits back down. She looks utterly shaken by the conversation.

"No, *Irene,*" she says in a daze. "She didn't die of natural causes at all. She was smothered with her own pillow. Someone let themselves into her house and killed her in her sleep. What is going *on* in this town?" Her eyes fill with tears.

I almost vomit from the revelation. That makes two, and possibly three, people who have been killed in Soberly in a short period of time, and in an identical manner to their death in a previous life. The knowledge feels like it's too much of a burden to bear alone, and in a moment of panic, I decide to confide in Sheena. She didn't tell anyone about the hidden room in the basement of the inn, and I hope she'll be as discreet with my secret as well.

"If I tell you something, do you promise to hear me out with an open mind?" She nods, my question shocking her out of her reverie. "All of them—Bill, Marnie, Irene—they all died the same way as they did in a past life. Except in the past, their deaths were accidental, or in the case of Irene, natural. Now they're being killed to make it look like it was the same." I pause for a moment to let it all sink in.

"What?" Sheena says, utterly bewildered. She shakes her head and I press on.

"When I was fourteen, I got really sick and was in a coma for a while. When I woke up, I had the ability to see bits and pieces of people's past lives any time I touched them." I give her a quick rundown of how the ability works and the types of things I tend to see. Although I do mention how the same spirits tend to find each other over multiple lifetimes, I don't tell her about the ongoing saga of the Russian village that's been unfolding amongst the people of Soberly. "I don't know why it happened to me and not other people, but I've been able to prove a few times that the visions I have are of real people and real events. Bill, Marnie, and Irene all gave me visions of a way they died in a former lifetime, and now they've died in the exact same way. That's not the way it usually works. In fact, that's not the way it almost *ever* works. Except in Soberly. I don't know what it means."

"That means...that means reincarnation is real," Sheena says. I take it as a good sign that she doesn't reject the idea altogether. On the other hand, maybe she's pretending to entertain me and plans on calling the psych ward as soon as she can safely get me out of her house. It's hard to read her body language, and her expression is still a mix of confusion and grief.

"Yes. People seem to reincarnate several times. At least six, from what I've been able to track in my research. My point is, there's someone else in town who can do the same thing as me, or at least I think there is, and they're using it in some sort of sick game to kill people. Now that Irene's death fits the same pattern, I'm more certain of it than ever. Ever since Marnie died, and I saw the connection to Bill, I've been hoping to be able to figure out who it is by using my own ability to look for some sort of pattern or clues from the past. To see if I can flush them out somehow."

"Have you come up with anything?"

"Not really." I can't tell her about the vision Kellen gave me of the man he killed. I don't want to believe he could be involved in anything like this. The idea makes me sicker still, and I hastily bring my mug up to my face to inhale the warm scent of peppermint. "Can you think of any way the three of them are connected, beyond the fact that they all live here? Someone they all have in common? Maybe that would help." Sheena contemplates the idea for a couple of minutes, biting her lip before eventually shaking her head.

"Nothing," she says. "They all knew each other, of course, but I can't think of something or someone specific linking them together. Have you...have you seen anyone else's death in the past? Have you seen *mine?*"

"No one's," I tell her, and she sighs with relief. "In

fact, somehow or another you and I haven't made any skin-to-skin contact yet. I don't know anything about your past lives at all."

"Really?" She seems to be thinking back for a moment, and shrugs. "Does it hurt when you do it?"

"It doesn't hurt at all, no. It's sort of like when you remember something all of a sudden, except it's not one of my memories. After a while, it does tire me out though, especially when I'm making contact with lots of different people all at once. I kind of lose myself in all the bits of other people."

"I've never heard of anything like that before." Now she looks dubious. I'm losing her. "I mean, there are mediums and stuff with their crystal balls, I guess, but I always figured they were hoaxes."

"They probably are," I say. "Everyone's some member of royalty when you visit one of those. They spin you a story to make you feel important. In all the people I've ever made contact with, I've never come across the past life of any member of the nobility or famous figures. Just normal folks like you and me." I fiddle with my teabag, dunking it up and down repeatedly in the water. I want to tell her how part of me wants to be able to prove it's real, to see what it looks like on an MRI when I touch someone. The other part of me thinks that if people know about this, everyone will think I'm some sort of freak. I've had enough social isolation in my life already, some of it my own doing, some of it not. Telling the police about my ability is not an option. Hopefully, the killer left clues behind and the case is already close to solved, but I can't count on it.

"Why are you telling me all this?" Sheena asks.

"You know the people here way better than I do," I say. "Maybe you can point me in the right direction or introduce me around so I can make more connections. You said you always wanted to be Nancy Drew," I add wryly. "Here's your chance."

"More like one of her sidekicks," she says, but my mention of the girl detective does bring a faint smile to her face, the first one I've seen since we sat down. "Seriously though, Audrey, I don't think we should get mixed up in this. This person has killed at least two people already. Let the police do the detective work."

"What if I can help? What if someone else dies while they're still trying to figure it out? I have an advantage they don't. I could make a real difference."

"You could also get yourself killed."

"I know." The thought is sobering. "I still have to try."

"Have you told Kellen about any of this?"

"No, and I'm not sure I'm going to. Please, Sheena, don't mention this to anyone. Besides the fact that probably no one else will believe it, it could put me in danger if the killer finds out."

"I won't, I swear," she says, but she frowns.

Having gotten a lot off my chest, I thank her for the tea and stand up to leave. She surprises me by holding out her hand as though to shake.

"Will you tell me? What you see?" she says hesitatingly. This is a new one for me. Not since I was fourteen and first started having the visions have I told anyone about my ability, and back then, the doctors I tried to describe it to brushed it off as vivid dreams or delusions as my brain healed. I've never been asked to describe someone's past life to them in the moment.

"Sure," I say, and grasp her hand.

REGRESS

The light of the small lamp on the desk beside him flickered as the oil began to run low, but he figured he still had another ten minutes by which to write, and he redoubled his efforts to get as many words down on the page as possible before he was forced to retire for the evening.

This tale he transcribed had been haunting his dreams for months—a future world where clockwork men replaced human ones in the factories, farms, and shops, leaving people indolent and without purpose. Now that the skies over much of the planet were dark with smoke from all the coal these mechanical creations consumed, the chief luxury on Earth was sunlight, enjoyed primarily by the wealthiest who could afford to rise above the smog in flying machines, and fresh air, which they trapped in bottles to bring back to the surface to breathe in the comfort of their homes. Crops were failing, people were starving, and still, humanity could not wean itself from the reliance on their clockwork men.

The writer saw the signs of this hellish world to come all around him—the locomotive, the steam engine, the weaving machines, and cotton gins replacing men's work already. The writer was an avowed Luddite, but rather than smashing machinery and burning down factories, his weapon was his words, the cautionary stories he wrote of what the future would hold if mankind did not return to its pre-industrial ways. He raged at the fact that none of the newspapers or periodicals would publish his stories, forcing him to print them himself as pamphlets and distribute them on the street to anyone who passed by. This—this was his masterpiece. This would be the story that persuaded people to reject these advances in technology before it was too late.

The irony was not lost on him that some of these modern inventions like moveable type and the printing press allowed him to create his tracts in the first place, but in service of the greater good, he swallowed his convictions to spread the word as widely as possible.

He wrote on, his quill scratching the paper, words packed tightly together to conserve the expensive material. He was running low on funds after leaving his job as a clerk to write full time. He had planned to support himself by selling his stories, expecting his name to be alongside the likes of Dickens in London's best-regarded magazines. With this, he would. There could be no way the editor would not see the value in this tale, see his skill as a wordsmith.

His protagonist, John, a young clerk like he had once been, was now about to duel a clockwork man who was trying to prevent him from setting fire to the machinery that operated the last coal mine on Earth. Without coal, the machines could not operate, and humanity would be forced to start working for themselves again. The owner of the coal mine, and the factory that produced the clockwork men, Viscount Magnus Munro, had ordered John's death. John had realized that if he could get the mechanical man to burn through its coal faster by pursuing him throughout the mine, it would die, and he could perform his mission. It would cost him his own life, naturally—the writer had a flair for the dramatic—when the writer's lamp sputtered out and he was swallowed by darkness. He pounded his fist on the desk, but there was nothing to be done for it—he was out of oil, and none could be purchased until tomorrow.

Laying his quill in the small box that also held his inkwell, gifted to him by his mother, the writer carefully stacked his papers together and locked them in his desk. Tomorrow at the first light of dawn, he would resume his work.

19

I have to laugh at the vision Sheena gives me, the paradigm between the way she immerses herself in objects of the past in this lifetime, and her obsession with the future in another.

"What?" she asks, looking like she's not sure if my amusement is a good thing. I tell her about the writer and how he envisioned the future to be, along with his struggles to have his writing acknowledged by society.

"I wonder if he was ever successful," she muses.

"Dunno. Without a name, it would be pretty hard to find out. If you had that, you might be able to find some surviving example of his work, particularly since he did self-publish. Unfortunately, it was as hard to get published in those times as it is today." In fact, it was probably harder, since everything was handwritten, and sent by snail mail. On horseback. Sheena's writer would probably love today's modern options. Two clicks and your novel can be on Amazon. I wonder what he'd think of the Internet. Of the world in general, really. It certainly hadn't turned out as terrible as he'd predicted.

I check my phone while walking back to the inn. There are fourteen missed texts and one missed call from Kellen. With a sinking feeling in my chest, I bring them up on the screen.

"u coming to the staff meeting?" reads the first one. Staff meeting? I don't know anything about a meeting being called. Maybe it's a regular weekly thing at the inn? If so, it's the first time I've heard about it.

"where are u? Checked ur office and u weren't there. Everyone's waiting"

"C is starting without u" C must be Cora. Cora called a staff meeting?

"Holy shit she just told everyone she's leaving"

"And that they can go to u from now on with their problems"

"Audrey where are u this is brutal"

"she's making it seem like we're all gonna be out of jobs in a couple months"

"says we're more than welcome to contact her for references and wishes us the best"

"did u even know about this?"

"mama and I tried to downplay it but everyone looks nervous"

"Jana's almost crying"

"now C's apologizing to us and said she tried her best but it's out of her control now"

"I don't know what to do but the meeting is over. C's glaring at me, think she knows I'm texting u" "text me back when u get these"

The beep of a car horn startles me back into the present, and I look up to see a Subaru stopped in front of me, beckoning for me to cross the street. I hadn't noticed I'd stopped at the corner, shaking with rage as I read Kellen's texts. I wave at him to drive on. I read through them again, clutching my phone so tight my knuckles turn white. I'm at a loss for how to reply. Even if I had gotten the messages in time, what could I have done? I do know one thing though. Cora and I need to have a conversation. Right now.

The bell above the door of the inn's lobby jangles aggressively as I push it open. Cora's sitting at the desk, chatting with a man and a woman holding suitcases. I stop short, not wanting to cause a scene in front of guests and see Cora glance over the rim of her glasses at me, taking in my narrowed eyes and heavy breathing. She knows I know, and that I'm not happy. Is that satisfaction in her eyes at my thwarted lecture? Not knowing what else to do, I stalk past her without a word of acknowledgment, taking the back stairs up to the office. To my surprise, Kellen's sitting on the couch. He jumps up when I storm in.

"You need a better lock," he tells me when I open my mouth to ask him what he's doing in here. "I opened the door with my credit card. Audrey, tell me you didn't freak out on Cora just now."

"You would have heard it if I did, she's right downstairs—"

"Good. Take a minute to calm down and think—"

"She's trying to undermine *my* authority here. She's sabotaging me before I even have a chance."

"I know, but do you think going off on her is going to help your case, either with the staff or your credibility?"

"I can't just let her—"

"You have to think smart about this. Losing your temper isn't the way to go."

"You should talk." I jerk my head at the cast on his hand.

"Yeah and look where it got me. Got *us*. There's twice the talk in town now about what's going on here. You're not going to reassure people that everything's going to be fine if you lose your shit on Cora, and word gets out that the two of you are butting heads. Let her spout her doom and gloom before she leaves, then *prove her wrong*. That's how you can win this."

"Dammit. You're probably right." I sink down onto the couch and drop my head into my hands. As much as I want to pull rank on Cora and tell her off, it's not going to help me. It might even cause her to quit on the spot. Maybe that's what she wants, and she's trying to maneuver me into a position where it will look like she has no choice. Either that or she wants to make me so angry I fire her, which would gain her untold sympathy with the townspeople and probably turn them away from me for good.

"Is your mom working right now?" I ask him. He looks confused but checks his watch and nods.

"She started about fifteen minutes ago. Why?"

"Can we go over to your house? I need to work some stuff out, and I don't want to be quiet about it." I check to see if he catches my drift. The slow smile spreading across his face tells me he does.

"That's a plan I can get behind. I'm at your service.

Let's go."

On the way past Cora's desk, I inform her that I need to be notified in advance of any future staff meetings, keeping my voice and expression as coolly neutral as possible, and then leave the inn before she can reply. While we manage to keep a walking pace on the way there, when we get to Kellen's house, he ushers me downstairs at almost a full run, his feet thundering on the steps, pulling me along by the hand.

"You made me a promise yesterday," he says as we burst into his room. His hands are already up underneath my skirt, and mine are busy at work on his jeans.

"Yes, I did," I recall with relish. "I want to start with that."

༉༉

Shortly before he has to leave for work, Kellen makes us an enormous stack of sandwiches and brings them down to his room. I'm lying on my stomach in his bed, naked, feeling sore in places I barely knew existed, and perfectly content, for the time being, at least.

"Looks like it worked," he remarks, setting the plate down and stretching his long body beside me. "You've got a goofy little smile on your face I've never seen before. Kellen Greene's perfect dick for the win."

"God, I'm never going to hear the end of that, am I?"

"Never ever." I swing a pillow at him, but he dodges it easily like I knew he would.

"You going to stay awhile? You can if you want," he asks after we're through eating. He's eying my prone position as he shrugs into his pub uniform shirt. It's true I don't want to move, but I shake my head and swing my arm over the side of the bed, half-heartedly fishing around on the floor for my skirt.

"No, I'll go do some work. If I stay, I'll fall asleep."

"That wouldn't be such a bad thing, coming home to find you already naked and waiting in my bed." He waggles his eyebrows at me, making me giggle.

"You don't have to go, you know," I tell him with an inviting look.

"Yes, I do," he tells me, and his voice loses its playfulness. "You don't think people are already talking about whether this"—he gestures back and forth between the two of us—"is causing any favoritism? I don't want to give them any fuel for that fire. You're my boss, Audrey. It's a fact, and we need to keep our personal lives completely separate from work. It all goes back to your credibility as the new owner. No skipping out on shifts. No fooling around on the clock. I won't be a part of anything that keeps you from succeeding. I'll quit first."

"You can't quit your *job*," I say, horrified.

"Well I'm not quitting you," he says, and bending over the bed, he kisses me deeply. His hands start to trace their way down my body, followed by his mouth. "I'm not on the clock yet, and I still have ten minutes before I have to leave. Let's see if I can put that smile back on your face before I go."

❦

The next day passes by uneventfully. Cora doesn't share any further information about the operations of the inn, but on Friday Naomi does, walking me through the kitchen's inventory and ordering system, staff scheduling, and the little things like what days the table linens get picked up for laundering.

"How come we don't wash them ourselves?" I ask her. "We've got the machines on the inn side that do the bedding." The question takes her by surprise.

"I...I don't know. We've always sent them out. They take the dirty ones away and drop off clean ones at the same time. It's convenient, I suppose." I make a mental note to see how much the service costs the inn, and whether switching to doing it ourselves would save money in the long run, once I factored in the extra labor, detergent, and the cost of buying our own linens instead of renting them.

Kellen goes over the bar operations in a similar fashion, showing me how he keeps track of the liquor stock, where we order from, and how the computer system that tracks food and beverage orders works. True to his promise, even when we're alone in the stockroom there's no groping or even whispered dirty talk about what we have planned for later. The inn has filled up now that it's the start of the weekend, and the pub is busy as the supper rush begins.

"Want to grab an apron and give us a hand?" Kellen says as I fiddle around with the computer system some more. I stare back at him incredulously. "It's easy," he says with a grin that doesn't increase my confidence at all. "Ask people what they want, write it down, and if it's a drink you tell me, and if it's food you tell my mama. Then you punch their order into the computer, and when it's ready, you bring it to them."

"Just like that, huh?" I swallow nervously.

"Just like that. Here you go." He pulls an apron from

behind the bar and I tie it on, stalling for time by trying to make the bow perfect.

"Wait, how do I know who's already been helped and who hasn't?"

"Here, Drew will know." He beckons Drew over as he emerges from the kitchen. "Audrey's going to help out for the rush," he says. "Any tables that haven't been served yet?"

"Three, eight and eleven. All have menus, no drinks," he says, slapping an order onto the bar and entering it into the computer. I look out at the pub, clueless. Kellen's arm appears over my shoulder, pointing.

"That one," he indicates a party of four to my left, close to the bar, "that one," a couple, "and that one." Another couple. They're all grouped fairly close together. "That's going to be your station tonight, all right? I'll let Livvy know." Livvy's the other server who works in the pub. I just met her tonight when Kellen introduced us. "You'll be fine," he tells me. "Now off you go." He gives me a push between my shoulder blades and I head for the table of four, pasting what I hope is a friendly smile on my face.

"Hi, I'm Audrey," I say, making eye contact with each of them in turn. *Should I shake their hands? No, servers don't shake hands, you idiot. Just keep smiling.* "Umm, what would you like to drink?" I write down each of their orders in turn and take the slip over to the bar. "That wasn't so hard," I tell Kellen as I pass him the paper.

"Couple tips. First of all, write the table number at the top of your order pad so I know where it's going, in case I send it with Drew or Livvy. You can also bring me the orders from all your tables at once. Goes a bit faster that way. Okay? You're doing great. I'll have these ready in a couple minutes. You go take those other two orders."

Taking the first couple's order goes off pretty seamlessly, but at the second, the man seated at the table begins firing questions at me.

"What beers do you have on tap?" he starts out with.

"Umm..." I turn to squint at the handles at the bar and name them off. I can't read the last one because it's too far away so I leave it off the list.

"Any of 'em local?" I freeze.

"Let me check," I say and scurry over to the bar. "Which of the beers are local?" I hiss at Kellen. He points out three and has me repeat the names back to him. "This should be on the menu," I tell him.

"We never update the drink menu," he says. "Just the seasonal keg and the daily special on the board." Crap. I haven't mentioned the specials to anyone.

"Well, we're going to start." I whirl back to my table and rattle them off. After what seems like an eternity's thought, he chooses one. Then his date asks me what label the house red is and I feel a headache start to come on.

"It's a merlot," I say, hoping that will satisfy her, but she insists on knowing the actual brand, which means I have to make another trip to the bar. She orders a beer instead, and I struggle hard to keep my expression neutral. Having delivered the two orders to the bar, I collect the first table's order, balancing the four drinks precariously on a tray as I shuffle between tables at a snail's pace. That's when I realize I don't remember who ordered what, or even which drink is which, in the case of two of them. *You suck so bad at this*. Sweat is starting to pool in my armpits.

"Okay, who had the gin and tonic?" I say with a giant smile. "And the IPA." Hands go up and I pass them around. "Now this one is the—" I glance up at Kellen, who's watching me and trying hard to keep a straight face. *Red ale* he mouths to me. "Red ale." I'm almost shouting and these people are looking at me like I'm a bit mad. I feel like I am. "Which means this last one belongs to you." I plunk the last pint down in front of its owner. "Awesome, folks. Enjoy."

"We're ready to order," one of them says.

"Right, yes. Food. The food is so good here. I mean, it's, like, the best," I gush. Now Kellen is openly laughing as he's pulling pints. *Table 8* I write at the top of a new slip. This time, I make a point of memorizing who ordered what, and after enthusiastically ensuring them they made some great choices—*what are you doing*—I make my way to the kitchen.

"Over with the others," Naomi indicates to me where to put the order slip. I give her the thumbs up and she nods in reply, busy at the stove.

The couple with all the questions about their drinks has even more about the menu. At least this I have more experience with, having eaten my way through most of it. They're particularly concerned with where everything comes from.

"We're *locavores*," the man informs me in a snooty tone. I tell him both the crab and the salmon are locally caught, and many of our vegetables come from area growers as well. I even mention the pies that are baked right down the street. Much of this I learned from

Naomi earlier today, but again, the information isn't featured on the menu itself. Another mental note: time for a redesign and new descriptions. "You don't have any non-seafood local options?" he says with a frown.

"Not entirely, no. The beef in the burgers is American—" I start, but he interrupts me.

"Beef is almost *always* American." He heaves an irritated sigh. "I suppose I'll have the burger." His partner chooses the salmon, and after confirming their sides, I take the order to the kitchen.

"These ones are cranky," I say to Naomi. She rolls her eyes but is too busy to ask for specifics.

Fifteen minutes later, not long after I've brought them their food, he beckons me over, pointing at his place with an angry expression.

"What is *this?*" he says, poking at the fried egg on top of the beef patty.

"It's an egg," I reply, not sure how else to answer. "It comes on the burger. It's in the description." I grab a menu to show him.

"Take it back," he says to me, shoving the plate away. "I despise eggs." Given that a moment ago I saw him sample a piece of his partner's salmon, which is served with hollandaise sauce, I have to wonder if that's actually the case. Maybe he's not the foodie he thinks himself to be.

"Do you want to take the egg off?" I ask. It seems like the most reasonable solution to me. I mean, when I don't like something on my plate, I leave it on the side and eat around it. It's a life skill I picked up when I was three or four.

"I want a new burger. With *no egg.*" I raise one

eyebrow but take his plate back to the kitchen.

"He doesn't like the fact that there's an egg on it, but he never told me he didn't want it on there in the first place," I tell Naomi.

"This is the same cranky table?" I nod. "Some people you can't please no matter how hard you try. I'll get a new one made up on the fly." True to her word, in less than ten minutes she has a fresh plate ready. As I take it from her, our hands accidentally brush.

REGRESS

Her hand was still shaking when she picked up the bottle of cheap red wine and poured herself another glass. She shouldn't have spent the money, but if she wasn't going to be able to make rent at the end of the week anyway, what would it matter if she was short another couple dollars?

"There's nothin' to do for it," she'd complained earlier to Mona, talking across the lane at the grocery store they both worked at. She'd pretended to be busy wiping down her counter so Joe, the manager, didn't get on her case about standing idle. "Frank's been out of work for almost two months now, and with Jamie needing to see the doctor twice on account of his damn ears, I don't know how we're going to manage. We got

no more savings left, and Joe won't give me any more hours. We barely got any food in the icebox."

"You can have my shift on Friday," Mona had offered.

"I'm already working Friday. I'm working every damn day between now and the end of the month. Besides, we won't get paid until after the first, and that'll be too late." Their landlord had warned Frank he wouldn't accept any more late payments. If they came up short again, they'd be evicted on the spot. It would be their third move in a year. She was tired of packing boxes.

"Can't Frank get some handyman work, or maybe do some day laboring?"

She'd shrugged, pressing her lips together until all that was visible of her coral-colored lipstick was a thin line. The truth was, Frank was a proud man, and too accustomed to an easy life. He'd never cut it as a laborer. He wanted to find work as an accountant again. To him, lowering himself meant taking a bookkeeping position, but he hadn't even been able to find that. Now he mostly sat around the house, watching TV, and minding the baby while she stood in the checkout line all day. Maybe she could sell the TV to make up the difference in rent money. That might wake Frank up. She, like Mona, felt he should be doing anything and everything necessary to support his family, even if it meant delivering newspapers door to door, or pulling sodas over at the drugstore. The thought of a big empty space in their living room where the TV now sat filled her with a sense of bitter vindictiveness. Hell, she'd sell *the radio too.*

She'd rung a customer through mechanically as she made her plans. Probably it would be easiest to offer the TV to their landlord in lieu of some of their rent money. It would certainly save her the trouble of lugging it all the way to the pawn shop.

"I'll be right back, Mona," she'd said. "I need to make a phone call." In the break room, she'd dialed their landlord's number, rehearsing what to say while the line rang. "Mr. Eastman, it's Mrs. Frank Garland, one of your tenants," she'd begun. "I'm calling because...well, Frank and I have a bit of a predicament this month. You see our son, Jamie, has been sick with an ear infection and with the doctor's bills, and the medicine, we're a little bit short this month, and—"

"Mrs. Garland, I told your husband last month if you didn't pay the full amount, on time, you were out. I have no time or patience for deadbeats," he'd interrupted.

"I know, Mr. Eastman, and I understand. We're only about fifty dollars short. What I was hoping was that you'd be willing to take our TV as part of the rent. It's a real nice one, only a few years old. We paid a hundred and twenty for it brand-new."

"I've already got a TV, and a kitchen table, and whatever else you might be thinking about offering me. What I want is cash, do you understand me? Now either you have your money to me on the first like you're supposed to, or you start packing your things. Is that clear?"

"Yes, sir, of course. I understand. I thought I would

ask, is all. Sorry to bother you. We'll have it all for you by the first, I promise." She'd dropped the receiver back into the cradle and sat staring at the wall for a long moment before walking back out to her register, mulling over her options. *In truth, she didn't think she'd get even half of what they needed by pawning the TV. Was she willing to sell her wedding ring to keep from having to move yet another time? She'd looked down at the thin gold band. It was probably worth less than the TV.*

"I give up," she'd said to Mona when there was no chance of being overheard again. *"I guess we're going to have to move. I don't know how I'll manage it, what with being here all the time. The stress is givin' me a headache already."*

"You need to relax, Jeannie," Mona had said, and came around to her lane, looking around to see if anyone was watching them. *"Here. Open your hand."* She'd pulled a matchbook-sized silver pill case out of her apron and gave her three bright red pills. *"Put those in your pocket, and after the baby's in bed, take one. I promise you'll have the best sleep of your life. In the morning, you tell Frank to get off his behind and either get a job or start packing up your things. You hear me?"*

She'd stared down at the pills, then slipped them into her pocket like Mona had instructed. *"What are they?"*

"My doctor gives them to me for when I'm thinkin' too much and can't get to sleep. They're marvelous, I promise."

Now she was staring at them again, looking like oblong droplets of blood in her palm. Frank was in the living room, staring sullenly at the TV, which was playing Gunsmoke. Rather than waiting until morning to give him her ultimatum, she'd brought it up as soon as the baby was down and they'd had their biggest fight in years, with her accusing him of failing their family, and him blaming everything on her for wanting to move out of the city in the first place.

She tossed back the wine, poured herself a third glass, and swallowed two of the pills. Mona had said they were good for when you were stressed; well, this was about the most stress she'd ever felt in her life.

It wasn't long before she started to feel woozy, and she stumbled down the hall into the bedroom, leaning heavily on the wall. Her hands no longer had the coordination to undress and put on her nightgown, so she fell onto the bed, fully clothed. Mona was right. All her cares seemed to have slipped away. Everything was going to be all right; she saw that now. She loved Frank. She loved baby Jamie. And she loved Mona for sharing her wonderful red pills with her.

She lay like this, staring up at the ceiling, until it became too difficult to hold her eyes open, and a short while later fell into unconsciousness, her breathing becoming slower and slower until it ceased altogether.

20

When my hard-to-please customers sign their bill at the end of their meal, there's a big zero with a line slashed through it in the "Tip" field. My face burns with anger and shame. I snag a twenty dollar bill out of my wallet, tuck it into the bill folder along with the credit card slip, and bring them both to the register.

"I saw that," Kellen says out of the corner of his mouth as I close out the order in the system. "He stiff you?" I nod, jaw set. "Put your money back. It happens sometimes."

"There's no reason why you all should pay for my mistakes. He's right. He got terrible service." I slide the twenty into the till before he can protest further and go to check on the next table.

Three hours later, there are only a few patrons left, and they're all loitering over their drinks under Livvy's supervision. Drew is busy wiping down tables, and I'm sitting at the bar rolling cutlery into napkins for tomorrow's service.

"Despite what you think, you did all right," Kellen says, busy with his own tasks.

"It's hard work," I say, glad to be off my feet for a bit. "I've never worked as a server before. When I was in college I used to do overnights at a convenience store. It wasn't as bad as you think," I tell him when I see his sympathetic wince. "It was usually pretty quiet, and I worked alone, so I could study in between customers."

"You ever get robbed?"

"Once, sort of," I say. "A guy came in with a knife and told me to empty the till, but I said he was screwing up his whole life, and he should be ashamed of himself. He ended up telling me all about himself, how desperate he was to feed his family, and he didn't know what else to do. In the end, I gave him fifty bucks of my own money in exchange for a promise he wouldn't go around robbing places anymore, and he left." I'm laughing at the naiveté of my twenty-year-old self. Kellen looks incredulous.

"You're an incredible woman, you know?" he says.

"Incredibly stupid, you mean. He could have stabbed me. I never did see him again. I've always wondered if he turned out all right." I move on to filling the salt and pepper shakers. "Thanks for encouraging me to do this," I tell him. "I learned way more about how the pub runs by being in the thick of it than by doing a walk-through."

"I'm glad. You up for anything later? Maybe try and finish that movie we started last night?"

I snort. We hadn't made it through more than twenty minutes before I flipped down the screen of his laptop and we rolled off the couch, a mess of tangled limbs, half-unclothed, and laughing hysterically. What was I supposed to do when he kept nibbling at my ear?

"Only if we're staying here, and if you'll rub my feet. They're killing me. Next time you're going to conscript me, warn me ahead of time so I can pick some better footwear." The ballet flats I'm wearing are cute but don't offer any support.

"Deal. See you upstairs in a bit." He winks as I disappear into the back.

It's been an exhausting day, but everything feels all right, I reflect as I stretch myself out on the couch, wiggling my toes, now free of their prisons. I'm happy, I realize suddenly. Genuinely happy with my life. It's an unfamiliar enough feeling that I need to reflect for a moment to make sure that's what I'm experiencing. Despite the uncertainty of the future, the challenges ahead, and the rollercoaster of emotions I've been through over the past two weeks, there's a solid core of warmth, of conviction, that's been growing inside me. It tells me I'm doing the right thing, and that maybe, just maybe, I've finally found my home.

The next two weeks pass by fairly uneventfully, at least for me. Bill Blackmoor, Marnie, and Irene Bell all have their memorial services at the church in Soberly. I pay my respects at them all, not only hoping it will increase my acceptance around town, but also because I had genuinely liked them during our short acquaintance. Learning about the inn takes up almost all my time—if I'm not sifting through the paperwork Roz left behind,

I'm shadowing various staff members on their jobs, from housekeeping to the man who comes twice a week to trim the grass and weed the garden beds. I'm surprised when he shows me the boundaries of the property. The inn is on a decent-sized parcel of land and has a large lawn alongside the pub.

"We should build a patio," I muse out loud to Kellen one day as I stare out at the lawn. He's persuaded me to take the day off and spend the afternoon at the beach with him, and we're just leaving the inn.

"This is supposed to be a no-work day, remember? No thinking about patios today," he chides me as we walk toward the lounge chairs. Both he and Naomi have mentioned several times that I'm going too hard, and I need to ease off a bit. Even Drew told me I looked tired yesterday.

To be honest, I am exhausted, and for the past few days when I wake up, I'm nauseous thinking about getting out of bed and facing the world. Cora's still a hair short of being openly hostile and is the only one who doesn't welcome my questions about the inn and its operations. It's been Jana who's trained me on the front desk services and the booking software we use. I also learn that, unlike what I assumed, she doesn't stay at the desk overnight, only until midnight, at which point the phone line is automatically forwarded to Cora's personal phone for any emergencies. I get Jana to switch it to my own number since I'm living here anyway. Sheena did renew her offer for me to stay with her, but she didn't seem as enthusiastic about becoming roommates when she mentioned it the second time around.

Sheena's been different since I shared my secret with

her. It's subtle, but I catch her looking at me strangely sometimes like she's trying to figure out if I'm mentally sound or not. I'm trying my best to ignore it, hoping that with some time, she'll see I'm the same person as always. Since that talk at her kitchen table, she hasn't brought up the subject of the killings once, although she did mention she'd had no luck finding her past self, the writer, via some Google searches. She didn't ask me to try and access another vision of him, and I didn't offer. From her body language—the way she's always aware of my proximity to her, and the way she holds herself a little apart—it's obvious to me that she doesn't want to make any skin-to-skin contact with me. It saddens me, but I have to respect it.

"What are you thinking about?" Kellen asks me as he drags an umbrella over to our chaises. "You look like you're a million miles from here."

"Nothing." *Everything.* The inn. The way most people in Soberly are still steering clear of it. I've hardly seen a local in the pub these past couple of weeks. Money. Time to do all the things I need to, like make a trip back to New Mexico to pack up my apartment and bring what few possessions I care about back here. All of it is weighing on me, and none of it I can delegate to anyone else. While I appreciate Kellen's desire for me to relax for a day, it feels like it puts more pressure on the rest of the week by leaving more things undone to catch up on later.

On top of it all, I have a vicious case of heartburn, which only worsens as I lay back in my chaise, a radiant pain rising up from my midsection all the way to the base of my throat. I toss and turn several times, trying to find a position that will make it abate even slightly. In the end, I have to bring the back of the chaise up to almost ninety degrees so I'm sitting upright before the pain subsides a bit.

"I need to cut back on the coffee," I say, rubbing my chest futilely. I thought I had been—I'm down to only a couple cups in the morning now. If I have to quit coffee altogether, I don't know how I'll function. I'm too reliant on it in the morning to get my brain in gear.

"Why don't you take my car and grab some antacids later today," he suggests. The pharmacy is still closed, and I've heard Marnie's husband Gord is planning on selling it and moving out of Soberly to be closer to family. In the meantime, the next closest drug store is in the big box store fifteen minutes up the highway. "Or do you want to go right now?" We'd rummaged in the medicine cabinet in his house earlier for any but had come up empty-handed.

"No, later is fine."

The fact that there haven't been any more deaths in Soberly is at least one thing that brings me a sense of relief. I had almost expected them to continue at the same rate of two or three a week, but there hasn't been a hint of violence at all. *Maybe it was just someone passing through town.* I've been repeating this thought again and again for the past few days, hoping it's true.

Although the news spread like wildfire throughout the town, Kellen hasn't mentioned a word about Irene Bell's death being a murder instead of natural causes like he had first believed, nor has he discussed Marnie's murder with me since the first morning we had breakfast at his house. Thanks to the way Sheena's pulled away,

I'm afraid to bring the subject up with him or fill him in on my ability. The thought of him silently questioning whether I'm stable or not and seeing him slowly start to become more distant fills me with dread. Yet, not being able to share such a fundamental part of myself with him feels like I'm cheating him out of knowing the real me. *He deserves better,* that dark voice in the back of my head keeps telling me, and I start to muster up the courage to tell him. Then I remember Sheena snatching her hand away from beside mine when I dropped into her shop to give her an update on some of the bootlegging research I'd done in my spare time, and to show her a book I'd ordered on the topic that had arrived. All my courage dissolves at that point.

I've been almost equally cagey with stories of my childhood. Kellen's probably figured out I didn't have a good one, and other than telling him I don't have any siblings and am estranged from my parents, he knows virtually nothing about my life before college other than Roz's visit when I was twelve. It's hard, sometimes, to see how he is with his mom, knowing I'm never going to have that sort of family relationship. I don't know if he picks up on it or not, but I'm pretty sure Naomi has. When we're at the inn she's strictly professional, like Kellen is, but in her home, I'm encircled with a mixture of warmth and sternness that feels like she's hugging me with her words, even when she's lecturing me about working too much, and reminding me that Roz wouldn't have wanted for me to make myself sick over learning the ropes.

It's Naomi that's finally been able to satiate my need for stories about my aunt. Having known her longer than pretty much anyone in town, she had countless anecdotes to share with me over cups of tea, and more often than not, a plate of homemade cookies. My favorite stories were the ones about all her growing pains and missteps when she first bought the inn, and how, eventually, she began to put her own mark on it.

"Now you're in her shoes," she told me one evening. "You'll make plenty of mistakes along the way, have no doubt, but you'll also make it your own. There'll come a time when people won't think of it as Roz's place anymore. They'll all call it Audrey's." Her words had brought tears to my eyes, both because I wanted badly to reach the point where I was accepted at that level, and also because I didn't want people here to forget about my aunt.

Maybe I could use some of that bare lawn space to put in a memorial garden for her, I consider now. A mix of perennials, medicinal plants, and kitchen herbs, something a little untamed, like Roz was, but with benches for reading and a shade tree or two. I grab my phone and start to type up some notes.

"Hey, put that away," Kellen says. His eyes are still closed, but he must have heard my nails tapping on the screen. "No work today."

"How do you know it's work?" I counter, stalling for time while I try and finish getting all my thoughts out.

"Pardon me. Is it for work?"

"Sort of. Sort of not."

"Does your brain ever stop?"

"Very rarely. This whole lying around doing nothing is hard for me. You could have at least let me bring a book." He'd been insistent that I'd have no distractions, but I've never been comfortable sitting with nothing to do.

"I was hoping you'd nap." He pauses for a moment. "You really don't look well, Audrey. I'm worried about you, for real. You're hardly eating, and you don't look like you're getting much sleep either."

"I'm not." I pinch the bridge of my nose with my index finger and my thumb. "I can't sleep sitting up like this."

"Sorry. This wasn't a good idea, I guess." He starts to pack up the bag we brought.

"No, I'm sorry. I appreciate the thought behind it. You can't help if I'm feeling gross right now. If this heartburn would ease up I'd be able to sleep better and eat too. Everything seems to set it off. I've never experienced anything like it before. Maybe I will go to the pharmacy now. I've been hoping it would clear up on its own. I hate taking any sort of medication."

He hands over his keys, and after slipping on a cover-up I drive myself to the next town over, parking as close to the doors as possible. The shock of the heat after having the air conditioning at full blast makes me wince.

I'm concentrating on getting a basket unstuck from the stack inside the door when someone slams roughly into my side, knocking me sideways.

Pavel stood staring at the knife sticking out of his chest, shocked by its appearance there. It felt as though he was looking at someone else's body, because there was no pain at all, nothing that indicated he had been stabbed, other than the leather-wrapped hilt in the center of his chest. 'What a strange thing,' he thought to himself. His legs gave out from under him, and he dropped to his knees, but there was still no sense of intrusion. He couldn't even remember why the blade was there in the first place—the entire notion was so perplexing to him. He opened his mouth to ask someone, but instead of words, a stream of blood came forth and ran down his chin, dripping onto the hilt. Pavel died with his eyes wide open, still trying to figure out what exactly had happened.

"Watch it, bitch," the person says as I narrowly keep myself from falling sideways. It's Aaron Glass, the man Kellen punched a couple weeks ago. He's leaving the store by the same door I came in, carrying a shopping bag in each hand and doesn't look back. I pick up the basket I dropped and try to shrug it off. I'm disturbed by the brief vision, both of its violent content and the fact that I'm once again reminded of Kellen's version as the man who inflicted the deadly wound. Curious that Aaron was Pavel in a past life, and that he and Kellen have found conflict again in this one. Upon further reflection, however, if people have positive relationships with others throughout their lifetimes, it makes sense that they can have antagonistic ones carry forward as well. I've just never seen it so plainly before.

Faced with a number of options for heartburn in the pharmacy section of the store, I grab the extra-strength version of the brand I see advertised on TV and give the directions a quick scan. This is the first time in my life I've ever suffered from the condition, and I have new sympathy for an old coworker of mine who had a terrible case of it all throughout her pregnancy.

The blood in my veins suddenly freezes. Pulling my phone out of my shoulder bag, I call up the calendar app, scroll back to the previous month, then count forward. Then I count forward again with my fingers to make sure. With trembling hands, I add another product to my basket and ring myself through at a self-checkout.

An hour later, locked in the bathroom of my suite, I have the answer to my heartburn source and my worst fears realized at the same time.

I'm pregnant.

21

It takes me very little time to make the necessary appointment, although I'm going to have to travel to Portland on Thursday for it. No waiting period, no ultrasound, no counseling session. Two courses of pills a day or two apart is all I'll need to do to solve this problem, much to my relief. I'd been worried my only option would be a surgical procedure. I'll probably feel a bit rough for a few days, but nothing that will keep me from functioning normally as long as I take it easy, armed with some Advil.

Once I'm done making arrangements, I give myself permission to be furious with myself. I'm *never* careless about birth control. For as long as I can remember, I've never wanted to have kids. Not only do I not particularly like them, I don't have any maternal instinct. Any time I've thought about my future, children haven't been a part of it. Yet here I am, growing another human. It feels like a parasite, leaching away my energy, stealing my nutrients, and making me sick. The sooner I can put this disaster behind me, the better, and once it's over and done with, I'm going to find a more permanent solution to my birth control slip-up so something like this can never happen again. Maybe an IUD. Maybe I'll opt straight for a tubal ligation and get myself sorted out for life.

In retrospect, I can't believe I missed all the warning signs. Besides the period that's more than a week late and the heartburn, my breasts have been aching for days—so sensitive that the last time Kellen spent the night I wouldn't let him touch them. I've also had almost constant nausea, which I'd chalked up to all the stress around the inn and tension with Cora.

"What's she done now?" Kellen asks when he comes up to my suite after the pub shuts down, mistaking the angry look on my face as being directed at Cora.

"We fucked up," I tell him. There's no sense in trying to hide anything from him. "I'm pregnant. I think it was the time on the beach. The night Marnie died." It's the only time I can't recall with one hundred percent certainty that we used a condom. "It's all fine though," I reassure him. He's as still as I've ever seen him, shocked speechless. I know the feeling—I was living it a few hours earlier when I saw the positive result come up on the digital screen of the pregnancy test. "I made an appointment with a doctor in Portland. I need a prescription and the whole thing will be taken care of. Really, no big deal. I caught it early enough that I don't need to have the...more invasive procedure."

"Wait. An abortion?" He sinks onto the couch and rubs his face with his hand.

"Well, yeah." I stare at him, perplexed. "What else would I do?"

"I don't know. We haven't even talked about it."

"There aren't any other options, Kellen. There's nothing to talk about. I don't want children. I really don't want one right now. And while we're getting along pretty well, we've only known each other about a month. We have no business having a kid together, even if I did want to be a mother. Which I don't."

"Not ever?"

"No." The word hangs heavily between us.

"How can you be sure?" he asks finally.

"How can you be sure you're straight?" I counter. "I just know it. Parenthood is not for me. I wouldn't...I wouldn't be good at it."

"You can't decide *not* to have kids because you had shitty parents growing up."

"We are *not* having this conversation right now and stop trying to change the subject. I can't believe you're even considering going through with this. Are you serious?"

"I would if you wanted to. I think we could make it work." He gives me a hopeful smile, but I turn away. What he's suggesting is preposterous for so many reasons.

"Well, I don't. I can't think of anything that would make me more miserable." He tries to hide it, but I can tell my words have hurt him deeply by the way his body goes perfectly rigid and he stares past me. "Not because it's with you," I add in a softer tone. "It's something I've never wanted."

"I understand." His voice isn't quite cold, but it's certainly not the same as the way I'm used to him speaking when we're alone together.

"Look, I get it if this is a deal-breaker for you. You shouldn't waste your time with me if I'm never going to give you the life you've envisioned for yourself." The possibility that Kellen would want to have kids with me someday has literally never occurred to me until this conversation started going so dreadfully sideways, and my voice trembles. The fact that what I thought was a frustrating, but solvable mistake might mean the end of our budding relationship leaves me almost breathless. The heartburn flares in my chest, and I pop another Zantac, leaning against a bookshelf for support. I wait for him to tell me that of course, it's not a deal-breaker, and we'll figure this out together, but that doesn't come.

"I don't know," he says instead, and I break out into a cold sweat at what might come out of his mouth next. "I need to think about it. I need some time."

"Of course." I swallow hard. He can't force me to have a baby with him; I can't force him to stay in a relationship with me if I don't. *Quid pro quo.*

Probably for the best you figure this all out now. You should have known it was too good to be true. That cruel little voice in the back of my head rears its ugly head. It's been virtually silent these past couple weeks, but time and disuse haven't made it any less savage.

"When's your appointment?" he asks. "I'll drive you."

"It's on Thursday. I can get there myself. I'd rather go alone." The gulf widens between us as the silence lengthens. "I need to go to sleep," I say finally. What I want is to ask him to stay, to hold me through the night, make me feel safe and wanted, but I'm afraid I won't be able to handle the rejection if he says he'd rather not. He moves mechanically toward the door, and I start stacking the couch cushions on the floor so I can pull out the bed, grieving the fact that he didn't offer to stay either. He said he needed space, and there isn't much space between two bodies curled up in bed together, each mourning an idea they didn't even know they'd have to face twelve hours ago.

"Audrey, wait," he says as I turn to go into the bathroom, holding the tears back by a sheer force of will I know I won't be able to maintain for much longer. He pulls me toward him and bows to press his forehead against mine. The vision he gives me is one of deep sadness, when the young man who lost his wife in childbirth says a final goodbye to her at her funeral. Is he saying goodbye to me now? I choke back a sob and run my fingers up his neck to twine into his hair. When we first met it was cut close, but it's grown out enough now that I can weave my fingers into it, something I love to do when he kisses me or when his body is stretched out on top of mine, moving deep inside me.

"It's going to be okay, all right?" he says, but I'm not sure. No matter what happens from this point forward, I can't help but feel there's something we can never get back.

♀♀

Tuesday and Wednesday each go by so slowly that I'm an anxious mess by nightfall, flitting back and forth between multiple tasks and distractions, none of which can hold my attention for more than a few minutes at a time. Kellen and I see each other rarely, and only under professional circumstances. Each time our eyes meet, I can see he's searching my face to see if I've changed my mind before looking away, disappointed by my continued resolve. Nor do I see any indication he's reached a point of understanding and acceptance. Yet, I keep hoping. I have to believe he will get there in his own time. If he doesn't, I'm not sure I can find the strength to keep going with the inn and all the rest of it.

If Sheena weren't still acting weird I would talk to her about it, but with the new distance between us, I'm no longer comfortable sharing my personal life with her. I'm struggling to hold up under the isolation of having no one to ask for support. In the past, I've always been able to shoulder my burdens on my own, but since coming to Soberly, I've had to face more new challenges than any other time in my life, and it's started to feel almost natural to reach out to someone else to help share the load. Hoping it will help me find a solution again, I ask the Roz inside my head what I should do, but she has no answers for me this time, other than to counsel time and patience, something I've already figured out myself. Time and patience can't stroke my hair when I'm crying into my pillow at night, though.

Thursday morning finally arrives, and I leave in my rental car before the sun rises so I can make it to Portland for my 8 a.m. appointment. It goes by quickly; I take a pill in the office. I'm handed one more to take at home tomorrow, and almost before I know it I'm back on the highway to Soberly. I don't hear from Kellen to see how the appointment went, and since he has the day off, I don't see him in the pub or around the inn. Not having his support or even his company over the past few days has made me wonder whether I should have even told him about the pregnancy in the first place. If I'd just gone ahead and taken care of it without him knowing, we would have never created this rift between us. On the other hand, I think if he ever found out about it after the fact, he would never forgive me for keeping it a secret. Either way, I lose. We both do.

Friday morning, I take the second medication, and about two hours later, the cramping starts. I take the maximum allowable dose of ibuprofen and try to distract myself with work but end up curled around a hot water bottle on the couch with a mindless movie on Netflix instead.

I spend a lot of the time thinking about Kellen, and his desire for a family someday. Everything I know about him makes me certain he'll be a wonderful father. He's the right measure of easygoing and firm, warm, loving and funny. In my head, I can see him playing with his kids, being involved in their lives, listening to them, and caring about their problems. He deserves to see that dream realized, and hopefully, he will. It just won't be with me, and the heaviness in my heart deepens at the inevitable end to our relationship. Even if we somehow manage to pull through this, and he decides to forgo fatherhood for now, at some point his need for the future he's planned out for himself will outstrip his need for me.

By dinner time, I feel well enough to make myself a can of soup and some toast. I haven't seen or heard from a single person all day. *Do they all know?* I imagine how this will further tarnish my reputation in the community. Would Kellen have told anyone? His mother, maybe? I can't believe either of them would share such a private thing. I'm being paranoid. Everyone at the inn probably assumes I need some space and quiet to work, or I've taken a day off.

I spend the evening alone as well, watching more TV to pass the time, wishing I had some company.

The police sirens awaken me just after three in the morning. Disoriented, I sit up in bed, confused at why my room is full of red and blue strobing lights. Then my phone starts ringing on the table beside me, the caller ID indicating it's a forwarded call from the inn's main line. I answer blearily.

"This is detective Andrea Chao with the Oregon State Police. To whom am I speaking?" I give her my name, and as an afterthought, tell her I'm the owner of the inn.

"What's going on?" I ask, walking over to the balcony. A sudden cramp almost doubles me over on the way, forcing me to hobble the last few steps. I peer down over the railing, but the lights are coming from the north side of the building, where the parking lot is, and I can't see around the corner.

"There's a body in your parking lot. We need to ask you some questions." I tell her I'll be down in two minutes, shove my feet into my Chucks, and wrap one of Roz's shawls around my shoulders. Even though the temperature's been reaching the low nineties each day, it's still chilly at night, especially when the wind comes in from the sea. Going through these steps keeps me from thinking about what the detective has just said, and what—who—I know I'm going to find when I meet her.

Until I can't avoid it any longer. I choke back a hysterical giggle as the old board game Clue comes to mind.

Aaron Glass, in the parking lot. With a knife.

22

"There's nothing to be concerned about, I apologize for the disturbance. Please stay in your rooms," I tell the man poking his head out his door. The sirens are no longer wailing in front of the inn, but the lights are still flashing, creating a weird disco-like effect around us as the red and blue bounces off the walls through the window at the end of the hall. For a moment, I think he's going to ignore my advice and have a look for himself, but after a moment he rubs his face, shrugs, and retreats back into his room. I breathe a sigh of relief and make my way downstairs and out the door.

"Mrs. Eames?" a tall, willowy woman leaning against one of the police cars approaches me, hand extended, and introduces herself as Detective Chao. I don't correct the title she assigned me, but I do ask her to call me Audrey.

"You said there's—that someone died?" I'm avoiding looking in the direction of the parking lot, but in my peripheral vision, I can see several figures milling around with flashlights, accompanied by the occasional flash of a camera.

"Yes, he was discovered by his girlfriend who went out searching for him after he didn't come home earlier this evening. She spotted his car in your parking lot, and him shortly afterward."

"My god, that's horrible," I say. My gaze strays to the parking lot against my better judgment. Most of the officers' attention is focused on one area on the far side of a silver Honda, but one is scanning the area around it with his flashlight, and another is walking around the perimeter with yellow crime scene tape. "Who is it?" The words come out half an octave higher than my normal pitch.

Detective Chao looks over at the scene for a moment, then back at me. *Maybe it's a tourist,* I hope against hope. *Maybe he was drunk and hit his head.* It could even be a guest, for all I know. My intuition tells me different though. "The victim has been tentatively identified as Aaron Glass, a resident here. Did you know him?" Even though I'd been expecting it, my heart stops in my chest for a moment.

"Not really at all, no. I spoke to him once briefly a few weeks ago. I'm fairly new to town. I've only lived here about a month," I add.

"Do you have any security cameras out here?"

"No, we don't." I shake my head for emphasis. We don't even have an alarm, although I don't mention that. Maybe we should. My mind drifts off to my mental to-do list, adding it as another item, and for a moment I forget why I'm standing outside at three in the morning in my pajamas.

"Were you at the inn this evening?"

I nod. "I didn't leave the premises at all today," I say. *Who uses words like premises?* I sound like Miss Marple. Or somebody who rehearsed the answers to these questions ahead of time.

"Did you hear anything unusual this evening between the hours of ten and 2:30 a.m.?"

"I don't think I was even awake then," I tell her, trying to remember what time I turned out the light. "I don't know exactly what time I went to bed, but it was pretty early, for me. Before eleven for sure. I...I wasn't feeling well. I didn't hear anything at all. I'm a sound sleeper. How did—what happened to Aaron?"

"He was stabbed." She speaks in a short, clipped voice, confirming my fear. It's like it was in the past. "We'll need to interview your guests here as well to see if they heard or saw anything unusual tonight, although it doesn't have to be at this time. Are any of these rooms occupied?" She points up to the windows which face down over the parking lot.

"None of those are rooms." I explain that they're located at the ends of the halls on the second and third floor. "All the guest rooms either face the beach or out into the town. Other than those, the only place you can really see the parking lot from is the pub. It closed at eleven, and I'm sure if he was out here then, someone would have seen him."

Detective Chao scrawls a few things in a small notepad she's holding and thanks me for my help.

"Oh, one other thing," she says before I can make my retreat to the front step. "Do you know anything about an altercation Mr. Glass had here a couple of weeks ago? His girlfriend mentioned he got into a fight with someone else who works at your inn." She's watching me closely. I swallow and nod, stepping back toward her.

"Yes. He—well, it was the one time when he and I met, and he was unhappy that I was taking over ownership of the inn." I explain as briefly as possible the circumstances that brought me to Soberly. "He didn't believe I had the experience to keep the inn open, and that I would end up hurting the other businesses in town. Which is fine, that's his opinion, and he's entitled to it. Then he made a rude sexual comment toward me, and my boyfriend hit him once, in the face. Aaron said he would remember it and walked away. That was the end of it."

"What's your boyfriend's name?"

"Kellen Greene. He had nothing to do with this though, I know it. He's not a violent person. The only reason he lost his temper is because of what Aaron said to me, and Aaron's history with women." *Stop talking,* my brain screams at me. I'm giving Detective Chao all the information she needs to suspect Kellen, and she's been jotting down everything I'm saying.

"Do you have contact info for him?" With a sinking heart, I give her both his number and address.

"Please, he didn't do this. I know it looks suspicious, but it wasn't him."

"Were you with him tonight?"

"No, I was alone."

"All right, well that's all I need from you for now.

You won't have access to your parking lot for at least the next day while we examine the scene, although if needed, we may be able to remove your guests' vehicles. Are you able to stay close by in case I have any other questions for you?" I assure her I'm not planning on going anywhere, and step into the doorway of the pub, wrapping Roz's shawl around my shoulders. Detective Chao ducks under the yellow tape and walks back toward the spot where Aaron's body presumably lies, and I pull out my phone. I figure this situation is serious enough to break the "need for space" rule.

"Aaron Glass was killed in the parking lot tonight" I text Kellen. "The police asked me about the fight you had" He charges his phone on his night table, so although he's almost certainly asleep, the buzzing of the incoming message might wake him up. I clutch my phone and will him to reply. Within moments, I see the bubble with three dots pop up, indicating he's typing something.

"Be right there." I don't know whether to be relieved he's coming, or worried because he might be a suspect. Maybe he'll be able to clear everything up right now and prove he had nothing to do with it.

He arrives twenty minutes later, on foot, and picks me out immediately even though I'm half-invisible behind one of the posts that holds up the awning above the entrance to the pub.

"I'm sorry," I say as he approaches. I speak low so my voice doesn't carry over to the parking lot. "They already knew about the fight."

"I don't care about that," he says. "How are you?" I can't form a reply, just shake my head. He wraps his arms around me, enveloping me with his warmth. I inhale the scent of him deeply and let myself collapse into him, finally finding the support I need. "C'mere," he says and leads me to the edge of the small veranda. He sits on the top step and positions me on the next step down, between his legs so he can maintain our embrace. I lean back into him, wishing we could be alone, or at least that we were together under different circumstances.

"God, I miss you," he says into my hair. I twist my head around to see if he means it, but in the dim light, it's almost impossible to read the expression on his face. "I'm sorry," he tells me. "Look, I know why you did what you did, and it was the right thing to do. There's no question we aren't ready to have a kid together. I should have been here for you these past few days. It was the wrong time to have that conversation with myself. It wasn't until I saw you just now, looking so alone, that I realized there was never really any choice to make at all. This is where I belong. If...if you still want me here."

"Yeah," I say. "Yeah, I do." Tension I didn't know he was holding releases, and I feel his body relax behind me.

"Why don't we let the future figure itself out, okay?" I nod, but a grain of sadness in my heart remains. From this point forward, I'm always going to be waiting for an ultimatum. How long until it comes, a few years at the most? I feel like I'm right back to where I started when I was still planning on selling the inn and leaving Soberly—and him—behind.

It doesn't take long for Detective Chao to notice Kellen has joined me, and she approaches the spot where we're sitting. He rises and introduces himself, and she pulls him away so I can't overhear what they're saying.

He's still wearing the bright pink cast; a color which he chose to make me smile at the ridiculousness of it, but now stands out like a neon admission of motive. She questions him for a lot longer than she did me, and for one sick moment I think she's going to put him into the back of a police car, but in the end, he makes his way back to me.

"She wants to interview me again later at the station on the record, but for now she says I'm free to go, as long as I don't leave town," he tells me.

"Does she really think you have anything to do with this?"

He shrugs. "Dunno. I had to tell her all about the fight and the history between us, and you. She wanted to know where I was tonight. Mama will be able to tell them I was at home, but I wasn't sitting up with her all night or anything. She also asked if I would be willing to hand over my phone for them to examine."

"Did you?"

"Hell yes, I did. I don't want to seem even the slightest bit uncooperative. Black men like me have been shot and killed by cops for less. I'm going to be the most compliant, helpful person that woman has ever worked with."

It's not until the sky begins to lighten in the east that I abandon my post on the veranda and return to my suite. The medical examiner's van transported the body away not too long beforehand, and I want to try and get an hour or two of sleep before I'm faced with the inevitable barrage of questions from both the guests and the townspeople. If they've been avoiding the pub lately as a sign they don't support me as owner, their morbid curiosity at the discovery of a body in the parking lot will surely change that. My guess is the place is going to be packed from the moment the doors open, to well after close. *Death is good for business,* I think, and immediately feel guilty for such an unsavory thought.

Kellen follows me upstairs and closes the door quietly behind him.

"You going to go back to bed?" he asks, and when I nod, asks if he can stay.

"We can't do anything," I tell him. Not that I'm even remotely in the mood. "For at least a week. Maybe longer, I'm not sure."

"That's not why I want to stay," he says with a wry look. "There are different kinds of need, you know."

A few minutes later I'm curled into his chest, tucking my knees up so he can mold himself around me.

"Are you afraid?" I ask him after we're all settled in. I've been waiting for his breathing to settle into its usual slow rhythm as he falls asleep, but he's tense and I can hear his heartbeat, not quite pounding, but not calm either.

"Yeah."

"Me too."

I spend almost an hour trying to calm my thoughts to the point where I can try and drift off before giving it up as a lost cause. Easing out of bed carefully so as to not wake Kellen, who's snoring softly, I crack open my laptop and draft a memo to the staff apprising them of the murder. After some reflection, I've decided to close the pub for the rest of the weekend out of respect for Aaron, and so the police can do their job without disruption from customers. As for the guests currently booked in, I'll leave it up to them whether they'd like to stay or not. Either way, I promise, no one will lose their wages because of this. I send the memo and pull on some clean clothes.

Cora is so surprised at the police cars and crime scene tape when she arrives, she forgets her hostility toward me. I hadn't included her on the email chain; I know I'm going to need her support this morning and wanted her to come in.

"What on earth went on here last night?" she asks, eying the parking lot and the two or three officers still working there from through the glass of the inn's front door. I fill her in as succinctly as possible, leaving out the fact that Kellen's a suspect.

"I don't know how to even begin to handle this with the guests," I confess. "There wasn't a "murder on the premises" section in any of those textbooks." Cora cracks a wry smile at that. "What do we say to them?"

"Just the truth, I suppose. That someone died, we don't have any more information, and they're welcome to stay or end their visit early without any penalty. I don't think there's anything else we *can* do. It's nothing to do with the inn itself, of course. People are usually understanding."

"I was thinking about maybe offering them a voucher for a two-night stay that they can use another time," I tell her, fully expecting her to shoot down the idea because it's mine.

"Yes, let's do that," she surprises me by saying, and I sit down at the laptop at the front desk, trying to remember Jana's instructions on making up a gift certificate. A few minutes later I have ten of them printed out on nice cardstock, one for each of the rooms—it's a full house this weekend. I also type up a letter explaining the situation, enclose both these in envelopes and slide them under the doors of each guest room. Then, I wait.

It doesn't take long for the inhabitants of the inn to trickle down to the lobby. Most want to leave immediately, others are morbidly curious about Aaron's death, and want as many details as I can provide. All the guests are questioned by an officer about whether they heard or saw anything in the night before they're allowed to leave the scene. Most of them pack up and leave afterward. I doubt many will bother to redeem their vouchers.

Kellen's gone when I find a moment to slip up into my suite. A note informs me he was going to go home, and to call him on his mom's landline if I needed him, but that he was supposed to go to the local office of the state police to be formally interviewed at noon.

Meanwhile, it's not just the guests who have me busy with questions. Word has spread through the town, and residents are milling around outside the parking lot, craning their heads to see if they can spot anything to feed the gossip mill further. Some come in to press Cora or I for details, then bring what scant information we have to offer back outside to their compatriots. A few make their annoyance known about the pub being closed, but I stand firm in my decision and hope the majority agree that it would be in poor taste to carry on eating and drinking steps away from where a local man lost his life hours earlier. Crumb's Cafe is probably bursting at the seams trying to make up the difference.

Around four in the afternoon, Detective Chao shows up at the inn and asks if we can speak again. My suite upstairs is a mess, with the bed still unfolded and dirty laundry on the floor, so I suggest we sit in the vacant pub.

"Can I get you a glass of water or a soda?" I ask, and she accepts water. I fill two glasses at the sink behind the bar and seat myself across from her.

She's an inch or two taller than me, with smooth, shiny black hair pulled back into a short ponytail. I judge it to be about shoulder length. Her fringe brushes the top of her eyebrows, softening the sharp angles of her face. She's wearing the same navy blue power suit as when we first spoke in the night, and I wonder if she's been working continuously since then. If she has, she doesn't show any signs of fatigue—no puffiness under her eyes, no weariness in her voice.

"Do you mind if I use this?" she says, putting a tape recorder on the table. I shake my head, wonder if I should have my reply on the record, and answer verbally as well.

She begins by going over the same information I gave her the evening before—where I was, whether I heard anything unusual, and the nature of my relationship with Aaron Glass. She also asks me to recount the events leading up to the fight between him and Kellen, including their exact words, if I could recall them. I answer as best I can. Did Kellen ever mention running into Aaron again at a later date? No, never. Had I seen Aaron since? My stomach sinks. There's no point in lying about it—there would have been cameras in the store for sure, and I'd look suspicious as hell if she found out about it later on, so I tell Chao about the encounter at the drugstore when I'd gone to buy antacids. Did I tell Kellen about that incident? No, I state. I didn't want to stir things up between them again. Why had I gone all that way in the first place? I tell her that since Marnie's death, the Soberly pharmacy has been closed.

"Marnie Decker, another recent homicide here, correct?" I nod. "Did you know her at all?"

"I'd shopped in her store a couple of times. Sunscreen, a paperback, stuff like that. We only talked a bit, but I liked her. She was friendly to me when I was new here."

"Have others been not so friendly?"

"Well, there was Aaron." I think for a moment about how I want to express myself. "I've heard that some people would prefer if I sell the inn to someone with more experience doing this job."

"That was the crux of your disagreement with Mr. Glass, wasn't it?"

"Yes."

"What about Irene Bell; did you know her?"

"I met her at church, that's it."

"There have been three homicides in Soberly in the past month, Ms. Eames. In a town of 400 people. What do you think about that?"

"I think it's awful. Like a nightmare." She doesn't know the half of it.

"You came to town about a month ago, is that correct?"

What? The blood is roaring in my ears. "Yes, I did, but you don't think *I* have anything to do with this, do you?"

"Can you account for your whereabouts on the nights of July 11th and July 17th?"

"I don't know." My mind is blank, heart pounding. I wipe my hands on my jeans. I have no idea about either of those nights, I don't keep track of my whereabouts for every single day. *Think back,* my brain commands. The night before Marnie was found in the storm pond. Was I at Cora's? *No. You spent the night here, with Kellen.* Yes. It was our first time together.

"The night Marnie died I spent the night here, with Kellen," I tell Chao. "It was the first time we hooked up. I don't know about the other night. What day of the week was it?" She tells me Irene died either Sunday night or early Monday morning. "Sunday, I went to church, which was where I met Irene. Kellen's mom, Naomi, introduced us. Afterward—" I rack my brain, trying to think about what I did the rest of the day. "Afterward I think I slept at Cora's. When I first got to town, she let me stay with her, on account of her being my aunt's partner. Yes, I think I did. I had a headache from the heat and didn't leave her place again that day."

"Can she confirm you were there all night?"

"I suppose so. I don't remember if we talked that night or not. We mostly kept out of each other's way." *Shit.* All Cora has to do is tell Chao she has no idea if I stayed in or not, and I'm screwed. At least I have Kellen to back me up for the night Marnie died. Why is Chao focusing on me?

"Do you recognize this?" Chao takes two photographs out of her satchel and slides them across the table to me. Both depict a large knife, and while the blade has been cleaned off, there's no mistaking the bloodstains on the leather wrapped around the hilt in the first photo. In the second, the leather has been removed to reveal the handle. It seems like an odd thing to do to what appears to be an everyday kitchen knife.

Wrapped in leather. Just like in the vision of Pavel's death.

"No, not at all." I can feel bile rising in my throat. "Is this the knife that killed Aaron?"

"Yes. He was found with it sticking out of his chest. He died of a single stab wound which severed his aorta. He bled to death in less than a minute. Kellen Greene tentatively identified it as being similar to the type of knife used in the kitchen here."

The room starts to spin, and I suddenly feel a sharp desire to get out of this room, to run as fast and as far as I can from this woman who's doing everything but accusing me outright of killing three people. My vision narrows until all I can see are the photos of the knife on the table. It's the pain of my fingernails digging into my palms that brings me partially back to my senses— enough to speak.

"That's impossible," I whisper.

"Mind if I check?" I don't know how I manage to stand, my knees feel so weak, but I lead her through the swinging doors into the kitchen. I've never been in here when it hasn't been full of the bustle of a busy service crew, all spitting grease, clattering plates, and calls for orders. Now the silence seems magnified by the stainless steel, which offers only muted reflections of my horrified face.

"I'm not even sure where the knives are kept," I tell Chao. "I've only worked in the front of the pub, never the back." She doesn't answer me because she doesn't have to—each of the three workstations have a large wooden knife block sitting in front of it, with the handles jutting out, at the ready. Naomi insists everything be left ready for the next day's work. The first two blocks have all their knives accounted for, but the third one—Naomi's own station—is missing its largest occupant.

23

"I don't know what to say," I tell her, leaning up against the counter to hold myself steady.

"Who else has access to this kitchen?"

"Well, all the staff here, of course. There are seven people who work in the pub altogether."

"I'll need to collect all their fingerprints so we can eliminate them from the scene. Who can access the kitchen after hours?"

"I—" It occurs to me that I have no idea who has keys to the pub. "Cora will know. I'm not sure how many key holders there are. At least a couple, plus Cora and myself." I'd inherited Roz's keyring the week I'd arrived in Soberly.

"Any signs of forced entry? Do you keep a log of when the alarm is set and deactivated?"

"We don't have an alarm system," I tell her. "I don't

know why."

While we've been talking, Chao has been photographing the empty knife block and the workstation around it.

"Was Mr. Glass drinking here tonight?"

"I'm not sure, but I doubt it." I tell her what he had told Drew when they'd run into each other after Kellen had punched him. "He was obviously still angry at me, based on what happened at the drugstore. I doubt he'd give me his business again." Just then her phone rings, and she holds her index finger up while she answers.

"What have you got?" She listens for a minute or two. "Okay, send me screenshots. I need someone back here who can print the kitchen in the pub. I think I found where the weapon came from." She disconnects and taps on her screen for a minute, reading intently.

"What's your mobile number?" she asks me. I rattle it off. "Is that the only phone you have?" I nod. "Will you consent to a search of your phone and its contents?"

"Yes, of course." I tell her the code to unlock it and pass it to her. I don't even care that any number of people might end up reading the steamy texts Kellen and I sometimes send each other—or see the photos either. Anything to prove I had nothing to do with this, with any of it. Chao makes a note of my password in her notebook and puts my phone in a plastic evidence bag.

"Mr. Glass was sent a series of texts last night urging him to come to the inn and finish the fight he and Mr. Greene had started," she tells me. "Since he doesn't have any other injuries, it appears he was lured here specifically to be killed. I assure you, Ms. Eames, if those texts came from your or Mr. Greene's phone, even if you changed out the SIM card and deleted the conversation, we will find them." Her voice is so cold and devoid of feeling. It's as though she's reading me the weather report.

"You won't find anything, I have nothing to do with this, I swear," I tell her. "I'll do whatever it takes to help you find the person responsible. Anything you need at all."

"Let's start with your fingerprints." I expect her to take out an ink pad and a card with a spot for each print, but instead, she plugs a small scanner into her phone's charging port and shows me how to put my fingers in, one at a time, to be scanned. After unplugging the device, she taps away for a moment and waits.

"Well, you have no criminal record," she says after a long minute, once the results are returned. "These prints will be kept on file to compare to any we find in the kitchen."

"Were there any on the knife?"

"I'm not at liberty to say."

Silence stretches out between us. "Are you going to arrest me?" I ask finally, my voice small. The thought of being hauled off to jail, in front of half the town, has me literally shaking with fear. I might as well sell the inn and leave town for good. Even though I'm innocent, I'll never regain what little trust I've built here.

"Not at this time, no, although that might change, depending on what we find on your phone. I'm also going to instruct that under no circumstances are you to leave the state without prior approval from me. Understood?"

"Of course. I'm not going anywhere, I promise. You can get in touch any time if you have any other questions, or if there's something else I can help with. There's someone killing people here in town. I want to find them."

"Leave that job to us, Ms. Eames. I'll be in touch." She motions me to exit the kitchen. "You should really get a security system."

"Believe me, we're going to. Cameras too."

The crowd hasn't dissipated at all when I slip out of the pub to make my way back to the inn side of the building.

"Audrey," someone shouts. It's Livvy, who, despite the memo I sent to the pub staff, is here anyway. Maybe she didn't check her email before she left for work—it's coming up on noon, the start of her shift today. But no, she's here to rubberneck along with everyone else.

"I got your email this morning. This is so freaky. Have the police told you anything else about what happened to Aaron?" The crowd quiets down, wanting to hear how I'll reply.

"Not really, no," I say. I refuse to be a part of the rumor mill, nor am I going to divulge details about the case that Aaron's own family probably hasn't found out about yet. Like how he was stabbed with a knife from the pub's own kitchen, or that the lead detective's line of questioning seems to be zeroing in on the fact that the murders started when I moved to town. No, I'll be keeping those things to myself for as long as possible, thank you very much. Suddenly I'm filled with a deep, burning anger. I want to tell everyone to go home and mind their own business. None of these people look sad, not like they were when it was Marnie's body in the storm pond that the police were investigating. This is pure sensationalizing of a man's death, and it makes me sick.

"Excuse me," I mutter, and push my way through the throng back to the inn, where Cora's holding down the fort at the front desk.

"What did she say?" she asks.

"Just more questions." Then, after a pause, "They think the knife might have come from the kitchen. There's one missing." Cora covers her mouth with her hand, and for a moment it looks like she's stopped breathing. Then, with a shudder, she gulps down a lungful of air.

"Why don't we have a security system?" I ask her, desperation in my voice. It feels like this one small detail could have meant all the difference in whether Aaron had lived or died.

"I brought it up once, but Roz didn't think we needed one. She said she trusted the people here, and it wasn't that kind of town. She was right—we've never had a break-in or even any vandalism, either from tourists or locals."

"Well we're getting one now," I tell her. "It might not have been that sort of town once, but it is now. You can trust people and still keep yourself safe. First thing Monday, I'm having someone out here to put in alarms and cameras."

"That's your call," she says with a shrug, and I can see she's back to being not all that impressed with me and my ideas by her frosty tone and was that an eye roll? "Seems like a case of closing the barn door after the horse has escaped though." I turn my back on her so she can't see my own exasperation, and head upstairs to my suite. I grab my journal from the desk drawer, and pore over the visions I'd noted from the three people who had died recently in Soberly, plus Kellen's version of Pavel's death. I hadn't gotten around to adding Aaron's side of things, so I do that now. It doesn't even fill an entire page, it was so brief. I read through them again and again, looking for ways they're related, both in the past and the present.

What if the thing they all have in common is the fact that they've all been seen by you?

The thought takes my breath away. Am I the reason why these people are all dead? How? I'm absolutely positive I'm not killing them myself during some sort of fugue state. None of these murders were by my hand. Of that, I'm certain.

What if they weren't murdered at all? What if you triggered them to kill themselves?

No. No, that can't be possible. That's not how the visions work. People don't get any sense of the images they show me when we touch. It's not a two-way street. I, and I alone receive the scenes from the past. The person I'm touching doesn't.

Are you sure?

Could I have unintentionally planted the idea in them somehow to recreate their past deaths? All four had died in the night. Might they have been sleepwalking, or even hypnotized into taking their own lives somehow, through some sort of subconscious suggestion I'd given them?

I won't make it to the bathroom in time. I grab the wastebasket sitting beside me and retch mouthfuls of bile into it, tears and snot streaming down my face. When my stomach stops contracting, I curl up into the fetal position on the couch, burying my hands deep inside the sleeves of my sweater, sobbing. What if I did? What if it's all my fault, and my seemingly benign ability is monstrous?

MY FAULT? I underline the words in my journal several times, scrawling out my thoughts and how I could have been responsible.

Wait, my mind instructs, a rational life raft trying to make its way through the dark miasma of self-loathing inside me. *Marnie got a call, and Aaron received texts the night they died so they would leave the house. Someone else is involved here.*

Perhaps, but perhaps those two things aren't related to their deaths at all and are merely a coincidence. Or maybe it was just the excuse the subconscious suggestion needed in order to trigger the fatal consequences. My thoughts are spinning so fast it's hard to make sense of what's real and what's not. All I know is that I can't count on there being a killer in Soberly anymore, and I don't know which is worse: hoping there is, or hoping there isn't, and that four people have only indirectly been murdered. By me. What I want to do is run, to protect them from whatever danger I might expose them to, but ironically, since I'm a suspect, I have to stay. Until I know for certain I'm not responsible, I need to take precautions, which means not letting anyone touch me at all, lest I trigger another death.

Why hasn't this happened before? My rational side is still looking for a way out of this. *Maybe it has,* the paranoid side returns. *Maybe you've been leaving a wake of the dead behind you all this time.* Grocery store clerks. Friends of friends met once at a party. Old coworkers I hadn't bothered to keep in touch with. How many of them could have died without my ever knowing, set upon their fatal path by an innocent handshake or accidental brush of the skin? The four people in Soberly had died shortly after they'd given me the visions of their past deaths, all within a day or two if I'm correct. Reading back through my journal confirms it. Is something different at play here? I'm balled up on the couch, shaking so hard I have to clench my teeth to keep them from rattling, my mind at war with itself.

"Audrey?" Kellen's voice at the door, along with a knock. I remain pressed into the couch, hands covering my face like a toddler playing hide-and-seek, hoping he'll go away. *If I can't see you, you can't see me.* I hold my breath, silently willing him to go away. Instead, I hear the snick of the lock releasing, and his steps entering the room a moment later. "Audrey? Shit, are you sick? Is it the—do you need the doctor?" I open my eyes to see him advancing toward me. In only a second or two he'll have me in his arms.

"Don't touch me," I rasp out, my throat still raw from retching. "Get *away.*" With my hands buried deep in the sleeves of my sweater, I ward him off, pushing him solidly back. He's caught off guard, and staggers into the table, knocking a glass of water onto the floor. It shatters, sending shards everywhere, but I barely even register it. All I have eyes for is the mixture of fear, confusion, and concern on Kellen's face.

"Tell me what's wrong," he pleads, reaching for my hand. I shrink back into the couch. I can't let him touch me, I can't be the one to set him on the path to his death. Not him. If it means I have to hurt him, have to break his heart even, so be it.

"Just leave me alone," I say, hugging myself tightly, refusing to meet his eyes. Mine are streaming. "I don't want you here."

"Audrey, what—"

"I said *get out,*" I scream. When his eyes start to water it nearly tears me in two, but he retreats toward the door, his shoes crunching the broken glass underfoot. He pauses at the door, out of my direct line of sight, but I can still see his shadow stretching across the floor.

"Okay, I'm going to call you later, all right? When you're not so...upset. I want to know what's going on."

"Don't." I spit the word out, make it bite like a bullet, even though I'm dying inside.

"Jesus, you're scaring me right now. I—whatever it is, I'm sorry. I'm sorry, Audrey. Please."

I press my lips together to keep from begging for his forgiveness and flinging myself into his arms—the safest place I've ever known, but now possibly the most dangerous. When a long, silent minute has elapsed, his shadow retreats and the door clicks shut.

24

The next morning Detective Chao comes by to inform me that the police are finished with the kitchen and the parking lot, and we are free to resume normal operations. It will still be a number of days until I get my phone back, however.

"Have you made any progress?" I ask.

"We're following up on some leads," she says evasively. Her pantsuit is beige this time, free of wrinkles, and she looks utterly unaffected by the fact that the temperature has already reached ninety degrees and it isn't even 10 a.m. yet. I, on the other hand, can feel perspiration beading on my brow and am suddenly aware of how pilled my old cotton jersey capris have become. Furthermore, while I brushed my hair this morning, I'm reasonably certain I forgot to put on deodorant. Between all that and the puffy, dark-ringed eyes from a sleepless night of crying, I'm an absolute train wreck.

A tow truck is pulling away Aaron's car as we speak, and for the first time, I set eyes on the spot where his body fell.

"Is that—" There's a dark stain in the pavement to the left of where Aaron's car had been parked. I close my eyes tight and press my nails hard into my palm to keep the band around my chest from tightening any further. I force myself to take slow, deep breaths until the feeling passes.

"Blood comes out of concrete fairly easily. If you have a pressure washer, that's usually best," she tells me, as though she's advising me on how to clean my silverware.

"I'll take care of it," says a voice behind me. I startle so violently Chao grabs my arm to steady me. It's Drew. Lost in my visceral reaction to the sight of Aaron's blood, I hadn't heard him come up behind us. "Sorry, boss lady," he adds with an apologetic nod. "Came by to see if there's anything that needs doing."

"Are you sure?" I ask. It feels like a job I have no business asking anyone else to do. If Aaron's blood is on my hands—and there's at least a good chance that it is—I should be the one responsible for cleaning it up.

"Yeah, it's no problem, seriously. We've got a pressure washer in the toolshed. I'll go grab it."

"Thanks, Drew," I say, relieved. He lifts his fist, and out of habit, I bump it with mine. The vision he gives me is of an everyday scene, an adult male I think I've seen before, sketching out plans and taking notes for a large display of insects at a museum. I sigh with relief while admonishing myself to be more careful. I can't afford to screw up even once.

"Jana wants to talk to you," Cora says to me when I walk into the inn. "I sent her to the staff room since I wasn't sure if it was...presentable upstairs." I bite back a retort because the truth is, my suite is in no way presentable at the moment, and I'd be embarrassed to have an employee see the state of it.

"Thank you," I tell her as civilly as possible, and thread my way through the halls to the staff room alongside the kitchen of the pub.

"Hey, Jana," I say. She's sitting at the Formica table as I enter, chewing at one of her fingernails. There's an envelope sitting in front of her, and as I approach, I see it has my name on it. Between that and her apparent nervousness, I'm pretty sure I know what this conversation is going to be about. "Cora said you wanted to talk. What's up?"

"I'm sorry, Audrey," she says. "I'm...I'm quitting. I'm going to work over at the Surfside Inn." She slides the envelope over to me. Inside is her letter of resignation, effective immediately, and her key to the main entrance.

"Is this because of what happened here yesterday?" I know it's not. She couldn't have come up with a new job so quickly, and on a weekend to boot.

"Not exactly," she confirms. "I wish you the best of luck, I really do, but I need job security. I'm the only provider for both my son and my mother."

"And you feel like you no longer have security here. Did you think I wanted to replace you? Because I promise you, I value you very much here, Jana. You're an essential part of the team. In fact, I don't know what I'm going to do without you. Will you reconsider and stay?"

"Thank you, that's kind of you to say. It's not that at all, it's just..." she shrugs and looks down at her hands. "You know what they're saying."

"That the inn's going to go out of business because I don't know what I'm doing." I struggle to keep my voice even.

"For what it's worth, I think you're catching on quick," she says, her expression earnest.

"Just not quick enough for you to stay." I try to smile to take the bite out of the words, but all I can manage is a twist of my lips that feels bitter and fake.

"I'm sorry," she says again.

"I know. Well, I wish you all the best. Thank you for everything you've done to help me since I've started on here." We both stand up and eye each other awkwardly. The moment feels like it should conclude with a no-ill-will-here hug, or at the very least a handshake, but I can't bring myself to do it. Instead, I slide my chair back into the table and gesture for her to lead the way out of the room. She does hug Cora when she passes through the entrance, and they make promises to keep in touch that sound sincere.

"Did you know she was leaving?" I ask Cora once Jana's left the inn.

She nods. "She asked me for a reference."

"You might have mentioned something," I snap. "We could have had a new employee lined up to replace her. Now, what are we supposed to do in the evenings? She turned in her key; she didn't even give a two-week notice. Fuck." I slump down onto the couch across from the desk. "Looks like I'm on the night shift," I say glumly, rubbing my temples. Just what I need. Cora shrugs, not looking all that sympathetic, and I feel myself boiling over with rage. "You know, maybe if you were more invested in keeping the inn up and running and less concerned with undermining me, we wouldn't be in this situation," I say through gritted teeth. "This is a deliberate act of sabotage."

"I didn't know she wasn't going to give notice," she says. "I didn't even know she got the job until this morning when she told me. How was I supposed to know they would want her to start right away?"

"You did know she was looking for a new job. You didn't think that was something worth mentioning? Would you have told Roz if she was still here?"

"If Roz was still here, Jana wouldn't have quit. All of these bad things started happening after she died and *you* came around, trying to replace her. Like you could ever be half the woman she was." The words, and the venom behind them are like a slap in the face. I actually lean back as though Cora had physically struck me.

Tears rise unbidden to my eyes, but before I can formulate some sort of a retort, she grabs her purse from underneath the desk and, after digging around in it for a moment, produces her own set of keys. *Good,* I think viciously, but another part of me is dreading what she's about to do.

"It's you or me," she says. "Call me when you're ready to call it quits." She presses the key ring into my hand.

REGRESS

He knew he had to work fast if he was to get everything concealed before the village council came to his home. Thanks to his friend and sometime fellow gambling partner Pavel, who sat on the council, he had gotten the heads up that there may be a mandatory sharing of food and grain to be rationed out amongst those who had less, now that it was apparent the storms were not letting up and the pass would not be open until spring. Because of that, although it was well past moonrise, he and Slava were working feverishly to dig a hole underneath the floorboards of their small two-room stone hut. They planned to stuff this small cellar with as many potatoes, beets, onions, cabbages, wheels of cheese, and ropes of cured sausages as they could safely without it being obvious that they were holding back. For now, the food they planned to set aside was hidden under the straw in the chicken coop.

"Kolya, take the bucket," Slava hissed to him and passed him up a pail of thin, dusty soil. They had to be careful to conceal the evidence of their project, so they carried the dirt outside, one bucket at a time, and scattered it in the few places that weren't knee-deep in snow, such as the space under the chicken coop and inside the small barn.

It was hard work, since the ground was frozen solid, but they persevered, taking turns crouching in the small hole and scraping at it with a pickax until there was enough dirt to scoop up. They worked in near-darkness, with only the light of one small candle. He was terrified of being caught, although the chances of anyone coming around at this time of night, especially a council member, were almost none. Nevertheless, he kept a close eye out the window while Slava dug and instructed her to do the same when he spelled her.

It had been Slava's idea to hide the food in the first place after the idea for the ration was first brought up in church this past week. He had resisted her urging to make preparations, telling her that surely people would not agree to have a portion of their hard-earned food, needed for their own families' survival, given away to others. When Pavel had all but confirmed it was going to happen, and would likely be a full seizure, not partial as they had first believed, she had doubled down, and he had finally relented. After all, she had argued, everyone else will be doing the same thing. Why should we be the only ones to suffer?

Although he'd given in, he still had mixed feelings about what they were doing. He knew some families were already doing poorly. He thought about his sister, Yulia, and his nieces and nephew. Did they have enough to eat every day? He felt ashamed that he hadn't checked on her recently—not since her husband left the village to see if he could make it through the pass. He would make a point of asking her in church this Sunday, he decided as he pulled on his heavy boots to take the bucket of dirt outside.

The wind slapped him in the face when he opened the door, stinging the small strip of exposed skin from his eyebrows to the middle of his nose. He trudged out to the barn, leaning into the gusts, keeping his head down. He dumped the dirt into a corner, scattered it around with his foot, and made his way back to the house.

"Do you think it's large enough?" Slava asked. She had climbed out of the hole and was peering over the edge. It was a good four feet deep and nearly as wide.

"I think so," he said after examining the space. They would know soon enough, he supposed. "Get dressed, woman," he told Slava, who was standing by the hearth, watching him. He'd be damned if he was going to lug the food inside by himself. This was her plan. She glared at him and looked like she was about to protest, but he gave her a warning look and she began to pull on her heavy woolen sweater.

Once all the food was stashed away, he replaced the boards over the hole and inspected the space carefully for any evidence that things were not as they seemed. Aside from some dirt around the area, which could be easily swept up, he could see nothing to give them away. All they had to do now was persuade whoever came tomorrow to collect their stores that what they'd set aside was all they had to offer.

"Clean that all up," he told Slava, indicating the dirt. Now that their deception was complete, he was angry—at Slava, at the village council, at the families who hadn't put by enough to support themselves through hard times, but most especially at himself. Perhaps his feelings would change once the hunger set in, and they were able to supplement their rations, but for now, it was hard to feel any pleasure at what they'd done. Without another word, he turned his back to his wife and went to bed.

25

It takes a while for my hands to stop shaking as I sit behind the front desk, staring blankly out the window. I check in a honeymooning couple who don't seem to have heard anything about Aaron's death, and another couple who are driving down the coast for their tenth anniversary and only staying one night. Those are the only guests the inn is expecting, so I use the rest of the afternoon to finish up the bookkeeping. I'll be able to send it all off to an accountant this week, which is a relief. I still have a ton of questions about things I can't reconcile, particularly the credit card statements. I've highlighted and added up all the unexplainable charges and they amount to over twenty thousand dollars over the eight-month span, which is a significant amount of money for the inn.

Cora's advice to file them as a miscellaneous expense

doesn't sit right with me, and I pick up the phone to call the credit card company. Pressing four to report a fraudulent transaction gets me a customer service agent immediately, and I outline the charges I want to dispute and ask if they can clarify what they might be for.

"It looks like they're using a mobile payment system, one of those devices you can plug into your cell phone to take payments on the go," the agent tells me. "They're easy to get. All you need is a bank account. Beyond that, I don't have any information on what sort of business it is." I tell him I want to open an investigation and cancel the card in the meantime. He says it will take several weeks to determine whether the charges are fraud or not, but he'll have a card with a new number issued today. It's the best I can do for now.

Now idle, and in a bit calmer frame of mind, I decide to read through my vision journal again to see if anything stands out or sparks a new thought. I flip back to my first entry upon arriving in Soberly and start to skim. The first two are both from Kellen, and my heart twists when I remember how I screamed at him last night. Next is Cora's vivid vision of her past life in the Russian village, the one where her former self had almost been caught stockpiling food. I read through it carefully, looking for clues. Is the solution to the mystery in the visions from that time and place? Aaron's death mirrored the one he suffered then, but none of the other three did.

Bill Blackmoor's is next, and this one corresponds to his death—still considered an accident by the police—in this time. Neither what I've written, nor what I remember of the vision, tells me anything new.

I keep reading, scrutinizing every entry carefully,

calling back my own memories of the visions for any details I might have left out. Some of them I barely remember having at all, others are as clear and sharp as the moment I received them.

When I get to the one about Kellen's Father Lvov finding his love, frozen to death under the tree, tears threaten to spill over, and I brush them hastily away so they don't fall on the page and mar the ink. Twice now he's lost his lover prematurely, and I can't believe I didn't see it sooner. It's no wonder he's so protective. He can't help but cling tight to relationships because, on some subconscious level, he knows they could end at any moment. Now I've gone and done it again.

I keep reading. There are plenty of visions from the people I know best, along with a smattering from others around town. The day I went to church fills six pages. Re-reading the entry about Sheena's past as a budding author brings a brief smile to my face. I wonder if she's done any more research to find the fellow.

Next is an entry from Naomi that had unsettled me deeply when I'd received it—when she'd overdosed in her sleep from combining pills with alcohol. I remember she'd given it to me in the middle of the first shift I'd worked in the pub, during the supper rush. I hadn't written down much about the vision—I remember I was pressed for time that evening—but I could recall all the details precisely, down to the exact wording of her conversations. I fill in the page with a few more notes and observations, now that I have the time.

Pavel's death, both from his own observation and from Father Lvov's, offers me no motive or any context leading up to the fatal stabbing, much to my frustration.

I feel like if I only knew more about what had happened in that moment, I could feel so much more at ease about Aaron's murder.

Once I reach the end, I jot down the latest vision from Cora. It's a struggle to keep my feelings about her in this lifetime from coloring how I relate to the scene from the past. No matter what my opinion of Cora, the truth is, her past self had felt some guilt about cheating his neighbors out of food rations.

It's late afternoon by the time I'm finished, and I close my eyes to think for a minute, letting it all sink in. I've marked the four visions that resulted in a death in Soberly and re-read them, looking for a connection. Nothing stands out. I've scrutinized every vision for clues to indicate the person could be a killer, either in their past or in the present. The priest has been the only person who exhibited a tendency toward violence, but I know in my heart Kellen has nothing to do with any of this.

Who did that leave? Why would anyone want these people dead? Nothing I could see connected them. Were they chosen at random? Was my hypothesis that it was somehow related to my ability correct? I still couldn't discount it entirely, but it was a huge leap of logic.

Opening my eyes again, I flip through all the pages I've marked with sticky tabs. All deaths. There are five, and only Naomi is still alive. I'm wracked with a sudden shiver as goosebumps rise all over my skin. Was Naomi in danger? All the others had died within a day or two of them giving me the vision of their past death, but Naomi's was dated three and a half weeks ago. What made her vision different from the others?

I pick up the phone and dial Sheena's shop. She should still be there unless she closed early today. She picks up on the fourth ring, just when I thought she was using caller ID to screen the call because she didn't want to talk to me.

"Out of the Attic Collectibles," she says, then, "Audrey?"

"Yeah, it's me. Listen, I think I've figured something out. About what's going on."

"Then tell the police. They know something's up now. Let them handle it."

"I can't. They won't believe me." I say bitterly. My voice is shaking. I tell her about how Naomi's past death is the only one I've seen that hasn't come to pass in this time. "I'm worried she's in danger. I want to keep an eye on her, to make sure she's safe. I couldn't stand it if..." my voice trails off. "Will you help me? I want to watch her house."

"What does Kellen say?" She's not going to do it, I can tell by her voice.

"I haven't—I can't tell him. Besides, we're not—I broke up with him. Last night. Please, Sheena. I don't have anyone else."

She sighs, and there's a long silence while she considers. "All we're going to do is watch the house?" she says finally.

"Yes. If we see anything, anything at all, we'll call the police right away, I promise."

"Okay." I can tell she still has doubts, but at least she agreed to help. Naomi's not done at the pub until nine, so we agree to meet outside her house shortly afterward. It will mean I'll be abandoning my post at the front desk and I'll have to hope the guests won't need anything that can't wait until morning. From what Jana told me when she was training me, nothing much ever happens at night unless there's a late check-in. All the guests have a key to get into the lobby after hours, so they can come and go as they please.

When the appointed hour comes, I duck upstairs, change into dark clothes, and lock up. It's no more than a fifteen-minute walk to Naomi's house. Twilight is falling—soon it will be dark, and Sheena and I can hopefully conceal ourselves somewhere in the yard where we won't be seen, either by Naomi or the neighbors.

Sheena's waiting on the far corner, looking anxious. She's dressed in black as well. Good—hopefully we can melt into the shadows.

"Girl detectives, back on the case," she says nervously, twisting a strand of hair around her finger repetitively.

"Think of us more like guardian angels," I say, hoping to reassure her. "Or bodyguards. Secret Service."

"We need those mirrored aviator sunglasses to be Secret Service," she jokes.

"I'll get some for next time," I promise.

"How long are you going to do this for, anyway?" Her use of *you,* not *we,* doesn't escape my notice. Looks like I can't count on her help beyond tonight.

"I...don't know." I know in my heart I'm going to be out here every night until the killer is caught. The thought of Naomi getting hurt terrifies me. "I'm so scared, Sheena. I can't think of anything else to do."

"Can't you tip the police off anonymously or something, without telling them about your—"

"What would I say? The only evidence that Naomi

might be in danger is because of my visions, and there's no way the police will take me seriously."

Sheena sighs. "What time does Kellen get back?"

"Probably around eleven-thirty, maybe midnight." I ask myself whether I feel Naomi is safe once he's home. Probably, if someone tries to break in. If Naomi is under the influence of a subconscious suggestion and tries to harm herself? He might not hear a thing from the basement, especially if she overdoses on pills. No, I'm going to need to keep an eye on the house all night.

"Look, here she comes," Sheena says suddenly, pointing down the street at the petite silhouette approaching. We duck out of sight behind a large oak and watch her walk up to the door and let herself in. "Now what?" she asks. "We can't see the house from here."

"I know. I'm hoping we can find someplace in the garden where we can see the house, but she won't see us." It's almost dark now, and we walk slowly up toward the house, trying to look casual. None of the neighbors have their porch lights on, but there's a faint flickering behind the curtains of the bungalow across the street. Hopefully, their television is engrossing enough that they don't notice us as we duck into Naomi's yard, keeping close to the tall hedge rounding one corner of the property.

"What about under there?" Sheena points to a large fir tree with drooping branches. There's space underneath it for both of us if we crouch. The house will be visible between the boughs. Unless you were looking specifically at that spot, we should be close to invisible. Still, I hesitate because it reminds me so much of the place where Father Lvov's young love Alexandra froze to death. Looking around the yard though, I don't see anything that would offer us even close to the same amount of cover and security.

"Works for me. Can you see Naomi inside?" Light is streaming from the big bay window. It doesn't reach the tree, but we'll have to cross it from our position near the hedge in order to get there. Sheena pokes her head out for a moment, scanning the house.

"No," she says finally.

"Okay, let's run for it." I count to three under my breath and we scurry across the yard, crouching, and throw ourselves under the fir. We both freeze, waiting for the wailing of alarms or high-pitched screams to come from the house, but all is silent, and there is no movement inside. I breathe a sigh of relief and make a mental note to tell Kellen to install one of those motion-sensor lights on his front porch. If we could pull this kind of stunt, someone with ill intentions could too. Knowing the small-town mentality, the front door probably isn't even locked.

I maneuver myself into a semi-comfortable position, squatting with my back to the trunk. By peering around the branches, I can see through the living room into the kitchen via the bay window. The lights are on in both rooms. Sheena is to my left, scoping out the same view. Naomi's bedroom, I know, is in the back of the house, along with Kellen's brother's for when he's home from college. Other than that, there's only a bathroom on the main floor—the entire house is less than a thousand square feet.

"There she is," I whisper unnecessarily. Naomi has

appeared from the hallway, now dressed in a comfortable sweater and maxi skirt. We watch her put the kettle on to boil and take a mug down from the cupboard.

"I feel really weird doing this," Sheena says. "Even if it's to protect her, it's still spying. Should we maybe tell her we're out here, keeping an eye on things?"

"We can't," I say. "We'd have to explain everything, including why we think she's a target." *Or why I think she might harm herself.* When she goes to bed, I plan on moving into the backyard so I can watch for her light coming on in the night, in case she sleepwalks and accidentally takes a handful of pills, but I'm not telling Sheena that.

Naomi settles down onto the living room couch with her tea and a paperback after slipping on a pair of reading glasses I never knew she needed. I agree with Sheena—it feels wrong to be peering into her home like this, watching what I'm sure she assumes is a private moment. All the same, I'm glad she hasn't thought to pull the drapes shut.

Nothing much happens for a long time except my knees start to ache as I alternate from squatting to kneeling in the mound of needles under the tree. Other than the occasional car driving by, the neighborhood is silent, and the sun has long gone below the horizon. Every once in a while, I see the faint glow from Sheena's digital watch as she illuminates it to check the time. Neither of us has said anything in over an hour, and Naomi hasn't budged from her position on the couch.

"It's after eleven," Sheena says eventually. "Kellen should be home soon. Can we go after he gets here?"

"Yeah, probably," I reply. From the frequency she's

checking the time, it's clear she's close to being finished with surveillance duty, and I don't want to push my luck by asking her to stay longer in case I need her help again. "He'll be adequate protection if anyone tries to break in."

"Only he's not coming home, at least not for a while," says a voice behind us, and it's all I can do to keep from screaming in surprise as the shadow of a person emerges from alongside the hedge and crouches down outside the perimeter of the fir tree. "Hello ladies, want to join the party? Come on out now, nice and slow." They're speaking in a low whisper so I can't recognize the voice, but there's no mistaking the glint of the large gun being pointed straight at me. *Maybe I should have screamed when I had the chance.* I edge my way out from under the boughs, Sheena hyperventilating at my side. My heart is beating so fast I feel lightheaded, and my legs, after more than two hours being constricted under the tree, are half-asleep and tingling painfully. A booted foot prods me forward roughly. I crawl the last couple feet, hoping against hope Naomi will choose this moment to look out the window, see what's going on in her yard, and call the police, but she doesn't. When I glance up at the house I can see the top of her head, bent down slightly, intent on her book.

"Get up," the voice says. I lurch unsteadily to my feet, holding on to Sheena for balance. I'm so focused on the gun pointed in my face it takes me a moment to register the person behind it, a person who now has a manic smile on his face.

It's Drew.

26

"Up to the front door," Drew says, motioning the way with the gun. His red headphones are around his neck, and he's carrying a backpack. Oddly, I'm hyper-focused on the newly-shaved pattern decorating the side of his head, a chaotic mix of zigzags and shapes.

"Kellen will be home soon," I say. "He won't take much longer closing up."

"Except he's off looking for you," Drew says as we walk up the steps to the door single-file, me in the lead, Sheena in the middle, and Drew behind us. "I told him you called and asked him to meet you way down the beach. Said you had some important stuff you needed to tell him." He's not whispering anymore, and I can hear the amusement in his voice. "Go ahead. Knock on the door." My hand remains stubbornly by my side, still trying to protect Naomi. "Do it, or I'll shoot her,"

Drew says, prodding Sheena with the gun. She lets out a whimper, and reluctantly I rap on the door. My eyes fill with tears as I hear Naomi's footsteps approach.

"I'm sorry," I say when she opens it, my voice breaking. Drew shoves us into the foyer and pushes the door shut behind him.

"What's the meaning of this, coming into my house with a gun? Just what do you think you're doing?" Naomi demands. She looks like she's going to slap Drew upside the head like an errant child. I've never seen her so furious. Sheena looks ready to faint, I'm crying, and Drew is still pointing the gun directly at me. The matte black weapon looks huge in his hand, and very lethal.

"So sorry to barge in on you like this, but unfortunately, I've got some loose ends to tie up. You can blame her, really," and he jerks his head in my direction. His voice has lost its laid-back, easy-come-easy-go tone. This Drew is sharp and menacing, and he's smiling like he's enjoying the moment. "As soon as you showed up and started poking around, I knew I'd have to get rid of you. Unfortunately for you, Naomi, you're caught in the middle of it. I guess you are too," he says to Sheena, who's leaning against the wall, trembling. "Didn't see that one coming. Nice to know there are still some surprises in life. Anyway, it's not personal, I never had a problem with either of you. It's her that's fucking everything up."

"You can't be serious," I say. "You're that against me owning the inn? You think I could screw it up that badly? I'm actually doing okay." Then something clicks. "Wait. The credit card. It's you who's running the fraudulent charges."

Drew uses his empty hand to mime pulling a trigger at me, confirming my suspicion. "I tried to run one through tonight, and it was declined. I knew you'd figured it out."

"And you thought killing those people would, what, scare me off?"

"Either that or you'd take the fall for it," he says. "Since you don't seem to be the scared type, I guess we're going to have to go with option number two."

"Fine," I say, taking a deep breath. "I'll go to the police right now and confess to everything. I'll tell them how I drowned Marnie, smothered Irene Bell, and used a burner phone to lure Aaron to the parking lot where I stabbed him with a knife from the kitchen. I'll even admit to pushing Bill Blackmoor down the stairs because you did that too, didn't you, asshole. Just let Naomi and Sheena go. I'll call Detective Chao right now. You can sit here and listen in on everything."

"Negative," he says. "I've got different plans tonight. Naomi, I think your bedroom would be a much more comfortable place to hang out. Lead the way, please."

"You sick fuck," I growl, clenching my fists helplessly as he pushes us forward into the house. "If you dare touch either of them, I will kill you myself."

"I'm not going to rape anyone. I'm not *that* kind of depraved, Audrey," he says, rolling his eyes. We enter the bedroom and he closes the door. "You two," he points at Naomi and Sheena, "have a seat on the bed. Audrey, into the corner over there." He sends me to the far end of the room, where there's a small space between the wall and a night table. There's a bedside lamp on it, and I wonder for a moment if I could throw it at Drew and knock him out with it. "I'll shoot one of them if you try," he tells me like he can read my thoughts.

"Look, if it's me you want, you've got me," I plead with him. "Let them go. They have nothing to do with this." Sheena is nodding vigorously. I should have never brought her into this, I berate myself. I know Drew is here for Naomi, and how I'm involved as well, but she's completely innocent of Drew's entire twisted scheme.

"Too late, they know too much," he says. "Besides, there needs to be a crime scene, and your hand needs to be on the smoking gun, so to speak."

"I'm not shooting them. There's nothing you can do to make me. I'll never do it."

"It was a metaphor, Audrey. I'm not stupid enough to hand the gun over to you. I am going to get you to help me though, and depending on how well you cooperate, your friends will have an easy death instead of a slow, painful one. Understood?" I nod, even though I don't have a clue what he means. Cooperate how?

Drew takes off his backpack and drops it to the floor beside him. With the gun still trained on me, he unzips it with his free hand and rifles around inside, pulling out a cardboard box not much bigger than a business card. He does a practice swing to make sure I know to catch it, then tosses it over to me.

"What's this?" My thoughts are racing so fast I can't focus long enough to read the words on the package.

"Fentanyl patches." My heart plummets into my stomach, and Sheena moans. "No, this is good shit," he says, as casually as if he was offering us a joint at a party. "As far as having to kick it goes, this way's pretty decent. You're going to feel amazing, then you're just going to nod off. I figure I'm doing you a favor."

This is the mirror to the drug overdose Naomi experienced in her past life, only instead of the barbiturates of the fifties, Drew is going to use the opioids that have spread like an epidemic all over the country.

"Go ahead, open it up and take a few out. Two each should do it. I'm guessing neither of you is a user?" He looks at Naomi and Sheena, who stare back blankly. "Morphine? Heroin? Anything like that?" They both shake their heads. "Good, because I don't want to have to use any more on the two of you than I have to. Like I said, this is good shit."

"Is this what you spent all the money on? You said you got cleaned up."

Drew shrugged. "That only lasted a few days. It was Roz's idea, not mine. I appreciate that she wanted me to be sober, but in all honesty, I'd rather not be. What you're going to do now is tear open the packages, and peel off the back. Then stick them on. The belly is a good spot."

"No," I whimper, shrinking back against the wall. I can't do this. I can't put my friends to death, even if it's under duress.

"Yes, or I tie you up and make you watch while I do it with a knife instead," Drew says. "Right now, Audrey, or I'm going to shoot Sheena in the knee." Sheena huddles against Naomi, who wraps a protective arm around her. They cling to each other while I stand behind them, paralyzed.

"You're the devil himself," Naomi says to Drew. "Pass them to me, child, I'll do it myself." She reaches her arm out toward me but Drew swings the gun in her direction.

"Nope, it has to be Audrey."

"Why?" I shout. There are tears pouring down my face.

"Fingerprints. When this is all over and done with, it needs to be clear you were the one responsible. Now no more stalling. Put the patches on right now."

With trembling hands, I slowly tear one of the paper wrappers open and pull the plastic patch out. It looks like a small, square Band-Aid.

"Naomi, lift up your shirt a little. There we go," Drew says, and motions me to come forward, instructing me to kneel down at the foot of the bed between Naomi and Sheena.

"Please don't make me do this," I whisper. "I'll do anything you want. Please don't make me hurt my friends. I thought you were a nice person, I thought you liked me, Drew, please. You don't have to do this. There has to be some other way. If it's money, I can get you some, everything I have, you can disappear." It's like talking to a wall. Drew doesn't show any indication that my pleas are having an effect. He presses the gun hard into the back of my neck.

"Right on her side there, above her hip. One beside the other. Come on, or things are going to start getting messy. You're the one making the choice, Audrey—are your friends going to have an easy death or a painful one? What do you want their last moments to be like?"

"It's okay, child," Naomi says to me. She strokes my hair, which only makes me cry harder. "Let's get it over with, all right?" She's so calm, and there's an expression of serenity on her face. Unlike Sheena, she doesn't look frightened at all. My hands are shaking so much I almost drop the patch, but I manage to stick the beige square onto Naomi's dark skin.

Jeannie opened her eyes to find herself in an unfamiliar room, a stark white ceiling stained with water spots above her. A blue curtain suspended by chains hung to her left, thin enough to let the light from a window on the other side through but preventing her from seeing what was beyond it. There were bars on either side of the narrow bed she was lying on. Hospital? she thought, with no recollection of how or why she was there.

"There you are," said a voice to her right, startling her. She turned her head to see a man in a white coat standing there. She'd never seen him before in her life. "I'm Doctor Mason, Jeannie. You gave us quite a scare there."

Her husband, seated in a hard, plastic chair alongside her, reached over and squeezed her hand. The dark circles under his eyes were a testament to his exhaustion, but he was smiling.

"What happened?" she asked.

"Another one," Drew barks behind me, making me jump. She survived. Naomi's past self hadn't died of an overdose after all. Does that mean history could repeat itself? Was there hope? I tear open a second package, and place another patch beside the first, this time careful not to make direct contact with her skin, then press my face into Naomi's lap and sob. She rubs my back in slow circles, making soft shushing sounds. "Come on, I don't have all night," Drew says, and he shoves me with his foot. "Sheena, lift up your top. Audrey, stick the patches on."

Sheena is shivering from head to toe and has her arms wrapped tightly around her middle. Her face is pallid, and I'm pretty sure she's going into shock. She doesn't make any attempt to move her shirt, so I pull it gently up for her.

"Don't, please, don't do it. I don't want to die," she whispers, and her voice is so small and sad I can't go through with it. Suddenly, Drew swings the handgun and hits Sheena on the temple with it, stunning her and causing her to unwrap her arms from her stomach.

"Last chance." He brandishes the gun at her again while she cradles the side of her head.

"*Stop*. Don't hit her," I yell, trying to put my body in between her and the gun.

"Then put the fucking patch on." Sheena whimpers, but doesn't stop me when I lift her shirt again, exposing an inch of flesh.

"Maybe it'll be okay," I murmur. Drew is directly behind me, but I don't think he can see my hands, so I quickly fold one side of the patch over slightly so less of the medicated adhesive will come into contact with her skin. Maybe it won't make any difference, but it at least feels like I'm doing something. I do the same thing with the second one, and let Sheena's shirt fall back into place, obscuring the patches. Drew doesn't seem to have noticed my small deception.

"Now what?" I say dully, still kneeling in front of the bed. "Two for me too?"

"No, in a short period of time, you're going to become

overcome with remorse and shoot yourself in the head. With my assistance, of course. In the meantime, you can go back to your corner." He prods me in the back of the head with the barrel of the gun until I stand up and step away from the bed. I breathe a silent sigh of relief that he's not going to drug me as well. Maybe I can still save us all. "Ladies, if I see so much as a twitch in the direction of those patches, I'll give you something to hurt about. Trust me, it's best if you relax, and let the drug take you away. It shouldn't take long. Ten, maybe fifteen minutes, tops. You might even find you enjoy it."

"Please, Drew," I beg. Sheena's crying softly again, but Naomi still looks peaceful, her hands clasped together in her lap. I wonder if she's praying. "It's not too late to fix this. Is this really the person you want to be? Naomi's your friend."

Drew shrugs. "I don't have much choice. I'm in too deep now. This is the only way I can fix it. Besides, I don't know why you're so broken up about it. You know they're coming back again. The circle of life, right?" He smiles knowingly and winks. "Honestly, it's helped me feel at peace with death. You'll all be born somewhere else and start all over again with a new life. Since you came along and showed me the truth, death has taken on a completely different meaning for me."

At that moment, I see the shadow of two feet appear from the crack at the bottom of the bedroom door. There's someone standing on the other side. Could it be Kellen? I have to keep Drew distracted, get him to drop his guard. I need to keep him talking.

"How do you know about that? About what I can see? How did you know the way they all died? Are you...

like me?"

"Not exactly." He's leaning against the wall beside the door, the hand holding the gun resting on top of the dresser beside him. "My sight is a lot more limited than yours. Like a finely tuned radio. I only pick things up from people who already have the gift. Everything you see, you pass along to me. Hence the fist bumps." He grins at me. "There are more of us than you think, but you're by far the strongest I've ever met. Most people have a vague sense of intuition or precognition. Some don't even realize they've got it. I've come across a couple people who have some weak telepathy. You— it's like going from an old black and white television to IMAX with surround sound. The whole past-lives thing is incredible. Can you do anything else? Move things? Control people?"

"Don't you think if I could I would have taken you out already?" I spit at him, furious that he's so glib, and that I was the one who made him so comfortable with the idea of taking peoples' lives in the first place, as well as the ideas for how to do it. I was practically an accomplice.

"Fair point. When did it start for you?"

"When I was fourteen. Meningitis. I was in a coma for a week, and it was there when I woke up. You?"

"Surfing accident when I was nineteen, in California. I drowned and had to be revived with CPR. They said I flatlined for almost ten minutes."

"What are you talking about?" Naomi says. Her voice sounds a bit slurred, and my heart seizes in my chest. The drugs are starting to take effect.

"Your almost future-daughter-in-law can see your

past lives when she touches you," Drew tells her. "I don't think it's something she really shares with others."

"She told me," Sheena retorts. Her voice is still strong. Good. Maybe that little bit I folded over *was* making a difference.

Drew raises his eyebrows in surprise. "And the whole town didn't find out about it the next day? I'm shocked, Sheena. I've never known you to pass up sharing a good secret."

"Past lives?" Naomi swivels her head around to look at me. I nod.

"Like little scenes from a movie in my head," I tell her. "Any time I make skin-to-skin contact with someone, I get a flash of their past. Usually normal stuff. Sometimes important events. Drew's been stealing them out of my head and using them to decide how to kill people. Bill Blackmoor fell down the stairs in his home on the day the Japanese bombed Pearl Harbor. Marnie drowned in a pond on her family's farm when she was a toddler. Irene Bell passed away in her sleep, probably from a stroke. Aaron Glass was murdered, stabbed in the chest."

"Ooh, this is a good one, tell her who stabbed him," Drew says with a malicious grin. "It was Kellen," he continues when I press my lips shut, refusing. "Kellen's past-self killed Aaron's past-self. Isn't that *wild?* We all keep finding each other, again and again."

"Praise Jesus," Naomi says. "You mean I'll see them again? Kellen, Marcus, and Graham?" The latter two were Kellen's brother and father, respectively.

"Yes," I tell her. "They may not be your children or spouse—maybe a good friend, or grandchild, or someone else you're close to. You've known Cora and Reverend

Trish in the past, too." At that, Naomi bows her head, and I hear her weep quietly.

"You forgot to tell Naomi how she died," Drew says. He's practically rubbing his hands together.

"I don't know," I shoot back. "She survived it."

"You're lying." His glee disappears as his eyebrows pull together in a frown.

"You don't have the most up-to-date information. She woke up in the hospital the next day. I saw it. All this—this is wrong. This isn't how it went down."

"Bullshit. Prove it." He holds out his empty hand to me, the gun pointed at my chest. This is going to be my chance. The shadows on the other side of the door are still there. I'm positive it's Kellen, waiting for the right moment. I advance slowly, my hands in front of me where Drew can see them. Drew's arm is stretched out toward me, and as I reach mine out to meet him, I shout and pull Drew forward with all my might. Kellen bursts into the room and throws himself at Drew. The gun goes off. I fall backward, caught off balance. Drew and Kellen hit the floor beside me, and in the scuffle, I take a hard kick to the stomach. Sheena's screaming, but Naomi bounds up, grabs the lamp and swings it at Drew's head like she's hitting a home run out of the park. He collapses on top of Kellen and lies motionless. Naomi uses the lamp's cord to tie his wrists behind his back.

"Take the patches off," I croak, trying to get my breath back. I'm lightheaded, probably from being winded—it feels like there's a heavy weight on my chest, preventing me from taking a full breath. I can hear sirens approaching, lots of them. I hope there's an ambulance for Naomi and Sheena. Relieved, I close my eyes, surprised at how sleepy I am. It's still hard to breathe, but it doesn't feel as important now. Naomi and Sheena are safe, and Drew's been incapacitated.

"Audrey, open your eyes, stay with me," Kellen says, grasping my hand and squeezing it tightly. Something flashes into my head, but I can't keep track of it before it's gone. Then someone presses hard on my chest for some reason, making me cough.

"Don't," I mutter. I want to sleep. It's been such a long night, and no doubt once the police arrive it'll take hours to answer all of their questions. Maybe I can rest here for a few minutes. The sirens are right outside the house now.

"Audrey, look at me, open your eyes," Kellen says. He sounds so frightened. I manage to crack one eyelid a fraction to see him looming over me. Naomi's the one pressing on my chest. "Hey," he says with a smile, but he's crying at the same time. He's still got my hand in a death grip. "Stay with me, Audrey, don't leave me, okay? I need you in this lifetime, not the next one. I love you." Both my eyes open at that. "Yeah, I said it," he says with a laugh. "Somebody had to first." I want to laugh too, but all that comes out is another weak cough. My eyes want to close again so badly. I hear the front door open, and footsteps pounding into the house.

"We're in here," Sheena yells. "Hurry, she's been shot!"

Who's been shot? I wonder before the blackness takes me.

27

Waking up is eerily reminiscent of Naomi's vision. I'm in a hospital bed, surrounded by sterile pale green walls and the scent of disinfectant. The sound of steady beeping comes from somewhere behind my head, and an IV tube filled with clear fluid snakes its way out of my left hand and up a pole. There's also a clip over my index finger. I feel like I've been hit by a dump truck, then backed over again. The last thing I remember is lying on Naomi's bedroom floor, with everyone kneeling over me. Reflexively, I groan as the scene replays itself in my mind. Drew must have shot me in the struggle.

Kellen's hand is wrapped around my right one, and the man himself is fast asleep in a chair beside me, his chin on his chest. There are smears of what must be my blood on his gray T-shirt. I squeeze his hand and feel his tighten in return, but he doesn't wake. A sense of warmth and safety envelops me, and I close my eyes again, knowing he'll still be here when I wake up.

There are only a few streaks of orange light left on the horizon when I open my eyes again. Just as I knew he would be, Kellen is still parked in the chair beside me, although he's got a clean shirt on and is awake, reading a paperback. He doesn't see that I've come to, so I spend a few moments watching him, drinking in the sight of his face, his chest rising and falling rhythmically, his long fingers as they hold the book. We are so lucky. Things could have turned out much worse.

He glances up over the pages and sees me looking at him, and I'm treated to his megawatt smile. Without a word, he leans over the bars on the bed and kisses me long and deep, cradling the back of my head so our foreheads press together. Some nebulous vision flits through my mind but I ignore it, wanting only the present. When we break apart I feel lightheaded in a way that has nothing to do with having recently been held hostage and shot by a serial killer.

"Hey," I manage, as my own face mirrors his wide smile.

"How are you feeling?" I consider the question. Better than when I woke up the first time—maybe the truck that hit me was only a half-ton.

"All right," I tell him. "Sore. Achy." He nods and leans over to press a button on the wall behind me.

"I'm supposed to alert the nurses' station when you wake up," he says. "You've been out for almost an entire day."

Only one day. I breathe a sigh of relief. I've got the same disorientation and sense of missing time as when I'd had meningitis.

"What happened?" I ask him. "I mean, I got shot, but after that?"

"You had a collapsed lung. The bullet hit here," he indicates a point on the right side of his chest, "and passed almost all the way through. The surgeon removed it. You lost some blood, but she said you're going to be absolutely fine. It didn't come anywhere near your heart or your spine." He folds my hand into his own, and not even the faintest hint of a smile remains on his face. I ignore the vision he gives me—it's full of fear and grief and things I don't want to feel right now. "I was so scared," he says. "When I saw you lying there, covered in blood, and your face was so pale..." he trails off.

"I'm fine," I reassure him. "It takes more than a bullet to stop me." It was true, I realize. I'd been shot, and I survived. The thought is sobering and freeing at the same time. "How are your mom and Sheena?"

"They're both great. One hundred percent. Ma was a bit woozy, but they both got those patches off before there was any serious risk of overdose. The paramedics checked them out and decided neither of them needed any treatment besides a good night's sleep."

"What about Drew?"

"They brought him here too. Ma clocked him so hard she fractured his skull. He's under police guard though, probably handcuffed to the bed. He can't hurt anyone anymore."

There's a knock on the door, and a nurse enters a second later, carrying a chart.

"My name's James," he says. He glances at the monitors and writes something down on the chart. "How are you feeling? You've had quite a day."

"Okay, all things considered," I tell him. "Pretty sore. Thirsty." Parched, actually. I also need to brush my teeth—the inside of my mouth feels all fuzzy. I can't believe Kellen kissed me with morning breath like this.

"You can have some water. I'll let the doctor know you're awake, and she'll be in to talk to you soon." He marks down a couple more things and leaves Kellen and me alone again.

"How did you know to come to the house?" I ask him. "Drew said he sent you off down the beach after me."

"I started out that way, but it didn't feel right. I jogged all the way down to where we sat before and didn't see any sign of you. The further I went, the more wrong it felt, but I couldn't text you because the police still had our phones, so I decided to go back to the inn and look for you there. When I got to the front desk, I saw your journal open and read through it. At first, I had no idea what any of it was about, but it was clear enough that it had something to do with the people who died in town, and my ma. You weren't up in your room, and I checked Sheena's place too. The only thing I could think of to do was see if you were with Ma. I heard the voices as soon as I walked in the house, and listened for a few minutes, figured out what was going on, dialed 9-1-1 from the kitchen phone, and left it off the hook on the counter. The rest, I guess you know. How did you know I was there?"

"Saw your feet under the door," I tell him. "I'm so glad you figured it out. If you hadn't been there, we all would have died."

"I wish you'd told me about all of that stuff," he says. "Reading your journal, I could tell how much it was weighing on you."

"I was afraid you'd think I was crazy. Or even worse, that you wouldn't. I told Sheena and she...changed. It wasn't that she didn't believe me—she did, but she was afraid of it, of me. If you'd felt the same way, it would have killed me. I couldn't bear to see that happen, to have you pull away from me."

"I'm not afraid of you. It's one of the things that makes you who you are. I always knew you were a remarkable woman." He smiles, and I wrinkle my nose at him. To prove it, he slides his hand into mine.

He put the final touches down on his next sermon, drinking in the warm spring air as he did so. It was the first night it was warm enough to sit outside and work. Memories of the long winter were still fresh, but the village was recovering, and the subject of his sermon was resiliency. He had closed his Bible and was about to step inside when there was the sound of loud scuffling in the street in front of his house. A moment later Pavel appeared, dragging Karina by the wrist. Her face was streaked with tears, and she fought to escape his grasp.

"Open the church, Father," Pavel said. "You're going to marry us, right now."

"Have you lost your mind, Pavel? It's obvious this woman does not want to be wed to you. Let her go at once."

Pavel pulled a knife out and held it to Karina's throat. She became very still. "Do it, Father. I will not be defied by a woman, or by you. Her father has promised her to me, and tonight I intend to take her."

He stepped forward toward Pavel almost unconsciously, and the man pulled the knife away from Karina to point it at him. He grabbed Pavel's arm, twisting his wrist until the man cried out in pain, even as the knife bit into his own forearm, drawing a thin line of scarlet, visible in the dim moonlight against the white of his shirt. He wrenched Pavel's wrist further, and Karina broke free and ran into the night, screaming for help. Pavel's grip on the knife loosened and Father Lvov grabbed the hilt, turning it toward the man's chest as he was tackled and knocked to the ground.

So, the Father *hadn't* intentionally killed Pavel. It had been an accident, an act of self-defense. I never truly believed Kellen, in any of his forms, had it in him to murder someone in cold blood, but it was reassuring to see how Pavel's death had come about. I weave my fingers into Kellen's and squeeze tight, and his smile broadens.

Doctor Danielsen pokes her head into the room a short while later to check on me, and I learn she's the surgeon who operated on me the night before. She checks my dressing, and I'm surprised to see I only have a small incision about two inches long, above my right breast.

"You'll hardly have a scar once it's healed," she tells me. I expected a gaping hole and a line of black stitches marching across my chest. Once she's finished applying new bandages, she shows me how to click a button for pain medication. I almost ask her if it's fentanyl but decide I don't want to know. "Don't be afraid to use it," she tells me, and I click obligingly. Seeing the incision has made the pain more acute, somehow, like it's real for the first time. The last thing she does is hand me a sleeping pill and a glass of water. "You need plenty of rest," she says when I protest that I only just woke up. "It's the quickest ticket out of here. Another day's observation and I'll probably be able to discharge you, but your body needs sleep to heal." She flicks off the fluorescent overhead light as she leaves, and I can already feel myself getting drowsy.

"Stay with me?" I say to Kellen.

"I'm not going anywhere," he reassures me. Gingerly, careful not to tangle the IV line or the monitor on my finger, I scoot over to make room for him in the bed. It'll be a tight squeeze, but I know I'll feel better with him beside me.

"You sure?" he says, hesitating. "I don't want to accidentally hurt you."

"You won't," I tell him. "You never could."

♈♈

The next day brings a steady stream of visitors, starting with Naomi, who brings me a plate of chocolate chip cookies, a pan of lemon squares, and another of brownies.

"I needed something to do while I was waiting on hearing about you," she says by way of explanation as I giddily help myself to all three. My breakfast of cold cereal and toast was woefully inadequate.

"Naomi, I'm so—" She cuts me off.

"You don't have anything to be sorry for, child, that's for certain. There was nothing you could do. You ended up saving us both and came out of it far worse than anyone else for your trouble. I don't want to hear another word about it." I don't dare disobey, not when she uses that tone on me. I know I still have a lot of processing to do, especially around my feelings of guilt and responsibility for Drew's actions, but Naomi isn't the right person to do that with. Maybe Doctor Danielsen can point me in the direction of a good counselor for victims of crime. Instead, we mostly talk about Kellen, who flees the room to go get some decent coffee when the conversation turns in that direction. It's painful to laugh, but I can't help giggling at some of the stunts he pulled as a kid.

As she's pulling on her sweater to go, her face becomes serious. "We didn't mention anything about your gift to the police, Sheena and I," she tells me. "Neither of us figured it was any of their business."

"Do you really think of it as a gift?"

"I do," she says vehemently. "However it came it to be, you have it for a purpose. It's nothing to be afraid of, least I don't think so, but I won't tell a soul about it so long as you want it kept a secret."

"Thank you," I tell her.

"You think you'll stay?" she asks, paused on the threshold of the room and the hall.

"Yeah. Yeah, I think I will."

"Good. We want you to, me and Kellen both." She nods approvingly and leaves.

Detective Chao is next, along with her video recorder to take my statement. We talk for over an hour about what happened in Naomi's room, leaving out anything to do with Drew's abilities or mine. The only sticking point is what Sheena and I had been doing at Naomi's in the first place—I told her we were waiting for Kellen to come home when Drew came along. It was almost the truth. I also explain the fraudulent charges on Roz's business credit card, and how Drew had said he hoped the killings would make me leave town before I discovered them.

"We searched Mr. Segura's apartment and found the disposable phone that contacted both Marnie Decker and Aaron Glass," Detective Chao tells me. "So far, it all lines up with what you've said. That, and his admission of the murders to you, Mrs. Greene, and Ms. Underwood, will be enough to charge him for at least those two killings, as well as the attempted murder of the three of you, and a variety of drug charges. It sounds like we'll be able to add theft to the list as well."

"Am I in any trouble for what he made me do, putting the patches on?" It's been weighing on me ever since she arrived, and I can't stop questioning myself on whether I could have done anything differently. If I should have stood up to Drew, instead of following his orders and nearly killing my friends.

"No," Detective Chao says. "It was clear from both women's statements you were acting under duress, only complied because you were under threat of your life and theirs, and you tried to talk him out of it. We have no reason to press charges against you, and in fact, you've been formally cleared of any suspicion."

"Okay, good. I'm glad." I mean it. Hearing that the police don't think I could have prevented what happened takes some of the weight off my mind.

"Oh, and I have something I'm sure you'll be happy to get back," she says and for the first time, Detective Chao smiles at me, reaches into her leather satchel, and pulls out my phone, sealed in a plastic bag. "If you're anything like me, you must have been going crazy without it." I try not to look too eager powering it up. It feels good to have it back in my hands again.

"Thank you," I say, and I don't mean just for the phone.

"You'll be called to testify as a witness when Mr. Segura goes to trial," she tells me, back to business. "Are you planning on staying in Soberly?"

"Yes, I am." It's the second time I've said it, and it feels right. It'll be an uphill battle to win people over to my side, but I want to do it, and I know I've got a few people in my corner.

"All right then. Take care and feel better soon." She packs up her video equipment and takes her leave. James comes in within seconds of her exit.

"No more visitors for a while," he says. "You haven't used your pain pump all morning. Doctor Danielsen's orders were clear: you're to stay on top of the pain and get plenty of rest." He clicks the pump for me and hands me a now-familiar-looking sleeping pill. "I'll wake you up for supper. Now, down the hatch." I swallow the pill obligingly, although I'm not sure I even need it. The heavy nature of my conversation with Detective Chao has left me exhausted. Within moments, the ache in my chest recedes, and minutes later I'm drifting away.

True to his word, James wakes me six hours later, bearing a tray of chicken alfredo, a roll, mixed fruit, and a juice box. It doesn't look appetizing, but I unwrap the plastic cutlery anyway. I'll reward myself with one of

Naomi's treats after I've finished it.

Kellen's in his usual seat beside my bed—he must have returned after I fell asleep.

"That was quite a nap," he says as I blow on a bite of pasta.

"They keep forcing me to take sedatives," I grumble. "Apparently I'm not getting enough rest." Remembering what James said earlier, I reach over and click the pain pump button. It hisses for a moment as it adds the drug to my IV and falls silent again.

"You, not following doctor's orders? I'm shocked," Kellen teases. I roll my eyes and change the subject.

"Shouldn't you be at work?" It occurs to me the inn has probably had to shut down entirely, with me in the hospital, Drew under arrest, Kellen here keeping me company, and Jana and Cora gone. There would be no one in charge, and both the inn and the pub would be severely understaffed. With the financials as precarious as they were, there was a chance the inn wouldn't survive. "It's not open, is it?" I say glumly.

"Everything's fine. I'll start back again once you're home. In the meantime, Cora hired a few temps."

"*Cora* did?"

He nods. "I think she feels pretty terrible about what happened to you, and about not listening when you tried to raise the alarm about Drew's embezzlement. As soon as she found out you'd been hurt, she jumped right in, took charge of everything at the inn, and made sure nothing fell apart. I guess yesterday was a bit hairy since she wouldn't let Ma come in, and every person in town stopped by to find out what went on, but everyone pulled through." He checks the time on his phone. "She said she was going to come by to visit tonight, actually."

"Oh," I say, unsure how to respond. I have no idea what to make of Cora's actions, especially after how angry she'd been when we last spoke. *And* she was coming to visit me? Suddenly what little appetite I did have disappears, and I push the tray of food away. Kellen pushes it back.

"Eat," he says. "It'll be fine." His assurances don't offer much comfort, and I only pick at the remainder of my now-cooled supper.

It isn't long before there's a hesitant knock on the door, and Kellen gets up to leave. "I'll be back in a while," he says before letting Cora in.

"Hi," she says, standing awkwardly at the foot of the bed. She's carrying a vase of sunflowers in her hands.

"Hey. Have a seat. Those are beautiful, thank you." She puts the sunflowers down on the small table beside the window and settles into the chair Kellen recently vacated. "Kellen tells me you've been holding down the fort," I say, deciding to plunge right in. "I can't thank you enough. You didn't have to do that for me."

"I— Oh. You're not angry?" She looks taken aback and stops fiddling with the hem of her shirtwaist dress.

"What? No, of course not. Why would I be? You're saving my ass. No one else could have kept things going after everything that's happened." A thought occurs to me. "Wait, were you *hoping* it would make me angry?"

A sad sort of smile appears on her face, and she sighs. "No, not at all. I was trying to make amends, I guess. Look, Audrey, I've been incredibly unfair to you, from the moment you first got to town. Before that, really, since I'd already made up my mind before you got there that I wouldn't like you, and you'd do nothing but cause problems. The truth is, you've done nothing of the sort. I should have given you a chance like Roz wanted me to. I'm sorry."

I somehow manage to keep my mouth from dropping open in surprise. This wasn't what I was expecting at all. Tears spring to my eyes, and I dab at them with the corner of my hospital gown.

"Anyway, if you want me to turn the reins over to someone else, I completely understand. I know I've burned a lot of bridges. I can probably get a fourth-year student intern here by the end of the week, and hire a temp until then—"

"No," I interrupt. "No, I want you to stay. Like, *stay,* stay." I hesitate. "If you want to." Instead of regretting my hasty words, I really do mean it. Cora and I should be running the inn together.

"How much pain medication are they giving you?" she asks, skeptical. I laugh, pressing down my chest where I was shot at the twinge of pain from the sudden movement.

"*Ow*. Not enough," I say, pressing the button on the pump. "I'm serious though, and dead sober."

"Well..." she pauses. "I'm willing to give it a try. Maybe we can agree on a short-term contract to make sure it really will work out."

"That sounds like a good idea. If you write one up, I'll sign it. I'm coming home tomorrow, but it'll be a few more days at least before I'm going to be up and around much."

Home. The word, and how easily it slips from my lips, catches me off guard. I can't remember the last time

I felt like I had one. The idea makes me smile.

"I'd better let you get your rest then," Cora says, and rises to leave, clasping my hand briefly. "I'll see you soon."

REGRESS

The sight of his nieces' and nephew's drawn, hollow faces had been haunting him since he last saw them while delivering firewood three days prior. He knew they were starving, that the rations weren't sufficient to keep them alive. His sister Yulia had been almost too weak to stand. He had been the one to stack the wood and build up the fire, bringing at least some warmth to the miserable scene in the cottage.

All of a sudden, he made up his mind. Pulling up the false floor, he filled his rucksack with all the food it could hold—potatoes, onions, parsnips, some cured hard sausage, and a piece of cheese, and slung it over his back.

"What are you doing?" Slava asked, watching him

in surprise from her chair, which she had pulled up to the hearth.

"Taking this to my sister's family," he replied as he pulled on his heavy boots.

"What if someone asks you what's in the bag? What if she reports you?"

"I don't care," he told her and left their hut.

"Kolya," Yulia said, her eyes wide when she opened the door. "I didn't expect you. What brings you here?"

"I have food for you. Children, come have some sausage and cheese." He opened his rucksack and began unloading its contents onto the table. The children, who had been sitting listlessly about the cottage, sprang up at the sight of the food.

"Has there been an extra ration?" Yulia asked, confused.

"No. This is food I set aside and kept back for us when the rationing was announced," he said, avoiding her eye.

"Kolya," Yulia said. He could hear the disappointment in his sibling's voice at his deception. "Is there more still?"

He nodded. "Grain, as well. I was afraid." He hung his head. The children were paying no mind to their conversation, tearing off hunks of cheese with their hands, barely taking the time to chew.

"What are you going to do?"

"I will make it right," he said. "Please, Yulia, eat something. Elena, put four of those potatoes in the ashes to bake." His niece complied quickly, rolling them carefully into the fireplace so they would cook without burning.

"I will see you soon," he told his sister, bending to kiss her gently on the cheek. As he left the cottage he reminded his nephew, Dragan, to make sure his mother ate something. "The biggest potato goes to her," he told him.

Walking through the village toward the church, he heard a commotion ahead of him and quickened his pace. It sounded like someone was cheering, but what was there to be happy about these days? It was as cold as ever, they were still drowning in snow, and there was no end in sight. He turned the corner and saw two men approaching, dragging something behind them. He couldn't see what because their bodies were in the way, but he could tell from the way they were leaning forward as they walked that it was heavy.

"Father Lvov?" he called, recognizing the man's hat. It was his uncle, Konstantin, with him. The priest was the man he was looking for. He rushed forward to see what they were so excited about. Both men were whooping at the tops of their lungs, and a few people had stepped outside to see what was going on as well.

He saw the antlers first and couldn't believe his eyes. There was an enormous buck on the sled, larger than any he'd ever felled.

"Meat! We have meat!" people were exclaiming as the two men pulled the buck up in front of the house where the priest and his uncle made their home. Everyone was smiling, hugging each other, and *clapping the two men on the back. For a moment, he contemplated staying silent about his deception, now that the village had this windfall, but he remembered his promise to his sister and joined the small crowd.*

"Well done, Father, Konstantin. He's a beauty. Can I assist you with the gutting and butchering?"

"Of course, thank you, Kolya," the Father said. "Brothers, sisters, spread the word—there will be meat for everyone tonight." There were cheers and laughter as everyone dispersed to share the happy news. Kolya grabbed the rope to help drag the sled around to the back of the house. For a few minutes, the three men worked in silence, laboring together to get the buck tied up by its hind legs and hung from a tree branch.

"Father, I have something to confess," he said finally.

"I will go get the knives," Konstantin said and walked toward the house so his nephew and Kolya could be alone.

"What is it, Kolya?" Father Lvov said.

"I have held back food that should have gone into the rations." He described how he and Slava had dug the small cellar and built the false wall to conceal their stores, and how they had been supplementing their rations since the long winter set in. "I acted out of fear of starvation and suffering, but by doing so I have caused greater suffering for others," he said. "It was cowardly and selfish of me. I knew it from the start, but I allowed the fear to control me."

"I see. Fear has caused a great many of us to do

things we later regret, myself included."

"I accept whatever punishment the village council metes out." He knew this would likely mean exile—he had little money to pay a fine, and the village had no means of imprisoning anyone. Those found guilty of minor crimes were often publicly flogged, but he had no doubt this was too serious for a mere whipping.

"Have you still some food left?" Kolya nodded and gave him a rough estimate of what remained. "Do you renounce your sins, and beg forgiveness from God?"

"I do, Father. It's why I decided to confess. My eternal soul is more important than my earthly sufferings."

"Then here is what I propose. You will surrender your food to be added to the rations. You will forgo any of the meat from this fine beast," the Father slapped the deer on its haunch, "and for the remainder of the winter, however long it may last, you will hunt and trap with me in order to add to the village's food supplies. Finally, should your sister's husband not return and is found to have died, you will support her and her children in addition to yourself."

"Of course, Father, that goes without saying. I have no children of my own—my nieces and nephew are the closest thing I will ever have. It was them that made me realize my wrongs. What of the council? What will you tell the people?"

"I will not say a word, so long as you hold up your end of the agreement. We all deserve forgiveness, Kolya, and I believe you are sincere in your remorse."

"*Thank you, Father. I am.*" *He embraced the priest, his heart lighter than it had been in months.*

Acknowledgments

For as long as I can remember, I've wanted to write a book. I mean, not just write a book, but write a book that people who didn't actually know me could pick up, take home and read. People like you (hi!). So first, thanks go to you for taking a chance on a debut author. It means the world to me.

I certainly didn't get to this point alone; I made the words, and then many people stepped in to help make the words great. The first eyes on Past Presence were my beta readers: my sister Jackie, my parents and the folks from WRITERS GROUP!—Lindsay, Saryn, Teresa and Tiffany. Your feedback was invaluable, as was your support along this journey. I owe a great debt of gratitude to my editor, Kylee Howells for pushing me to make Past Presence the book it is today, the team at Literary Wanderlust for shepherding this noob through the publishing business, and the organizers of the #DVPit pitch party on Twitter, both for your support of diverse voices, and for hosting the event that connected me with my publisher.

My parents, Allyson and Rod, have been supporting my writing since I was able to grasp a pencil. Without their support and undying belief that I could be an author, I would not be writing this today. They are my first and best cheerleaders. Mom and Dad, I'm so sorry you had to read my sex scenes. Thanks for not making it weird.

I am fortunate beyond measure to have a village of women who hold me up with love, wisdom, and sarcasm. To all the members, past and present, of the OKGS: shoulder bumps. You're welcome in my shed anytime.

Finally, this book wouldn't exist if it weren't for my family: My husband Darcy and my children, Mairead and Finley. You gave up time with me so that I could write, and encouraged me the whole way. Thank you for seeing that I could be Writer as well as Mom and Wife. I'm so lucky to have you. And to Oliver, my feline soulmate—I'm glad I'm your hooman. Please stop sitting on my keyboard.

About the Author

Nicole Bross is an author from Calgary, Alberta, Canada, where she lives with her husband, two children and one very large orange cat. When she's not writing or working as the editor of a magazine, she can be found curled up with a book, messing around with her ever-expanding collection of manual typewriters or in the departures lounge of the airport at the beginning of another adventure. *Past Presence* is her debut novel.

CPSIA information can be obtained
at www.ICGtesting.com
Printed in the USA
LVHW031623030419
612842LV00003B/631/P